"You're leaving?"

Gil hoped there was a note of regret in her words. "Yeah," he said. "Those 7:00 a.m. practices come awfully early."

"Wait a minute." Lesley got off her chair, stopped and teetered on one foot.

"What's wrong?" Gil asked. "Did you step on something?"

"No. My foot's asleep."

"I hate it when my foot falls asleep," Gil said, glancing at the Scottie dogs that ringed the ankle of her sock. "Then it's awake all night."

Lesley laughed, then grew serious. "I don't know why I'm laughing. I thought you were going to explain.... I was curious about what you said."

Gil touched her shoulder, and she returned her gaze to his. "I want more," he said for the second time that day.

ABOUT THE AUTHOR

Brenna Todd grew up in West Texas, where *All the Right Moves* takes place, but moved to Oklahoma while attending college. There, she met her husband of fourteen years and lived out her own romantic dreams when he encouraged her to write her first book. Now, Brenna is a volunteer for the Young Authors program at her son Benjamin's school, and she hopes to encourage young people to enjoy books every bit as much as she does. Naturally, her favorite subject is romance!

All the Right Moves

BRENNA TODD

Harlequin Books

TORONTO • NEW YORK • LONDON
AMSTERDAM • PARIS • SYDNEY • HAMBURG
STOCKHOLM • ATHENS • TOKYO • MILAN

Published November 1991

ISBN 0-373-70474-7

ALL THE RIGHT MOVES

Copyright © 1991 by Brenda Hamilton. All rights reserved.
Except for use in any review, the reproduction or utilization
of this work in whole or in part in any form by any electronic,
mechanical or other means, now known or hereafter invented,
including xerography, photocopying and recording,
or in any information storage or retrieval system, is forbidden without
the permission of the publisher, Harlequin Enterprises Limited,
225 Duncan Mill Road, Don Mills, Ontario, Canada M3B 3K9.

All the characters in this book have no existence outside the
imagination of the author and have no relation whatsoever to
anyone bearing the same name or names. They are not even
distantly inspired by any individual known or unknown to the
author, and all incidents are pure invention.

® are Trademarks registered in the United States Patent and
Trademark Office and in other countries.

Printed in U.S.A.

This book is dedicated to memory of my father, Wayne Thomas, who was always a shining example of excellence for me.

I miss you, Daddy.

Love, Kidrock.

CHAPTER ONE

A DUST STORM HAD ROLLED into West Texas an hour ago. Football practice should have been canceled. But in Warren, the number-one priority had simply been moved indoors to the basketball court. Lesley Tyler hesitated only a moment, then opened the field house door to the sights, sounds and smells of football.

The noise level was deafening. Deep-voiced shouts, squeaking court shoes and the squeal of a whistle reverberating around the walls assaulted Lesley from all sides. Energy radiated from adolescent athletes as they passed, blocked and bounded. Their exuberance was a marked contrast to her end-of-the-day weariness. Nevertheless, she urged her feet into motion, disregarding the rule of no street shoes on the gymnasium floor.

Approaching the first man crouched on the sidelines, she shouted, "Where can I find Coach Fielden?"

He looked up, irritation lining his craggy, bulldog features. "Who?"

"Gil Fielden," she said, cupping her mouth with both hands.

He pointed to the other side of the room, then turned back to the play being executed in front of him.

Wonderful, just wonderful. There was no way she'd attempt crossing their makeshift football field. That left the long way around. Lesley squared her shoulders, gave her waist-cropped jacket a straightening tug and started her trek around what looked like miles of wood floor.

She rounded the corner and scanned the sideline with a frown. It was crowded with coaches. Lesley propped her free hand on her hip and eyed the note she held in the other, not relishing the idea of going from one beefy-necked coach to the next, shouting Fielden's name until she found him.

She stopped short, her attention arrested by a man trotting toward the sidelines. He gestured wildly to one of the other coaches, then pushed light blond hair from his forehead. He looked over his shoulder with annoyance at one of the formations on the floor and mouthed an expletive.

He had to be Fielden, Lesley decided. That kind of intense emotional involvement, she knew from personal experience, was what it took to win championship titles. And Fielden had won his share. During the seven years he'd coached at Warren, his teams had won the state title four times. Yes, that intensity was the giveaway, all right; it certainly wasn't his looks.

He was younger than his colleagues lining the sides of the gymnasium, probably closer to her thirty years than their fifty. He was also in better condition. *Much* better condition, she noted, peering over the top of her glasses. The fleece sweatshirt he wore was not unlike those worn by his staff of assistants—black and gold with the Warren Wildcats emblem emblazoned on the front—but his didn't stretch over a rounded midsection. Instead, it fit as the manufacturer had intended, emphasizing the muscular proportions of the top half of his body. The lower half was just as impressive, clad in shorts rather than baggy sweat pants. Midthigh-length, snug-fitting, athletic shorts. At the very peak of physical fitness, he was a prime example of what shorts could do for the masculine physique... and feminine pulse rates.

Lesley's pulse rate had certainly perked up, which was strange. She'd never been attracted to blatantly physical men. Her preferences usually ran to the tailored jacket and sharply creased slacks type of man, the type that blended neatly into the crowd, the type whose subtlety was the only blatant thing about them.

Fielden swore again, this time audibly, and shook his head, pointing at one player. "You, Crenshaw," he shouted. "Off the field."

"Athletes," Lesley muttered, watching the boy, his helmet in his hand and dejection in his eyes, as he ambled toward a bench. Correction, athletes who molded other athletes in their own images. She resumed her march and came to a stop beside the man. Just as she reached up to tap his shoulder, a close-range screeching made her start, and she pulled her hand back. She should have known. He was the one with the overactive whistle.

It fell from his mouth and bounced against his impressive chest as he launched into action, sprinting forward then grabbing a player by the shoulders. "Tuck the ball! Get that ball in your hands, then tuck it! Son, you're a fumble waiting to happen!"

Glancing heavenward, he made his way back to the sideline. Frustration was evident in his expression. He swiveled, hands on hips, his attention solely on the players. She tapped him on the shoulder.

"Huh?" His concentration on the action in front of him never wavered.

"Coach Fielden?"

His gaze swung slowly from the court to her. His brows drew together over startlingly clear blue eyes.

"I need to speak with you, Coach."

"Practice isn't over for another forty-five minutes," he said, his brow still creased.

"I'm aware of that. I need to speak to you before it's over."

"Well, I'm a little busy at the moment."

A football sailed by, stealing his attention again. He followed its high arc with his eyes, then grabbed a nearby clipboard from the floor. Raptly he studied a diagram of Xs and Os, ignoring her.

Lesley's patience dwindled. "Coach—"

"Yeah, in a minute. Clarke," he yelled, his authority obvious when the assistant came sprinting over. "If Tucker can't find his receiver, then find someone who can."

"Right." Clarke took off to deliver the message.

Before she could detect which boy was Tucker, or see if he'd taken the news as badly as his teammate Crenshaw had, a football came hurtling toward Lesley from out of nowhere. She blinked then dodged, but not fast enough. The ball clipped her arm hard, so hard she knew there'd be a bruise there later. She grimaced and rubbed at the spot.

"Hey, are you okay?"

She was surprised that he'd remembered she was there. "Yes, I'm fine. But I need to discuss something with—"

"What kind of formation is that, Clarke!"

For the second time that afternoon, Lesley wished that this could wait until tomorrow. It was obvious that she'd never accomplish anything as long as they stayed in this field house. But she'd come this far....

"Coach Fielden," she said in a firm voice. "I need to speak with you out in the hall, if you don't mind. It's important and I—"

"Right." The shrill blast of his whistle pierced the air again and Lesley's fingertips went to her temple. "Tuck it!" he shouted, then threw his hands into the air as if asking for divine intervention. "You're brilliant, Ellis, simply brilliant!"

"Mr. Fielden, really. Don't you think a little positive reinforcement would get the job done better than all that yelling?"

She regretted the remark the moment it left her mouth. She might object to his teaching methods, but she'd wanted to get things started off on the right foot with this man. When he turned, giving her a look that was just this side of annoyed, Lesley wondered if she'd blown her chance.

"I'm sure that wasn't what you came here to talk to me about."

"No. No, it wasn't. What I need to speak with you about is—"

"Hold it a second." He motioned to his assistant. "Clarke, have them run through this and...this." He handed him the clipboard then indicated the side door with a dramatic flourish of his arm. She'd accept the gesture as payback for her remark, Lesley decided, walking with him out of the gymnasium and into the hallway. Lord knows the ground was fertile enough for a troublesome relationship between the coach and herself as it was. It wouldn't do to get miffed over every little thing.

"Coach, I'm sorry to intrude on your practice," she said once the door closed, shutting out the noise and confusion. "And if this could have waited..."

Lesley's words trailed off. When she turned, he was closer than she'd expected. And though she had stood right next to him in the gym, all the commotion going on must have served as something of a buffer to the senses.

Her senses were unimpeded now.

Lesley had heard all about Gil Fielden's blond good looks and fine form from the women in the teachers' lounge. He'd been a favorite topic of conversation since school had begun last week. And while there was no reason that she should be any less observant than all of the other women on the faculty at Warren, Lesley reminded herself that she had a job to do.

She slid her glasses off, placed them in her jacket pocket and handed him the piece of paper. She watched as he read it, predicting his frown even before it formed. It prodded the speech she'd practiced all the way from her office to the field house door.

"Coach Fielden, I know it was policy in the past for students with extracurricular activities to make up their detentions later, when it wouldn't interfere with practices or tournaments," she said, "but as you can see from the note Mrs. Quinn has written me, we have a special situation with Devin Michaels. He's been tardy to her first-hour English class three times this week alone. He was late two times last week. This being only the second week of school, Mrs. Quinn feels Devin is setting a bad precedent, so she assigned him a week of detention. I would've waited until after practice to talk to you, but Mrs. Quinn is adamant that Devin be pulled from practice now because he has a paper due tomorrow."

"And you are . . . ?"

"Lesley Tyler," she said, careful to keep her eyes locked on his. While she'd made her little speech, her eyes had slipped once or twice to the whistle draped around his neck and resting smack dab in the middle of his chest. Beneath it, bisecting the front of the sweatshirt, was a faint line of perspiration that brought to mind one of the more racy remarks she'd overheard in the lounge. It had to do with sharing a locker-room shower with him after a long, arduous practice. "I'm the new principal."

"Oh. Right. Listen, I would've been by to meet you sooner, but with fall practice and all, I've—"

"It's perfectly all right, Coach. I've been a bit busy myself."

His hand went to his hip, and his frown was back. "Look, Michaels is starting lineup, so I can't do without him in practice with this week's game only two days away. Tell you what—I'll talk to him. I can assure you that he won't be late again. You talk to the teacher. Tell her . . . I don't know, tell her that he'll do double D-hall in the spring or something. Just fix it."

Lesley felt she knew coaches pretty well. She'd worked with several of them in the Austin public school system. She'd expected this sort of response. She also expected him to be none too pleased with what she had to say next. "I can't do that, Coach."

His eyes narrowed, and he propped his other hand on his hip. "What do you mean, can't? I gotta have Michaels at practice. It won't be earth-shattering if he doesn't attend D-hall until this spring, and Mrs. —" he jerked the page up, scanning it quickly "—Quinn knows it."

"She also knows that policies like delaying detention for football players or the band are no longer acceptable."

"No longer acceptable?"

"Coach, I'd truly hoped to forestall going over this with you until I could call a faculty meeting next week and discuss it with everyone, but it appears I have no choice. I've been going over the no-pass, no-play policies here at Warren—"

"Oh, jeez," he said, rolling his eyes. "No pass, no play. I should have known. Listen, can't I get a break here? At least until the kid actually makes a bad grade?"

She wanted to inform him that it wasn't so much a matter of whether *he* got a break or not but of the student getting a better education. She refrained from doing so, certain that her positive view of the law would probably go over like the proverbial lead balloon.

"You're right, he hasn't made a bad grade yet, but there's a good possibility that he will. As well as being late, Devin has failed to hand in the first two assignments in that class. The sooner we get a handle on his problem, the better, Coach. It's to your team's benefit that we confront it now, before he makes a failing grade and is forced to forfeit not only an occasional practice, but games as well.

"Now, I'm scheduled to talk to Devin tomorrow morning because I'm concerned that his class load may be too heavy for the grade point average he maintained in his first two years of high school. If that's where the problem lies, then it's easily solved by allowing Devin to drop an unnecessary subject."

"Good. Discuss it tomorrow. For now, what's the harm in letting him finish practice?" He glanced down at his watch. "There's only thirty minutes left."

She sighed, feeling more like a strict schoolmarm of old and less like a fellow faculty member with each second that passed. "I can't allow it, Coach. Mrs. Quinn is insisting."

"Perfect," Fielden said, slapping the note against his outer thigh and sending his gaze to the ceiling in frustration. "Just perfect." He muttered deprecations about no-pass, no-play along with gripes about students who couldn't get up on time for school.

"It's not his fault, Dad," came a voice from behind them.

As one, they turned toward a girl who looked to be sixteen or so. Lesley remembered someone mentioning that Fielden was divorced, but she didn't remember hearing that he had a daughter. Blond and brown eyed, she hugged her books to her chest as she came toward them with a slow, wary step.

"Coby?" he asked. "This is a private conversation, honey. What are you doing here?"

"I missed my ride and decided to come here to wait for you to take me home. I heard what you and Miss Tyler were talking about, and...Dad, it's not Devin's fault." She glanced from her father to Lesley then back again. "I think maybe I might be to blame."

"You're to blame?" he said.

"Devin's a friend of mine, Daddy. I was the one who talked him into taking drama this year, and even trying out for the play. He's working really hard on his lines for the audition and...and maybe that's why he's missing assignments. I mean, I didn't know it would overload his schedule or anything. I just thought he'd like it as much as I do." Turning to Lesley, she said, "I'll help him make up those assignments, Miss Tyler."

Lesley smiled, liking Coby immediately. She reminded her of her youngest sister, Linda. Lesley remembered with pride how Linda had always come to the aid of anyone lucky enough to be called her friend. Lesley was ready to praise Coby for offering her help to Devin when Coby's father spoke.

"Honey, I think that's nice, your wanting to help Devin," he said, placing his arm around her shoulders and giving her a gentle squeeze. "But listen, I don't want you to be too disappointed if drama doesn't work out for him. It's like Miss Tyler said. His class load is too heavy and he might have to drop an unnecessary course. Isn't that right?" he asked, clearly bouncing the ball right into Lesley's court.

Lesley folded her arms across her middle and gave him a dry look. Somehow she didn't think the drama teacher would feel her subject more unnecessary than his. "I did mention that alternative. However, Devin's schedule lists two elective courses. One is drama and the other is football."

He looked surprised at first, as if he'd only just been told that credits in football weren't required for graduation. Then he gave her a slow smile. It was off center, a bit self-deprecatory…and every bit as potent as Lesley had heard it was. She felt the funniest sensation, tingles actually, that started low and rose the length of her spine.

That shouldn't be surprising, she told herself. Just because she wasn't usually attracted to his type didn't mean that she was beyond simple appreciation. Not stopping to admit that simple appreciation didn't normally result in tingles, Lesley turned her attention to Coby. Unlike her father, she wasn't smiling. "Don't worry about Devin, Coby. I'll talk to him tomorrow morning. I'm sure we'll straighten things out. And I agree with your father—it's so nice of you to offer your help. I know Devin will appreciate it."

Coby nodded but still looked troubled. She started for the door to the gym but stopped, glancing back at her father. "Devin loves drama, Dad. It would be a mistake for him to give it up."

Gil continued staring at the door after it had closed. He exhaled a heavy sigh and ran his fingers through his hair, then turned back to Lesley. "He may love drama," he said, "but he's also got several colleges interested in him for football scholarships."

"Yes, I'd heard that."

His hands went to his hips again, and he looked at her in a manner that Lesley could only describe as a sizing-up-the-enemy look. It shouldn't have been disconcerting, but it was. The skirt-and-jacket combination she wore, the comfortable pumps and pinned-up hairstyle no longer felt practical or sensible. They felt so...so schoolmarmish. Her hand went to the collar of her blouse, and she cleared her throat.

His gaze came back to hers. "Just how rough are you going to be on me with this law thing?"

This law thing. She'd encountered the same attitude at the school in Austin where she'd been vice principal before accepting this position. Coaches, understandably, took great exception to no-pass, no-play. Even though it had been passed several years ago, they were still lobbying the Texas legislature to get the restrictions softened.

Lesley knew that one of the main reasons she'd landed the position of principal at Warren was because she'd successfully instituted the law at her former school. Overall grade point averages had gone up, and the extracurricular activity departments had adjusted. She'd been told by the new superintendent of schools who'd hired her that Warren High School had been bending the no-pass, no-play law ever since it had been passed. He wanted that to change. Lesley wanted that, too. She'd hoped it could be accomplished without having to go to war with Gil Fielden, but that didn't look likely.

"I consider myself a proponent of fair play, Coach. I can promise you that it won't be any rougher on you than it will be on the other extracurricular departments."

Though his expression remained neutral, his reaction was apparent as his eyes went quickly from sky blue to stormy gray. Lesley nodded a goodbye and turned to head down the hall, deciding she'd said all that was necessary on the subject. Almost. She stopped short and looked over her shoulder. "But, Coach, that's not to say that it won't be rougher than you've had it in the past."

GIL STARED AFTER HER, listening to the oh-so-efficient tap of her heels as she walked down the hall.

Efficient.

Yeah, that was a good word to describe the new principal. She would be efficient to a fault...and a real pain. A pain who would enforce no-pass, no-play to the letter. And that was too bad, Gil thought, noticing the length of leg revealed by the demure slit in her skirt. She had great legs.

He went back into the gym and signaled for Clarke. While telling him to pull Michaels and send him to D-hall, he caught sight of Coby sitting on the collapsible bleachers, waiting for practice to end. He gave her a little wave and a smile but got nothing but a steady, cool look in return. He unconsciously patted his shirtfront for the cigarettes he'd given up almost six months ago. Days like this one made him wish he'd never given up smoking.

CHAPTER TWO

FORTY-EIGHT HOURS LATER, Gil stood at the foot of the stairway in his apartment. The urge to light up a cigarette had never been stronger.

What an absolute loss the past two days had been! He'd virtually beat his head against a wall, trying to get his team ready for tonight's game. They weren't. He'd tried to negotiate a compromise with the new principal in order to delay her detention hall rule. She wouldn't. If that wasn't enough—and it was—now he faced problems with his daughter.

But he didn't have to wonder whether it was the pressure at school or the situation with Coby that had him suffering this nicotine fit. It was definitely Coby—she'd lied to him.

God, how he hated this. His stomach was tied in knots and, even after seventeen years of coaching adolescents, he was facing his first real discipline problem as a full-time father. It gave him sweaty palms and jangled nerves. In all his time as a coach, he'd never been intimidated by a teenager. He'd always handled them with ease, combining a bit of psychology with a firm yet understanding manner. So why the hell should this feel so different?

Before ascending the staircase, he glanced over at the evidence of Coby's ritual after-school occupation of the living room floor. A tolerant grin stretched his lips. A drama script and schoolbooks were spread in a wide arc on the floor; MTV flickered on the screen of his small portable; a half-empty glass of cola sat on the coffee table. She might not have grown up with him as an everyday example in her life, Gil thought, but heredity obviously counted for something. Coby had definitely inherited his lax attitude where house-keeping was concerned. He wondered if Cecelia still blew her stack at every sock left on the floor....

Looking back up the stairs, Gil wiped the grin from his face. This was not the time to get sentimental over father-daughter traits. He reminded himself that Ceil, for all her nitpicking, had done an excellent job of single-parent child rearing. It was up to him not to drop the ball.

Know when to love; know when love means discipline. His ex-wife's words of wisdom sounded in his head, fueling his resolve as Gil climbed the steps. Now that *he* was the full-time parent, they were words to live by. It was in Coby's best interests that she follow a set of rules and regulations in this household. If he'd instituted them sooner, this lecture might not have been necessary.

"Coby," he called out. As he turned the corner leading to her bedroom, he noticed the lavender phone cord. It stretched from her room, down the hall to the closed bathroom. He shook his head, following the trail it made. "Coby?" He knocked.

"*Da-ad,* I'm on the phone."

"Are you decent?"

"Yes."

Gil opened the door and walked in. Perched on the vanity, the phone receiver on her shoulder, Coby applied blue shadow to one eyelid. She looked up at him in the mirror, gave him a brief smile, then held up a hand to forestall him when he started to speak.

"No, no, no, Devin. That's when he's discovered the first body in the window seat and he's trying to hide it from his aunts," she said. "Think about your motivation."

Coby's eyes met his in the mirror and he read the challenge there. He forced himself to look stern. "Finish your conversation," he mouthed.

Coby placed her hand over the mouthpiece and turned toward him, the look in her eyes slightly wary. "Is anything wrong?"

"I have something to discuss with you. Five minutes," he warned.

Once inside his bedroom, Gil threw his duffel bag full of gym clothes on to the unmade bed, feeling exhausted from the day's practice. The chances for a state title didn't look so good this year. Last year's state championship team was history. This year he was faced with a quarterback who was nearsighted at best, receivers—except for Devin Michaels—bent on fumbling that quarterback's passes and, to top it off, a principal with a list of new rules.

As he sat on the bed untying his court shoes, he thought back over the past two days since he'd met the inimitable Lesley Tyler. She was a pain, all right, and she was making his job that much more difficult. He'd had to grit his teeth as he'd watched players miss practice because of detention. He'd held on to his temper when a strategy meeting with his assistants had been canceled in deference to a mandatory faculty meeting she'd called. Maybe she was a long-lost cousin of Ceil's, Gil mused. Or possibly another football coach in the district had planted her at Warren to undermine his program.

He rose, shuffling to the closet for the slacks and polo shirt he'd wear to tonight's game. His thoughts drifting to Coby again, he frowned. Miss Tyler and all the complications she brought with her were nothing compared to what his home life could be if problems with his daughter cropped up. Ceil had warned him that things might not be rosy, warned him that she and Coby hadn't been getting along as well as—

"Daddy?" Coby stood in the doorway, her fingers twirling a long strand of blond hair. "You wanted to talk, Dad?"

Tension tightened his shoulders as he remembered the lie. Tersely he motioned toward the bed. "Have a seat," he said, then watched as she crossed the room and settled on the bed's edge. She looked up at him, brown eyes large and questioning.

"Your mother had some reservations about your coming to live with me, Coby. Do you know why?"

Her face transformed. Where there had been questions before, there was now a sullen frown. "I know that she doesn't understand me anymore."

"Now, Coby, I think she understands more than you give her credit for."

"I'll give her credit for nagging. She does that really well. That and come up with new rules every other day."

Ceil had mentioned that Coby was pushing for more freedom these days. In fact, she felt it was their daughter's prime motivation for wanting a change of household. Gil had been so thrilled at the thought of having more time with Coby that he'd dismissed the comment. He'd figured Ceil's apprehension was due to a typical mother-daughter clash. Now, after witnessing Coby's attitude, and after what he'd overheard at school today, he had to wonder.

"Is that the reason you wanted to live with me? Did you think that there'd be no rules to follow here?"

"Of course not," she said quickly. "I told you, I want to spend more time with you." Her eyes narrowed. "Did *she* say that was the reason I wanted to live here?"

Gil braced one untied shoe on the footboard of the bed and leaned toward her.

"As a matter of fact, aside from the few reservations, your mother was all for us spending some time together before you go off to college next year. Your mother loves you very much. You know that, Coby."

"Well, sure, Dad." She ducked her head, plucking at the bedspread with her fingertips. "But we're not very good friends anymore. Not like you and me."

Gil felt a twinge of guilt. Weekend parenting had given him an advantage over his ex-wife. Unlike Ceil, he'd never had to be the bad guy, handing out lectures or instituting guidelines. He and Coby had always had the luxury of being friends first and foremost. He saw now that things might have to change.

"Coby, friendship is important between parents and their children, and I'm glad we have that going for us, but—"

"You don't know just *how* important, Dad." She glanced down and scuffed one sneaker against the carpet. "Mom operates in two modes these days. The first is her grades mode. 'Have you done your homework? What tests are you supposed to be studying for? Remember how vital making National Honor Society is when it comes to college scholarships.'" Coby rolled her eyes. "Her other is the household-chore mode. It's like I'm some kind of machine to her, programmed for straight A's and a clean bedroom."

Gil knew how intense Ceil could get when she felt strongly about something. In fact, their basic personality differences had been one of the major factors leading to their divorce. But he'd never known her to badger Coby. Hell, she'd never needed to. Coby had always brought home perfect report cards. One thing the girl hadn't inherited from him was the ability to make sterling grades with ease. So if Ceil was hassling her, there had to be a reason.

"Have your grades dropped? Your mother didn't mention anything to me about it."

"She didn't mention anything because there's nothing to mention," she said. "I mean, do you feel all A's and two B's are anything to freak about?"

"You got two B's last year?"

"Don't tell me you're going to freak, too."

"No," Gil said with a rueful laugh. "No, that's a perfectly respectable report card as far as I'm concerned. It's just that I wasn't aware you'd ever made a B before."

"I haven't. That's why Mom..."

"Freaked?"

"Yeah. Big time."

Gil gave her shoulder a gentle squeeze. "Well, honey, maybe your mom was upset because she thought that you hadn't lived up to your potential. Didn't you explain that you'd simply come across a couple of subjects that gave you trouble?"

"That's just it, Dad. I *could've* made A's in those classes. But something had to go."

Gil's encouraging smile faded. "Explain 'something had to go.'"

"Now, Dad, don't you get crazy, too. After all, you're the one who's always saying that I need to lighten up, get a hobby, do something besides bury myself in schoolbooks all the time."

"Yes. But what's that got to do with—"

"Well, I did...find a side interest, that is. The drama club."

Gil nodded, careful to keep his expression free of anything that might indicate he wasn't supportive. He might not be thrilled about Devin Michaels's involvement in drama—the boy had decided to keep the course on his schedule—but that was different. Devin might not be able to handle such a heavy schedule, but Coby could.

Gil remembered the pride he'd felt at watching his daughter perform on stage. She'd gotten the lead in

Pygmalion on her first tryout last year. She'd been terrific.

"I love it, Daddy. I love everything about it. I was so nervous the first time I stepped onstage, but after my first few lines, everything just seemed to fall into place. I was hooked from that moment on. And it was the strangest feeling. It was like . . . like I'd always belonged there but had just never known it. Like I was born to be doing that and that alone." Her animated gestures stilled and her expression became thoughtful. "I think I'm really good at it."

Gil smiled. "Of course you are. I was sitting in that audience. I thought you were brilliant."

"That wouldn't have anything to do with the fact that you're my dad, would it?"

"Hey, I may not be an expert, but the way you mastered the accent alone was brilliant in my book. The transformation from West Texas to Cockney was great!"

Coby laughed, her eyes shining with happiness at the compliment. "Do you really think so, Dad?" At his answering smile and nod, she went on, "Because it's . . . become more than a side interest. It's—now you're going to think this is a pipe dream, but I've decided it's what I want to do with my life."

"Acting?"

"Oh, see I knew it! I knew you'd think I'm dumb to believe that I could make it as an actress."

"Coby, I believe that you could do anything you set out to do. It's just . . ." Gil struggled for the right words. He didn't doubt her ability, it was just that this had come as sort of a shock. He'd always pictured

Coby doing something different, something more... scholarly. Besides, the acting profession was synonymous with disappointment and rejection. How could any parent offer a blanket seal of approval?

In conflict with his apprehension was the memory of how his parents had reacted to his own choice of career. Being college professors, they'd disapproved of his involvement with sports from the start, wishing he'd chosen an academic vocation, as had his brother, Gregory. Looking back, he knew he'd been right to stick to his guns. Especially after what had happened to Greg.

"It's just what?" she prodded.

"Coby, if you're serious about this, my thoughts are that you should go for it, but—"

"Really, Dad?" She got off the bed and launched herself into Gil's arms. "Oh, Daddy. You don't know how good it makes me feel that you approve. I thought you'd be just like Mom, thinking that I have my head in the clouds and worrying that I'd devote too much time to drama and not enough to my studies."

Gil patted her back, then broke the hug. "I'm not worried about your grades. That's not to say I'm completely thrilled about the acting. You've picked a career that's got a lot of ups and downs. I don't like to think of all the difficult times that might lie ahead."

"Will it help to know that your daughter, known for her levelheadedness, is approaching this sensibly? I've thought it through. I'll need to find a university with a good drama department. I'll need to diversify, take some singing and dancing lessons. And I'm not going to just head out for Hollywood with stars in my eyes and nothing but lint in my pockets, Dad. I'm going to minor in business for something to fall back on. I don't want to live like a bohemian all my life just waiting for my big break."

"Well," he said, ruffling her bangs, "it's good to hear that those two B's don't mean that your brain stopped working."

Coby gave him a light punch on the arm. "Jeez, Coach, I'm glad you aren't as hyper about those grades as Mom. If she had me doing marathon cleaning, I can imagine what your punishment would be. Probably something like wind sprints." She gave him a kiss on the cheek, then glanced down at the multicolored watch strapped to her wrist. "Oh, no! Look at the time! Daddy, I have to finish getting ready. See you at the game tonight."

She was halfway to the door before Gil remembered what he'd originally wanted to talk to her about. "Hey, wait a minute. There's still the matter of why I called you in here."

Coby stopped, turning toward him. "Oh. You didn't just want to talk about our new living arrangements?"

"No. I wanted to discuss something I heard today at school, something that has me pretty disturbed."

"What is it?"

"I thought you were going to be spending the night with girlfriends after the game tonight, Coby."

"Well...I am. What did you hear at—"

"And that's all."

"Uh, yeah. Why?"

"I overheard some of the football players discussing their after-game plans today. They're meeting girls at the Pizza Palace. Devin Michaels mentioned your name."

Coby's eyes widened infinitesimally. "Oh, right. I forgot to tell you that. It's okay, isn't it?"

"I don't have a problem with your going, but I'm not exactly thrilled about being told so late. You didn't fill me in on all the facts, Coby. I felt like you'd lied to me."

"Oh, no, Daddy. That's not the way it was. Really. I didn't even know the part about the boys until today. Susan changed the plans at the last minute. I was going to tell you, but then we started talking about my grades and stuff and it completely slipped my mind." She walked back to him and took his hand. "I would never lie to you. Honestly."

Gil's stomach slowly unknotted as relief seeped in. It had been a simple misunderstanding. Leave it to his insecurities on the single-parenthood front to blow it out of proportion. He squeezed her hand and dropped a kiss onto her forehead. "Good. But let's make sure it doesn't slip your mind in future, okay?"

"Okay," she said.

"Listen, Cobe. This, uh...this thing with Michaels and you. You aren't getting, well, serious about him or anything, are you?"

She thought about it a moment, then said, "I don't know, Dad. We've always been friends, you know. But ever since I realized that there was more to life than just studying, it's like I've started noticing boys more. Especially Devin." She gave him a grin. "Me being almost eighteen, I'd say it was about time, wouldn't you?"

He wanted to shout, No, no! It's not about time. Forget I said anything about getting an outside interest. Bury your nose back in those books! But he set aside protective instincts and faced reality. It was bound to have happened sooner or later, this noticing-boys stuff. And Coby had said it herself, she was levelheaded, more so than many of the teenagers he knew. He just wished he didn't feel so... so panicked about it.

"I wouldn't say it's about time. I'd say the older and wiser you are when you start dealing with feelings about the opposite sex the better."

"Yeah, I guess so," she said. "Well, I'm gonna get moving." She started for the door again but turned back around before she reached it. "I can still cancel my plans if you want me to. I don't want you to feel that I misled you on purpose."

Gil gave her a smile and a wink. "Nah. Fifty wind sprints oughta cover it."

THE DUST STORM of days ago was a memory now; mild seventy-degree weather had taken over. With the end of the workweek, a familiar attitude reversal occurred in the small oil-field community of Warren. After five days of grueling dawn-to-dusk hours, the citizens were ready to play. And Friday nights in the fall were reserved for their favorite form of recreation. Football.

Lesley lifted her face to the warm September breeze, somewhat glad that she'd decided to come. Somewhat amazed, but somewhat glad.

Football had never been her idea of a favorite form of recreation. She'd tried to make it a point to support her school's team, but it had always been an effort.

Lesley had never been one to buckle when challenged, however. And she'd definitely been challenged, Lesley thought, remembering the short meeting she'd had with Fielden just yesterday. Unlike their first meeting that day in the field house, the second one had taken place on her turf, in her office. He'd come asking for a compromise on her new detention ruling, but Lesley had refused to accommodate him. That had been when he'd made the veiled remark about favoritism. He had said that he would bet good money that she wouldn't make it to a single football game but wouldn't miss a slide-rule competition or science fair.

That had rankled; Lesley didn't play favorites. Never had, never would. It had also pushed her to accept office secretary Stacey Blevins's invitation to attend tonight's game.

"This row, Les," Stacey said, pointing toward enviable fifty-yard-line seats.

Lesley nodded and led the way down the row, careful to avoid the feet of several fans who were already seated. Once settled, she looked around, smiling ruefully at the large crowd of people in attendance. This community, like the one she'd grown up in, took its football seriously. Lesley had seen college and professional games with fewer people in the stands.

"You see? I knew you'd enjoy yourself," Stacey said.

Lesley laughed. "The game hasn't even started yet."

"But you're already smiling. You needed a night out."

"You're right," Lesley admitted. She'd been overwhelmed by the amount of first-month-of-school paperwork her new job generated. Compounding that was the fact that she did things differently, a lot differently, than her predecessor, Mr. Moore. From what Lesley could tell, he had been rather careless about his paperwork, and his filing system defied logic. She, on the other hand was... well, her sisters had always referred to her as an organization freak, a list maker extraordinaire. They also thought she spent too much time thinking about work. They were probably right.

Slipping a long strand of hair behind her ear, she let the noise of the crowd surround her and push all thoughts of work from her mind. She stretched her jean-clad legs in front of her and watched the pregame festivities unfold, marveling at the lavish new stadium they were in. It had artificial turf, a large glassed-in press box and, in place of the wooden bleachers found at most high school stadiums, a concrete shell with individual built-in fiberglass seats. A glance toward the end zones revealed beautiful landscaping that swept up the sides of man-made hills. "This is some stadium," Lesley murmured.

"Impressive, huh? Several oilmen in the area put up the financing about eight years ago. That, of course, was before the oil boom went bust.'' Stacey brushed at the curly blond hair that had blown into her face and gave Lesley a knowing look. ''You know oilmen *love* their football.''

''Mmm-hmm.'' Lesley sipped at her Coke. ''My father coached football for a small college in East Texas. It's the same all over the state.''

''You grew up in East Texas?'' Stacey asked.

''Yep.''

''I'd heard you came from Austin.''

''I taught in Austin after graduating from UT,'' Lesley told her. ''I heard about this position opening up from someone who knew the new superintendent in Warren.''

The band started the national anthem, and they rose to sing. As the final note faded and the crowd sent up a cheer, Stacey nudged Lesley, pointing toward one end zone. ''How about that scoreboard,'' she shouted.

Lesley turned. Her eyes widened. The scoreboard was state-of-the-art electronic. A locomotive chugged across the screen with a wildcat in an engineer's cap grinning from the caboose. Her first reaction was amazement; exactly how much had this stadium cost? Then words came marching across the screen beneath the picture, and she had to smile. Texas football fans were notorious for ignoring price tags when their favorite teams were involved. One of the teachers at school had told her about a man in Odessa who flew his private plane over the stadium during games, with the Permian High School mascot, a panther, painted on the underside of one wing.

"Oh, isn't that cute! 'Wildcat Express,'" Stacey said. "That's a new one. You should see some of the stuff they come up with for that board."

"I can imagine," Lesley said, taking her seat with the rest of the crowd.

Lesley had taken an instant liking to Stacey. The girl was young, maybe twenty-two or twenty-three, but a hard worker who virtually held the office together. She had a vivacious personality, and her enthusiasm for her job had drawn Lesley to her.

"Since you're single, you've no doubt noticed another attraction that the Warren football team has to offer," Stacey said.

"Another attraction?"

"The coach." Stacey indicated the sidelines with an insinuating nod. "Here. I brought these for more than just watching the game." She held up a pair of binoculars.

"Oh, Stacey," she said, "you've got to be kidding me. We see him every day at school."

"I know, but this is different. *Here* you get to see him in action. Sort of like seeing a beautiful animal in the wild . . . you know, in its own habitat."

"You're outrageous, you know that? An animal in the wild, for heaven's sake?"

"So turn me in to Female Chauvinists Anonymous. But don't tell me you don't think he's yummy," Stacey said, thrusting the field glasses toward her.

"Yummy or not, I'm not going to stare at him through—"

"Oh, come on. How can you expect to contribute to our conversation in the teachers' lounge Monday morning? You won't even know what he was wearing,'' Stacey said with a laugh.

"Oh, give 'em here,'' Lesley said with resignation, deciding to join in with Stacey's good-natured fun.

She'd also decided that she would just see what he was wearing, then hand the glasses back. When she focused in on the female faculty members' idea of physical perfection, however, she changed her mind.

Though he was dressed more conservatively tonight than he'd been in the field house, the result was still the same. From the black polo shirt he wore to the slacks that fit so...well, so nicely, he presented an image of pure masculinity.

"You know, if all these women didn't already go to every game with their husbands,'' Stacey said, indicating the number of women seated around them, "I bet they'd come just to get a look at him.''

Probably so, Lesley thought, her gaze traveling back up his body.

He turned slightly, presenting his profile as he placed a hand over his headset and spoke into the small attached microphone. A force beyond her control drew Lesley's eyes to his mouth. His expression was all business now, yet she couldn't help recalling the smile she'd witnessed that day in the field house.

Lesley lowered the binoculars, then handed them back to Stacey.

"Was this a good idea, or what?'' Stacey said, grabbing up the glasses.

Oh yeah, a great idea. Lesley glanced skyward, not believing she'd been staring at the man through binoculars. Discomfort settled in, the same disturbing feeling she got every time she had come in contact with Gil Fielden. It was crazy. The man was definitely not her type, so why was she so strongly attracted to him?

The crowd came to life, and Lesley's gaze darted to the action at the end of the field. She turned to Stacey, then almost laughed out loud. The girl was still "coach watching." There was comfort to be taken in that, Lesley thought. Her own control over her libido might be lacking, but Stacey's, it seemed, was nonexistent.

"Hey," Lesley said, tapping her on the shoulder. "You just missed the first touchdown."

"Oh, rats!" Stacey shifted in time to see the football sail through the goalpost for an extra point.

HIS HANDS ON HIS HIPS, Gil faced a halftime locker room full of jubilant young athletes. Their faces lit up in smiles of victory, they were good-naturedly pushing and shoving and slapping each other on the back. The only problem was, victory was still far from theirs.

When their roughhousing subsided, he pulled off his cap, propped one foot on the bench in front of him and gave his assistant a sidelong glance. "Well, Coach Clarke, I'd say we've got this game won, wouldn't you?" he asked.

Catching Gil's drift, Clarke nodded. "Yep, fourteen points oughta do it."

The players had caught their coach's drift, too. Faces sobered. Smiles fell. Silence reigned.

"Come on, Coach," a boy from the back moaned. "Fourteen to nothing at the half's not so bad."

The boy who had spoken up was only voicing the opinion of the entire team, and that worried Gil. Not only did their skills need to be honed, but these boys lacked experience—most of last year's state championship team had been made up of graduating seniors. Gil was glad of the fourteen-point lead, but he was more concerned with the attitude of overconfidence these points had inspired.

"You're right, it's not so bad. But we got those TDs as a result of two fumbles. Are you forgetting that?" He paused, letting that sink in. "The scoreboard isn't telling the whole story tonight, and you and I know it." His gaze swept the room, and he noted several solemn nods. "It's too soon to celebrate, and much too soon to get cocky. Especially since those points were put on the board by the defensive squad. Am I right?"

"Right, Coach," several of the boys answered grudgingly.

"So. We know what we have to do, don't we?"

Throughout the rest of his talk, they listened attentively, studied the plays he diagrammed on the chalkboard and discussed game plans as if they hadn't scored at all. Then, as halftime activities on the field neared an end, they rose from their benches. Expressions of grim determination had replaced their bravado.

Gil kept his smile to himself. Watching them trade encouragements as they filed toward the door, he felt the first glimmer of hope for this team. Attitude was half the battle, and theirs was improving. He walked to the front of the group. "By the way, guys," he put in just before they left the room. "Congratulations on that lead."

Their shouts, a combination of war cries and laughter, rang out as they ran from the locker room onto the field. When he reached the sidelines, Gil took the headset that was handed to him, absently glancing into the stands as he put it on.

That was when he caught sight of Coby standing with two girls on the first row of seats. That was when all thoughts of game plans and diagrams were nudged aside by parental anxieties. Had he said the right things this afternoon? he wondered with a sigh. Had he reacted the right way? Most important, what about the decision to let Coby go with her friends to meet the boys? There was so much more to worry about now that she was living with him.

Who, for instance, were those girls she was talking with? They weren't the same two friends she'd ridden with to the game. That shouldn't be cause for worry. But whether he wanted to admit it or not, Coby's convenient absentmindedness had him bothered.

He narrowed his gaze on the two, wondering if he'd met them before. The one with curly blond hair seemed familiar, but he couldn't place her. And he was certain he hadn't met the other one, the one standing with her back to him. She had waist-length black hair—something he surely would have remembered.

The second half began and Gil turned, trying hard to keep his mind where it should be—on his job. But it wasn't an easy task. The image of Coby's blond friend kept nudging at his memory. He'd seen her somewhere, but he was sure it wasn't in Coby's company.

At school! He knew her from school. But she looked a little too old to be a high school student. His brows drew together in a frown. She wasn't a teacher, either.

Glancing back up into the stands, he chewed at the inside of his lip. He watched the girl's animated face as she talked, watched the way she smiled and gestured effusively with her hands. Suddenly his memory kicked in. It was Stacey, the office secretary.

The brunette turned to the side, and Gil blinked. That couldn't be who he thought it was, could it? She swept her hair behind one ear, and Gil had to clamp his jaw to keep it from gaping open.

That was no girl. That was Lesley Tyler!

He narrowed his eyes. Lesley Tyler at a football game? Because of what he'd said in her office yesterday? he wondered. He was surprised that she'd taken him seriously. The wind ruffled her hair, drawing his attention. Long, silky straight and unbound, it was gorgeous, a shining curtain of midnight that fell to her waist, stopping just short of her belted...*jeans?*

Well, well. Would wonders never cease? Gil tilted his head, watching her and Stacey head for the stairs. As they made their ascent, his eyes were on the principal alone. It might have defied the imagination that she was at a football game, might have defied the imagination that she was wearing jeans, but it definitely *captured* his imagination the way those jeans looked on her! He'd noticed that she had great legs the first day he'd met her, but . . . it hardly seemed possible that this was the same woman—

A voice came over his headset, jolting him back to awareness. "What?"

"I said, first down, Gil! Didn't you see it?"

"Uh, yeah," he lied, returning his attention to the field. "That's . . . great."

"They've shifted right, Gil. Don't you think now's the time to run it around the left side?"

"Uh . . . right, I mean good. I'll send in the play." He did just that, then watched as the play was executed for a substantial gain. It was a damn good thing Clarke had been on the ball up in the press box. Gil rubbed at his forehead with the back of his hand. That particular opportunity could have been missed because he'd been watching the new principal.

The irony of the situation hit him and he chuckled softly. Of all the women to make him lose his concentration. . . . He wouldn't have guessed it would be his nemesis, Lesley Tyler. Lesley of the prim skirts and jackets. Lesley of the proper, pinned-up hair.

What a difference denim made.

CHAPTER THREE

GIL SHIFTED in his chair, then tugged at his tie. He cleared his throat, garnering several looks of annoyance from faculty members seated around him. A surreptitious glance to the left found Clarke as engrossed in Lesley Tyler's speech as everyone else in the small auditorium. Everyone, it seemed, but himself.

She was dressed in her school uniform, one of those skirt-and-jacket combinations, and her hair was pinned up in the style she always wore with the suits. She was discussing something that sounded important, something he probably should be listening to. But try as he might, his attention wasn't on what she had to say. It was on her, and that had been happening a lot lately.

Irritated, he tapped his pencil on the clipboard that lay in his lap, then stopped when Clarke looked over at him, his brow raised.

Sitting quietly, he told himself that noticing things wasn't so unusual. He worked with her. Just like every other teacher at Warren, he saw her frequently. But since the football game last week, when he'd seen her "out of uniform," he'd been noticing more and more about her, little things that he wouldn't normally notice about a co-worker.

Her eyes, for instance. He knew they were green, that much he had discovered when he'd first met her. But they weren't just green. What he'd missed was that they were a clear, emerald green. They were almond shaped and deep set, and the richness of her black hair enhanced their startling color.

Gil propped his chin on his palm to look up at her. He couldn't get over it. She had damn beautiful hair. Why did she feel the need to hide it with a prim, matronly style? Granted, the hairdo went perfectly with her wardrobe, but it was beyond him why any woman with hair like that would want to conceal it. Or, for that matter, wear clothes that concealed such a knockout figure.

Those jeans she'd worn to the game hadn't concealed anything. She'd been all angles and intriguing curves. He'd gotten a hint of that on the day in the field house, but her everyday dress merely suggested what her casual clothes revealed so emphatically. Not that the suits weren't nice or stylish; she coordinated them with scarfs and shoes in subtle matching shades that...

God, what was he doing? What had *she* done to him? He wasn't a man to think of a woman in poetic terms or review her wardrobe like some fashion columnist.

He shifted in his seat again, totally at a loss as to why his thoughts had been so filled with her. It wasn't as if she'd encouraged them. Hell, she didn't even smile at him. She had plenty of smiles for the other teachers, and loads of them for students, but him? Every time he saw her, a businesslike, almost forced blandness altered her expression. She wasn't impolite. Far from it. She was politeness personified, courteous to a fault. He was sure that if he looked up *cordial* in the dictionary, her name would be there.

Gil sat up straight abruptly. Had he hallucinated, or had she smiled at him just then? Lord knows it would be a first if she had. Realistically the smile had probably been aimed at the crowd in general. He brushed a hand casually through his hair just in case. Maybe she had smiled at him, was smiling even now.

Gil's thoughts were interrupted when the teachers around him began to stand. Apparently the meeting was over.

He rose with everyone else and watched Lesley intently. He watched as she closed her notebook and reached up to switch off the small microphone on the podium, watched as she left the auditorium by the side door.

In a roundabout way, he'd spent the past thirty minutes coming to terms with the fact that he was attracted to Lesley Tyler. He hadn't realized it at the time, but he recognized it now.

With recognition came the need to take the next step.

THE MAN HADN'T LISTENED to a word she'd said! With a deadly calm Lesley opened the closet door in her office. She reached for her purse and coat, then shut the door. She went to her desk and picked up her nightly stack of homework, a list of what needed to be done for tomorrow sitting on top.

Stacey poked her head around the door. "Les, I'm leaving now unless—is something wrong?"

Lesley tempered her expression. "Oh, no. Just... tired, I guess."

Stacey looked unconvinced. She moved out of the doorway, stepping into the office. "How'd the meeting go?"

Lesley shrugged with as much nonchalance as she could muster. "As well as could be expected."

"No fuming coaches or enraged band directors? Crazed drama teachers?"

"No, quite the contrary, actually. There weren't any objections from the athletic department, and I, uh, I couldn't tell if Mr. Sibley or Mrs. Higgins were upset or not. They... I think they were seated toward the back." Lesley turned away from Stacey and stared out the windows overlooking the student parking lot, deciding she was more comfortable with a lie than the admission that she'd been too busy watching someone else to register the band director or drama teacher's reaction to her changes.

"That's a surprise," Stacey said. "I thought all hell would break loose."

"So did I."

"Well," Stacey said, "at least you've gotten it out of the way. That ought to be a relief."

"Yes, it is."

"If there's nothing else you need, I guess I'll be heading for home. You're sure nothing's wrong?"

Lesley gave her a smile. "No. I'm fine. See you in the morning."

"Okay, see ya," Stacey said, closing the door behind her on the way out.

Damn, Lesley thought, her mind still back in the auditorium. That had been an important meeting! Still too angry to leave, she strode back to the window. She'd dreaded making that speech for a week, knowing full well that the extracurricular departments would not be pleased with her changes. She'd tried as hard as she could to keep the changes to a minimum, tried to be as fair as possible while keeping to the letter of the law.

She drummed her fingers on the windowsill, watching a group of students as they made their way to their cars. In this football-manic town, one particular department head's job just might *depend* on how she'd augmented school policy. Several of her changes were guaranteed to make it difficult for Fielden.

And he hadn't even listened!

He'd squirmed in his chair and fiddled with a pencil and clipboard. He'd even stared off into space! She'd worried over decisions for an entire week, *and he'd been bored.*

"Do you have a minute?"

Startled, Lesley turned. "Yes, Coach. I have some time," she said, wondering as she had in the meeting why he was wearing a suit today. She also wondered about his furrowed brow and the determined set of his jaw. Was it possible that he'd been paying more attention to her speech than she'd given him credit for? "Have a seat, Coach. I assume this concerns my changes." She arranged her coat over the back of her chair, then sat behind her desk. "If we're going to have problems over them, perhaps it's best we go over them now," she said.

"Problems?" Gil eased into a chair facing her, wondering if this was such a good idea after all. When he'd opened her door, he'd half expected to find her already gone. When he'd felt an unnamed emotion stir at the sight of her standing and staring out the window, he'd felt glad that he'd decided to come. But, he thought as he watched her slide her glasses on and pull a notebook from a drawer—the same notebook she'd read from in that auditorium—if she thought he was here to discuss a meeting he knew nothing about, she was in for a surprise.

"Considering our history, I'm positive we're not entirely in agreement over what I said today."

Her cool tone matched the look in her eyes. He no longer had the problem he'd had in the auditorium; now he was sitting close enough to see that she was looking directly at him. He just didn't like the way she was doing it.

"Our history, Lesley?" He crossed his legs at the ankle and leaned back in his chair. "We've known each other the sum total of a week and a half."

Lesley looked up from the notebook, feeling inexplicably disquieted by his use of her first name. He looked different in a suit, she thought. Different, but still wholly masculine. His jaw was square, his features strong. Swallowing, she pulled her gaze back to her notes. "Be that as it may, Coach, we seem to have some basic differences of opinion about this law."

"Gil."

Her eyes lifted. "Pardon?"

"Coach is the occupation. My name is Gil."

"Oh. Well, Gil, then. Which of my changes did you want to talk about? We can go over . . ." Her words trailed off when he rose from his chair and took up her former post at the window. "Gil?"

He turned back to her, a cocky grin lifting one side of his mouth. "You don't like me, do you?"

"Don't like you?"

He propped a hand on his hip, pulling the jacket back to reveal a dressy cordovan belt slipped through the loops of his gray slacks. "As in, you don't like what I do or say or the way that I look or act."

Her eyes widened. "Oh, no, I don't . . . I mean . . . is this because of what I said to you that first day?"

"No, it's not just that. Granted, our first meeting wasn't the friendliest in the world, but I wouldn't call it the worst in the world, either. Since then, though, you've treated me pretty coolly."

Lesley lowered her gaze to the desktop. She was all too aware of the way she treated him. After that night at the game when she'd lost all dignity by staring at the man like a Peeping Tom with the binoculars, she'd decided that the best defense against her attraction was indifference. She'd attempted to deal with him impersonally ever since. She hadn't thought that he'd noticed it, however, and was amazed that he cared one way or the other.

"I'm sorry if I've seemed rude, Coach, but I—"

"You see. You just did it again."

"Did what?"

"You called me Coach. You call every other teacher in the building by name." He gave a mirthless laugh.

"And how come you can't even spare a smile when we see each other in the hall? You don't seem to have any trouble smiling at everyone else."

"I..." She was so confused she didn't even know where to look. Her eyes traveled quickly from the expression of annoyance on his handsome face to the hand still resting on his hip, then back to the desktop. "A smile?" she said weakly.

"Among other things." He stepped forward, bracing his hands on the edge of her desk, then leaned dangerously close.

"Listen, I know I must have seemed impatient the first time we met. And the next day in your office, too," he said. "My only excuse is that I've got a team that has a long way to go in a short period of time. But I'm not always like that. In fact, I'm not such a bad guy. People seem to like me. At least they don't mind talking to me, and some even smile at me once in a while."

"Maybe I have been rude," she said quietly. "And I apologize. But I've been so wrapped up in all the details of this new job. I'm sure you understand."

"Maybe I could if you acted the same way with everyone else."

"I guess, to be quite honest, I was rather put out with you that first day." She toyed with the corner of a page in the notebook. "It's understandable that you'd want that behind us. After all, if we're to maintain any kind of good working relationship, a strained atmosphere isn't conducive—"

"Good working relationship," he muttered, then pushed himself away from the desk. He shoved his hands into his pockets and moved back to his seat. Lesley watched in confused silence as he studied the arm of the chair with great interest, seeming to come to some sort of decision. Her heart picked up speed when he came striding back.

"I want more."

Lesley's throat went dry. "What . . . did you say?"

"I said—"

"Ms. Tyler," came a strident voice, interrupting them. Lesley's gaze jerked to the doorway, where she saw an angry Mr. Sibley. "I think you and I need to talk."

She closed her eyes and placed her fingers against her temple. "Mr. Sibley, as you can see, I'm rather busy at the moment." It took every bit of patience she could summon to keep her voice calm. "I'll have time to discuss whatever you want during your free period tomorrow morning."

"Oh, no," he said, rhythmically tapping his palm with a baton. "That won't cut it. My band goes to marching contest in four short weeks. Four! And I won't have all this nonsense about new tutorials and detentions affecting that!" He glared, arching his brow in Gil's direction. "You and I both know that law is more for his football team than for my band!"

Gil rolled his eyes and walked back to the window, his hands at his waist.

"Mr. Sibley, please," Lesley said, her gaze still on the coach as he stared out her window. "I, uh, I'm sure you want to extend Mr. Fielden the courtesy of allowing him to finish what he started."

At that, Gil moved away from the window. "Look, if Sibley insists on giving you a piece of his mind," he said, his words clipped, "then don't let me stop him." He walked to the door.

"No, wait," she said a little too quickly, then glanced at Sibley and sat straighter, trying to recapture her decorum. "I'll...be back in a moment." She edged around her desk and followed Gil outside the office, catching him by the sleeve. "You can't just leave," she whispered urgently.

Gil's gaze dropped to her hand and Lesley stepped back, releasing her hold on his jacket. He lifted a brow.

"I want an explanation."

"Yeah?" Gil sighed, glanced down at the toes of his shoes, then looked back up at her. "Well, I guess I need to think of one."

Boy, did he need to think of one.

"'SOME' ASSEMBLY REQUIRED," Lesley muttered, picking up the instruction sheet and scanning its confused diagram for the fifth time. Rubbing the back of her neck, she cursed the pieces of unassembled bookcase that littered her floor. The hour she'd spent trying to put this thing together had been a real pain in the neck—literally.

She'd needed something to concentrate on, something that would keep her from thinking about this afternoon. It hadn't worked. Between the confusing instructions and looking for unidentifiable parts, she'd found her mind filled with thoughts of the unsettling events of the day.

An unproductive train of thought, she scolded herself. There was no sense rehashing any of it. She'd made her decisions, and although she was more than willing to discuss viable alternatives, she would not throw her plans out the window for anyone. Not even a hysterical Mr. Sibley.

Lesley rolled her eyes, picturing again his mottled complexion as he'd ranted and raved. She'd worried that he might go into cardiac arrest right there in her office. And all because he wasn't able to hold extra marching practices after school for the next month. The man was nothing if not intense.

Intense.

It was a word she wouldn't have associated with her other after-school visitor, except maybe in connection with football. But Gil Fielden's strange statement, and the look in his eyes when he'd made it, had changed her mind.

I want more.

Lesley bit her lip at the realization that he'd popped back into her mind so easily. If the truth were known, Mr. Sibley's hysterics had had little to do with her need for a project. Her true motive had been to stop the incessant replaying of that moment with Gil. She'd wanted to put an end to dwelling on the glitter of intent in his eyes when he'd said it, and the sound of his voice, low pitched and determined.

Lesley's confused thoughts pitched back and forth once more as she wondered what he'd meant, then wondered if it was wise to even want to know. She must have misunderstood him. He couldn't have meant what she'd thought he'd meant. Surely there was an explanation. But then, he himself had said he'd need to think of one.

The ring of the telephone was a welcome interruption, and Lesley rose from the floor, making her way to the phone in the kitchen. She smiled in anticipation as she lifted the receiver. It would be Linda, she thought, glancing at the call chart next to the phone. Though her sisters had teased her good-naturedly about the chart of scheduled phone calls she'd presented them before moving, they had agreed with the logic behind it. What with Linda's studies, Gayle traveling hither and yon and Kelly's new business, the chart would bring some organization into their hectic lives. "Hello."

"Hi, it's me, right on schedule."

"Hi, you." Lesley pictured her little sister in a classic Linda pose, flopped down on the bed in her dorm, her jean-covered legs dangling off the side. She smiled. "How's UT's newest medical genius?"

Linda laughed. "Genius was two weeks ago when I could still remember holding that Bachelor of Science diploma in my hand. I didn't know what I was getting into then."

"We'll modify your status to merely exceptional then," Lesley said, her smile growing.

"Yeah, merely exceptional, that's me. My anatomy professor might have to disagree with us before it's all over, though."

"A tough one, huh?"

"The toughest. He gets his kicks by watching the amazed reactions on med students' faces when he assigns mammoth reading assignment after mammoth reading assignment. I have a hundred and fifty pages to get through tonight. That, you understand, is in addition to all my other studies."

Lesley's worry was evident in her slight frown. On top of a full class load this semester, Linda was working a part-time job. "Honey, maybe you should think about dropping a course for now. Or better yet, reconsider my offer. Quit the part-time job and let me help. Like I told you, with my raise in salary, it won't be a financial strain for me to send you some spending money."

"No way, Les. We've been over this before. I won't accept any more money from you. You've already paid the balance of my tuition after the government grants. I mean it, the time for big-sister sacrifices has come to an end."

"Linda, it's not a sacrifice. I told you, with the raise—"

"No, I mean it. Let me do this for myself."

Lesley bit her lip, realizing she'd done it again. She had trodden on Linda's independence. All three of her sisters were grown women now—Kelly was twenty-five and owned her own travel agency, Gayle was twenty-three and a stewardess, and Linda was twenty-one and had just started med school. But it was so difficult to treat them as adults. It was difficult not to feel protective, almost impossible not to... mother them. After all, it had been her role for nearly twenty years.

"Linda, I'm sorry. I know it must frustrate you at times, but I worry—"

"You don't have to apologize. And you don't have to worry anymore. I'm handling things on my own just fine now."

On her own. Her sisters hadn't done anything without her to guide them since their mother had the nervous breakdown so many years ago. Their father, a workaholic who hadn't been the most involved parent even before his wife had "gone away," was less involved afterward. His contribution to raising them had been to hire a woman to look after the girls until Lesley became old enough to do so. She knew her sisters were capable of leading their own lives now, but it was difficult letting go after all that time.

"Hey," Linda said, "let's talk about something else. Like your social life now that you don't have the three of us hanging around your neck. Have you found a man to be miserable about yet?"

Lesley chuckled. "Not yet. But I could put that on a list. You know, bread...milk...eggs...man to be miserable about."

Linda laughed. "I think Kelly's decided Stephen is Mr. Right. She says she's in love."

Lesley frowned. "Do you think she's been dating him long enough to know that?"

"Yes, Lesley. Come on, he's an okay guy."

"I'm sure he is, it's just that—"

"Look, there's something else you don't have to worry about anymore, Les, our love lives. Just think of all the time it'll leave you to concentrate on your own."

"Very funny."

"Listen, I'd better get to those books. Sitting here staring at them isn't accomplishing anything, so I guess I'd better go."

"Yes, I guess you'd better," Lesley said with a sigh. "Listen, it was good to talk to you, kid. Take care, and if you need anything—"

"I know—call."

"Yes, right. Call. I love you. See you at Christmas."

"Okay. Love you, too. Bye, Les."

"Goodbye."

Lesley cradled the receiver, wondering for a moment if she should place a quick call to Kelly. There wasn't any harm in simply finding out more about this new boyfriend, was there? She picked up the phone, punched out the first three numbers, then decided against the call. Okay, Linda, she thought as she put down the phone, I'll try. I'll try.

But trying and doing were two different stories. It was damned difficult to completely sever her mothering instincts after all these years. And being so far away from her sisters was making it even harder.

Her doorbell sounded, and Lesley padded across the room. It was probably her next-door neighbor, Edith, she thought, remembering with a grin the way the woman had introduced herself. Her arms laden with peach preserves and back issues of the *Enquirer,* the silver-haired woman had been a delightful neighborhood representative. Lesley reached for the doorknob, happily anticipating Edith's next visit. When she opened the door, her smile froze.

CHAPTER FOUR

"COA—GIL?"

"Hi." He pushed windblown hair from his forehead. "Is this a bad time?" he asked, glancing past her into the living room.

"Uh, no. It's ... no, it's not a bad time."

"I know I should have called, but—"

"Oh, no. Really, it's ... okay." But was it? Was she ready to find out what he'd meant this afternoon? An odd sense of panic had Lesley holding the doorknob in a death grip.

"Got kind of cold on us all of a sudden, huh?" He dug his hands deep into the pockets of a disreputable-looking letterman's jacket.

"Oh, here." She opened the door wider. "I don't know where my mind is," she said, following him into the living room.

"You'll have to excuse the mess. I was trying to put this bookshelf together, and, well, as you can tell, *trying* is the operative word."

Gil began taking off his jacket, and Lesley's babbling faded into conspicuous silence. He'd changed out of the suit, she noticed, and into a sky-blue oxford shirt and dark indigo jeans that fit like a second skin. "Um . . . let me hang that up for you," she said, reaching for his jacket.

"Thanks."

Gil slipped his hands into his back pockets, hoping he'd made the right decision about this impromptu visit. After seeing that Coby had plans and he wasn't needed at home, he'd called Clarke and found out about the meeting he'd daydreamed through. Now he had two reasons for being here.

She closed the closet door and turned back to him, her hands busy smoothing strands of hair back from her face.

Gil's gaze drifted downward and he read the words staggered on three lines across the front of her T-shirt. He chuckled. "I Came, I Saw . . . I Took A Valium. Great shirt."

"Oh." Lesley plucked at the fabric self-consciously. *He* might look great in casual, knock-around clothes, but she knew it wasn't her best look. The jeans she wore should have been discarded long ago, and she'd picked the oversized T-shirt with comfort, not company, in mind.

"It . . . was a gift," she said. "When I got the job as principal here, the teachers where I worked in Austin thought it might be appropriate."

"Ah, yes," he said, nodding. "I'm no principal, but even as a department head, I've had times when the thought of taking a Valium has been at the top of my list." Like after the meeting he'd had this morning with the new superintendent, Gil thought. By the end of it, his head had been throbbing and his tie had been at the threatening-to-choke-him stage. "Know where I can get a shirt like it?"

His boyish grin brought a smile to Lesley's lips. "No. Sorry."

Silence wove a web of tension around them, and both stood in the middle of the room, at a loss for anything to say. Moments passed. Gil shifted his feet, aware of each interminable second.

Lesley worried the hem of her shirt between two fingers, experiencing a crazy urge to shatter the silence with a shout of, *Well, are you going to explain that little remark you made this afternoon, or what?*

"Um...have a seat," she said finally. She indicated a chair and took the one opposite him. "So..."

"Yeah...so..." Gil said, wondering where this case of nerves had come from. He took a deep breath. "Look, I know you must have questions about today."

Lesley's pulse quickened a fraction. "Yes, I do."

"I thought it would be best if we went over it in private...to, you know, avoid any more interruptions."

"That would...yes, probably that would be best."

Gil tapped his fingers against his knee and dropped his gaze to the floor. "I...I disagree with the fact that we need more stringent measures as far as no-pass, no-play is concerned, but I think, well...I think you did an admirable job on those proposals nonetheless."

Proposals?

He was here to talk about that damned faculty meeting? What had happened to *I want more?* What about all that you-never-smile-at-me stuff?

This afternoon, in her office, she hadn't been able to get a word out of him on the subject of the law. Now that he had her completely crazed over something else entirely, she couldn't believe that he wanted to discuss no-pass, no-play.

She drummed her fingers on the chair. Okay, they would talk about the meeting. They would discuss it to his heart's content. But he wouldn't escape this house until she had the explanation he'd promised. "I'll just get my notes," she said, and left for the bedroom where she'd put them.

Gil shut his eyes. What in the world was wrong with him? He'd been so anxious to see Lesley, anxious to take that next step. But now, for some reason, he was as nervous as a kid on his first date.

He frowned, glancing around the room abstractedly. Her house was another indication that there was more to Lesley Tyler than the tailored clothes and her cool-as-a-cucumber exterior. From the outside it was similar to every other bungalow on the block—small, plain brick and frame, neatly landscaped but unspectacular. Nothing out of the ordinary. The inside, though, was vividly colorful. The furniture was modern and vibrant, and there were several vases of silk flowers of varying hues placed artfully on low tables. Oriental rugs overlay burnished hardwood floors, and the walls were strategically covered with tasteful paintings.

He edged forward, reaching for one of the laminated boards that lay at his feet, needing to occupy his mind. He quickly found the part that connected with it and pieced them together.

Lesley walked back into the living room, her notebook open in one hand. She peered over the top of her glasses at him, her annoyance momentarily forgotten. "I don't believe it! You mean there are two pieces to that thing that actually go together?"

"Yeah." He lowered himself to the floor and grabbed another section. "I put one of these things together for my daughter not too long ago. Do you mind if I try?"

"Be my guest," she said, taking his place on the chair. She watched him connect two more shelves and shook her head in amazement. "I thought they might have put the wrong instruction sheet in the box. Nothing seemed to fit."

"Don't feel bad—I've had practice. I was just as confused as you when I put Coby's together."

Probably not quite as confused, Lesley thought, being completely honest with herself. Her distraction over his cryptic comments that afternoon had definitely added to her confusion. "I, uh, spoke with Coby last weekend at the football game."

Gil's hands stilled on the shelving. "Oh, you did?"

"Yes. She seems like a delightful girl."

He set a finished portion on its feet. "Well, I won't argue with that."

Lesley grinned. "She's what, seventeen, eighteen?" she asked, setting the notebook on an end table.

"Seventeen." He aimed a smile at her over his shoulder. "I was a child bride."

He had a beautiful smile, Lesley thought. From the mischievous twinkle in his blue eyes to the dimple coaxed from hiding on one side of his mouth, it was by far the most infectious masculine smile she'd ever witnessed.

She smiled back.

He should badger her for a smile more often, Gil thought. Hers was beautiful. And in the span of a heartbeat he understood why he'd been nervous earlier, understood why he had avoided what he'd come here to say. Something about Lesley called out to him and made him crave her smiles. It left him feeling frustrated when she talked about the importance of a smooth working relationship just as he was beginning to feel an inward push for something more. Part of it was physical, he'd admit to that. But he would be a fool not to admit there was something else that drew him to her. Mere physical attraction had never made him feel this strongly about a woman.

Which meant he'd need to go slow.

He thought about the other subject he'd come here to discuss, the no-pass, no-play law. Just how much of a stumbling block would it be for them? Considering the strength of what he'd felt when she smiled at him, he knew he was going to make sure that it *wouldn't* get in the way.

Slow and sure—hardly his usual way when it came to women. But then, what he was feeling was very *un*-usual.

He cleared his throat and picked up the threads of their conversation. "Actually I was too young—*we* were too young," he said, turning back to his task. "Ceil—Coby's mother—and I were married right out of college, then Coby came along the next year. We were babies raising a baby.''

Lesley nodded, understanding what that felt like.

''And the fact that Ceil and I were the mismatch of the century didn't help matters. Ours was a classic case of falling in love with love rather than falling in love with each other. In time we accepted it and parted friends, which was important where Coby's concerned.''

Lesley shouldn't have been surprised that he would disclose such a personal detail about himself and his ex-wife to someone he hardly knew. After all, from what little she'd seen of him, he wasn't exactly one to hold back. Since the information had been provided, however, her mind couldn't help but play wondering games. Had he fallen in love since the divorce—not in love with love, but truly in love with someone? Had he considered marrying again?

''Stacey tells me that Coby lives with you now. Single parenthood must be quite a challenge,'' she said.

''Well, it's not as easy as I thought it would be, that's for sure.''

''Time-consuming?''

''Oh, yeah, but that's not a big problem.'' He stopped for a moment to appraise his work. ''I wanted more time with Coby. I mean, she's my daughter, right? But even living in the same town as her and her mom all those years, I never had the chance to really get to know her like I'm doing now. Those weekend visits were just that. Visits.''

Lesley was glad for Coby's sake that Gil's idea of parenting was different from her own father's. She took off her glasses, setting them aside, then tucked one foot beneath her thigh on the chair.

Catching sight of a bolt that Gil was searching for, she leaned forward and pointed. "It's right there by your shoe," she said.

"Thanks." He grabbed the bolt, put it into place and tightened it, then glanced up with a thoughtful look. "You know what the hardest part is?" he asked.

"The hardest part of what?"

"Of being a single parent. I'm discovering I have to be the bad guy now. The one who says no when Coby has her heart set on the wrong thing, the one who sets curfews." He rose up on his knees and faced her, propping one hand on his waist. "I *hate* being the bad guy."

Lesley couldn't help but smile. The big, tough football coach looked absolutely forlorn at the thought of having to be strict with Coby. "Aw, are you an old softy, Dad?"

"Hey, watch who you're calling old. Remember I was—"

"Oh, I remember," she said with a short laugh. "You were a child bride."

"You have a knock-out smile, you know that?"

For a moment Lesley thought she might not have heard him correctly. But she had. It was as clearly stated as his "I want more" had been earlier this afternoon. Her smile turning self-conscious, she said, "Well, I . . . thank you, Gil."

"You're welcome."

Silence again. If she'd thought it awkward before, that had been nothing compared to this. She pulled her gaze from his, wondering if something was wrong with the thermostat. The room temperature suddenly felt several degrees higher. "It, um . . . it looks like you're almost done," she said, nodding toward the shelving unit.

"Yes." He gave the shelves a cursory glance. "I'm finished."

"I . . . can't thank you enough. I'm so mechanically inept and I—"

"More than glad to do it," he said.

"Well, then . . ." She reached for her glasses and notebook as if reaching for a lifeline. "We can discuss that meeting now."

Coward, her mind accused. This would be the perfect time to demand explanations. He'd finished the bookshelves, and they were more relaxed with each other. At least more so than they'd been when he'd first arrived. Still, she rifled through pages, stopping when she found the place she needed.

"Ah, yes. The meeting." Gil eased back to the floor, this time facing her. Though it would be more of a distraction this way—watching her as they talked—it was necessary. He wanted to judge her reactions to what he had to say, wanted to understand just how big a stumbling block he'd have to tackle with their opposite stands on no-pass, no-play. "Okay, first of all, I want you to know that I respect all the work you put into those proposals you talked about today. You obviously spent a good deal of time on them."

"But you have objections, of course." She closed the notebook.

Gil leaned back, supporting his weight on his arms. A wry grin pulled at the corners of his mouth. "Considering the fact that I don't think the law should have been passed in the first place, yeah, I do. Mind you, I once said that out loud to a newspaper reporter, and ended up in print sounding like some kind of sports fanatic." He gave a short, rueful laugh. "He stopped just short of saying that I felt the primary reason for school is to fill up those hours of the day before afternoon football, basketball or track practice. Which is ridiculous.

"But for what it's worth, I'll give you the same speech I gave him the day that bill was passed." He took an exaggerated deep breath. "Are you ready?"

Lesley chuckled and nodded, saying, "Ready."

"Okay. Here it is. Surprise of the century: I don't happen to think that my department is any less significant than the academic ones. Team sports are a vital part of a well-rounded curriculum. The way I see it, math and English and history prepare a student academically, but what about socially? How about the importance of experiencing teamwork or learning to lose gracefully? Sports programs don't just develop muscles, you know. They help develop social skills, rules of fair play, even values. Many of the lessons learned on a playing field are useful in later life. Believe me, I know.

"My grades were—" he raised a hand in a so-so gesture "—well, let's just say I got by. Barely. But in sports? I guess you could say that I had a natural talent."

"So, it was a source of self-esteem for you, then?"

"Right. And I think every kid needs that," he said. "Not everyone can be a scholar—I'm certainly not. But people should take pride in their accomplishments no matter what they are. But, in my opinion, the Texas legislature is punishing athletes by denying them what they do best if they fail at something else." His gaze locked with hers, Gil waited for what she had to say.

Lesley sat back in her chair. She slid off her glasses and held them in her hand.

"Well, I can certainly understand why you feel the way you do. And I have to admit that you have a point. One that I'd never considered before."

Good, Gil thought, his tension beginning to ease. Understanding was the first step to putting this issue behind them.

"As you might expect, however, I don't see it quite the same way you do."

One side of his mouth lifted. "Are you agreeing with the reporter I mentioned?"

She shook her head. "No. But I don't think the legislature had punishment in mind when they passed House Bill 72. I don't think they had in mind the particular type of student you spoke about, either. Ready for *my* speech on the subject?"

"Ready, Madame Principal."

"Okay. In my opinion the law is a deterrent. The student the legislation is directed at is the one who *is* capable of making the grade but, for whatever reasons, isn't doing so."

"And you feel that sports is one of those reasons?"

"Not sports specifically. Extracurricular activities in general. I feel that students sometimes get their priorities rearranged. A prime example would be Devin Michaels."

"True, but I'm still not convinced that you didn't jump the gun in his case. He hasn't made a failing grade yet."

"The likelihood is there, Gil. And that's what this law is all about. Making sure *before the fact* that students aren't overextending themselves or that they haven't gotten their priorities mixed up."

"Okay...there." Gil sat up straight. "What you just said. That's my biggest complaint with this whole business. The phrase 'getting their priorities mixed up' is what I object to most. Why is it that educators don't consider sports as a viable career choice? I mean, we live in a country, no, a world, that's fitness and sports crazy. It's a big business these days. There are so many professional opportunities for young people who are sports oriented, yet the educational system in this state wants to ignore that fact completely."

He leaned forward, propping his palms on his knees. His eyes, still trained on Lesley's, were snapping with enthusiasm for his side of the debate.

"And since you used Devin Michaels as an example," he said, "I'll use him, too. He's a superior athlete who has a chance for a brilliant career in pro ball. If the state of Texas has its way, he could be sidelined and have his chances diminished severely. One bad grade—and haven't we all made a bad grade or two in our time?—and it could affect whether or not the right colleges want to recruit him. Which in turn could possibly affect his career as a pro.''

Lesley nodded and leaned forward as he had. "Okay, I can't argue that, but I can bring up this point. What happens if a career in pro football falls through for Devin? What if he's hurt, say in his last year of college? He's going to have a difficult time of it if we educators have allowed him to pass through the system with poor grades because he has a chance at a pro career. Think of the disservice we'll have done him. The state of Texas has. It's trying to deal with it the only way it knows how—by demanding higher standards at the secondary school level and deterring students from ignoring the academic side of their education."

Gil knew two things. One, he disagreed with just about everything she'd said. Two, he was really enjoying himself and could cheerfully continue their friendly argument for the rest of the night were it not for the fact that they would both eventually need some sleep. It certainly made a difference who your sparring partner was. He frowned, remembering the discussion he'd had this morning with the new superintendent on no-pass, no-play. Enjoyment hadn't figured in that conversation. Not by a long shot.

"Gil..."

"What?"

"I'm ready for your next point."

"Oh. Right." He pushed thoughts of the polite lecture he'd received this morning to the back of his mind, focusing instead on her last comment. "The only thing I can say about that last scenario you mentioned is that it could, has, happened. Injuries are an occupational hazard. If we're going to speculate, though, the law of averages says there's a better chance that it won't happen.''

His look bordering on cocky, he leaned back on his elbows again.

Lesley shook her head, smiling. "We could toss this issue back and forth for days, you know.''

"Mmm-hmm. And I also know that it won't change a thing.''

"Right. The law's the law.''

"How well I know it. I talked with the superintendent today. He's pretty adamant about Warren faculty following your new strictures to the letter.''

"Oh. Yes, I know.'' Lesley didn't know why the word stricture suddenly sounded so harsh. Being honest with herself, that's what her new proposals were, restraints for a situation that had gotten out of hand. "But, as I said in the meeting, I welcome any alternatives that you or the other faculty members might have....''

Gil's look was wry. "Do you welcome the suggestion that we do away with some of the proposals altogether?''

"Well, no. I'm sorry, but that's impossible. It was my job to straighten out the situation.''

"Right.''

Lesley studied his expression. While he didn't appear overjoyed, he wasn't angry, either.

"Well, at least I got my two cents in.''

"And?''

"And that's it. There's not a whole lot more I can say, is there?"

"Well, no. But..."

"But what? This is the way it's going to be, and I'm going to have to live with it. I'll need to adjust some of my practice schedules, have a good long talk with my players about keeping their grades up and keeping their butts out of D-hall, and... live with it."

Well, good then, she thought. But she wasn't completely convinced that there wasn't going to be trouble over this somewhere down the line. "We're going to have more battles about all this sooner or later, aren't we?"

"Yes. I'm betting we will. But I want it understood now that it has nothing to do with us personally."

Personally. As in "I want more?"

"Well, now that you've heard my speech—" he rose and patted the top of the bookshelf on his way to get his jacket "—and got some slave labor out of the deal to boot..."

"You're leaving?"

Gil stared into the dark closet, hoping that had been a note of regret he'd heard in her words. Now that they had the discussion of no-pass, no-play behind them, he'd like nothing better than to stay longer, but wisdom overruled impulsiveness. Hadn't he told himself that he'd need to go slow with Lesley? "Yeah. Those 7:00 a.m. practices come awfully early," he told her.

"Oh. Yes, of course." She glanced down at her notebook then back up again, watching him slide his arm into the leather sleeves of his jacket. Damn, there was nothing to do but come right out and ask.

"Wait a minute." She got off the chair and took a step forward, then grimaced. She stopped, teetering on one foot.

"What's wrong?" Gil came forward and offered her an arm. "Did you step on something?"

"No. My foot's asleep."

"Good. I thought you might've hurt your foot on a leftover screw the master carpenter here could've missed."

She gave a short laugh, then winced a bit at the pins-and-needles sensation.

"Here. Hold on to my shoulder." Gil went down on one knee beside her and encircled her foot with his hands, massaging it gently. Noticing the little black Scottie dogs that ringed the ankle of her socks, he smiled to himself. "Love the socks, Tyler."

"Thanks," she said, "that's helping. And thanks... about the socks, I mean."

He lingered over the massage, careful to keep the pressure light. "How's that? Better?"

She nodded.

"You know, I hate it when my foot falls asleep," he said glancing up at her with a crooked grin. "Then it's awake all night."

She laughed, then jerked slightly at the renewed tingling when her foot touched the floor. "Oh, you!" She shot him a look of mock anger along with a punch on the arm. "I don't know why I'm laughing at you. You come over here wanting to talk about proposals you wouldn't discuss this afternoon to save your soul...which doesn't make sense, because there wasn't anything to discuss. As you said, there's nothing that can be done about it anyway." She shook her head. "Honestly! Do you moonlight as one of those bookcase instruction-sheet writers? And what about this afternoon? I thought you were going to explain...."

Her eyes met his, and she released her hold on his shoulder. "I...was curious about what you'd...about what you'd said."

Her gaze dropped and she stepped back. If her glasses had been within reach, Gil thought, she would put them on again. She seemed to use them as some sort of defense mechanism. He'd seen the gesture enough tonight to recognize it. And, he thought as he rose from his crouching position, he wanted to see the last of that gesture after tonight.

He touched her shoulder, and she returned her gaze to his. Slow was one thing, he decided, but a snail's pace was a whole other story. He took a deep breath, and, lowering his head, he touched his lips to hers.

He kept the kiss light, a soft, gentle savoring. His hand rose to her cheek, then slid into her hair. Moments passed, moments that dulled Lesley's shock and left her hands clenching his jacket sleeves. He allowed himself another moment to enjoy her warmth and feel, then lifted his head to meet her stunned gaze.

"I want more," he said for the second time that day.

CHAPTER FIVE

COBY GRABBED the two cans of cola she'd been searching for, then bumped the refrigerator door shut with her hip. She walked to the kitchen table and placed one can in front of Devin, then sat in the chair across from him, folding her legs Indian-style on the seat. "I can't stand the suspense any longer," she said, popping the top on her soft drink and taking a sip. "What did you get on those two assignments?"

"Well, I didn't make A's like you thought I would."

Coby sat down her can. "I can't believe that! You worked so hard on those papers. Mrs. Quinn must really have it in for you."

Devin tipped back his chair to balance on two legs. "Nah, not really. She had to take points off because I handed them in so late. Otherwise they would have been A's, she said."

"Oh. No wonder." Coby took another drink and reached for her drama script on the stack of books in front of her. "Well, since your next paper will be on time, it'll be A material, no sweat."

"Yeah, no sweat." Devin set his chair back on all four legs and slid his script forward. When he reached over, covering her hand with his, Coby glanced up.

"Listen, thanks for what you're doing, Coby. You and I both know that anything I turn in wouldn't be A material without your help. You don't have to do it, and well . . . thanks."

"Oh, hey, it's no prob," she said with a smile. "Since you decided to stay in football and still keep drama on your schedule, you'll need some extra help. I don't mind being the one to give it."

And she meant it. She would never have to think twice about helping Devin. As she'd told her dad, she and Devin had always been buddies. They'd lived next door to each other ever since her mom and dad had divorced when Coby was a baby. She was certain Devin would do the same for her if the situation was reversed. Besides, she felt responsible. She had encouraged his interest in drama, the reason he'd been late for those assignments in the first place.

Devin gave her hand a squeeze and returned her smile. It was the smile her girlfriend Susan had dubbed "simply irresistible," after the title of one of their favorite Robert Palmer songs.

Simply irresistible.

There was no arguing that, Coby thought, slipping her hand from his and turning back to the script. And there was no arguing the fact that Devin wanted their buddy status to change. Last night he'd asked her to go with him to the Get Acquainted dance this coming weekend. While that in itself might not mean that he was interested in her as more than a friend and study partner, the fact that he'd almost kissed her last night did.

Her thoughts backtracked to that moment. They'd finished studying for the night, and Coby had walked Devin to his car. One minute they'd been talking about the play, and the next Devin had surprised her by taking her hand and asking her to go with him to the dance. She'd accepted, then he had leaned back against his car and gently tugged her along with him. There had been only seconds for her startled senses to realize, Whoa, he's going to kiss me! before he'd slanted his head, lowered his mouth to hers and . . .

And that was when the headlights of her father's old Mustang had swept across them as he'd pulled into the parking space beside Devin's car. That was when Devin had jerked up his head and dropped her hand as if it were loot from a bank robbery and her father were the police.

She glanced up at him and, catching the thoughtful expression on his face, wondered if he too was remembering the "almost kiss." "Is, um, something wrong, Devin?"

His gaze jerked to hers. "No. Just . . . thinking."

"Oh." She was dying to know. Dying to ask. Was his mind on last night, too? But she couldn't bring herself to form the question. Somehow, even though he hadn't actually succeeded in kissing her, his intent alone had been enough to make things between them feel different now. She wasn't as comfortable, didn't feel the same ease around Devin now that he was a potential boyfriend. "Are you thinking about the play?" she asked.

He didn't answer immediately. His eyes lowered to her mouth, and Coby tensed. She waited, wondering if he would pursue the topic that she'd avoided.

He didn't.

"Yeah," he said, looking away. "I was thinking about the play."

"Oh. Well, if you're nervous about it, there's no need to be. You're terrific!"

"I don't know about that. You really think so?"

"Well, sure. Don't you? I mean, Mrs. Higgins told you how well you did today, didn't she?"

"Yes, but... you think she really meant it?" He laughed, shaking his head. "This'll probably sound weird, but I guess I'm not used to the way things are done in that class yet. It's not like football, where you get more attention for doing something wrong than when you do it right."

Coby frowned. She had sat in on some of her dad's practices, both at Warren High and when he'd coached at the junior high school in town, and it would have been difficult not to notice all the shouting that had gone on. But then, she'd heard that Mr. Sibley, the band director, was worse than her dad when it came to losing his cool. Still, it was kind of hard to believe her dad could be a tough teacher; he was such a teddy bear with her. "Is my dad pretty rough on you guys?"

"Who, Coach? Nah."

"But you said..."

"Fielden—I mean, your dad—he's okay. It's just different in sports than other things. You don't expect the coaches to be nice, you know?"

"Why not? I don't see why they can't coach football and be decent at the same time."

Devin chuckled. "Coby, football's a rough game. Your dad's not a monster or anything, but coaches can't be wimps, either. Don't you think it would be kind of ridiculous for him to ask us nicely to watch out for those two-hundred-pound linesmen who want to pulverize us into dog food? Come on."

"Oh, gross. Pulverize you into dog food? Does he really say things like that?"

"Actually, that's pretty tame compared to what your dad says. All coaches talk that way. We don't think anything of it, though, because they're telling it like it is. Those linesmen really do want to put you out of commission."

"I don't get why anyone would want to play football then."

He shrugged. "It's not so bad."

"Not bad? That's a pretty unenthusiastic way of describing your future career. You still want to play pro football, don't you?"

"Well, sure. The pay's great, and several colleges are wanting to sign me, so I'd be a fool not to want to, right?"

Right, Coby thought. But from the way he was talking, she wondered who he was trying to convince, her or himself. "What I asked was if you *wanted* to play, not if it was the right career choice or if the pay was good."

"Well, right now might not be the best time to ask me if I want to play in the pros." He sighed deeply.

"My parents are probably right. It's just a phase I'm going through or something."

"A phase?"

"Yeah. I'm sorta tired of playing ball."

Coby was surprised. Devin? Tired of playing football?

Devin looked up from the pencil he'd been rolling on the table beneath his flattened palm. "A shock, huh?"

"Well, sort of."

"I know. I once heard someone say, 'You know Michaels, don't you? He plays football.' It's who I am."

"It's not who you are, Devin, it's something you do."

"Whatever. Anyway, I know I'll get over it. I have a cousin who's going through the same thing right now. We think it might be because we're seniors this year and feel kind of itchy to get on to the next stage. I introduced you to Todd Owens, didn't I?"

"Yes."

"He's played trumpet in the band as long as I've played football, ever since junior high. He made first chair Texas All-State last year and he was only a junior, which is a pretty big accomplishment. So he's been getting all these letters from places like Texas Tech and UT, offering him scholarships if he'll major in music. But he doesn't know if he'll take those offers. He told me that he's burned out, tired of devoting all his time and energy to music. And that's sort of the way I've been feeling, too."

"I can understand that."

"But, it's like I told Todd. We'll get over it."

Coby thought about that. What he said made sense in a way. Being tired of something now didn't mean you'd be tired of it forever. Still… "What if you don't get over it, Devin?"

"I *will* get over it. Todd will, too. We have too much invested in music and sports. We'd be crazy not to take scholarship offers seriously."

Coby reached over and stilled the hand that was now tapping an erratic rhythm with a pencil. "Or maybe you'd both be crazy if you did take the offers seriously. Maybe Todd's right. If you're already burned out, what's going to happen after four more years of football?"

"Nothing's going to happen, Coby, because it's just a passing phase. Like my Dad says, I *will* get over it," he said in a voice that told her his commitment to sports was firm.

But the look in his eyes didn't match the tone in his voice. Coby wondered if it was *his* convictions that were so firm or other people's. Like his parents, or the colleges that were hot to sign him. Or even her father, his coach.

Would a friend keep her nose out of it? Coby wondered. Or should she dog him about it until he realized that he needed to listen to his heart, not everyone else's plans for him.

This friend, she decided, would be here to listen, when and if he needed to discuss it any further. She gave him a smile. "You're probably right. But hey, you've got a whole year to think it over. A lot can happen in a year."

His expression was still too serious, so she tried for a lighter note by taking the pencil from his hand and bringing it to her mouth like a cigarette in a holder. "Just think, Ed McMahon could call us tomorrow to say we've won that sweepstakes." She took a drag of her imaginary cigarette and gave him a lofty look. "We'll be rich, we'll drop out, we'll be in one of those stupid commercials."

Humor did the trick. Devin laughed. "Open that drama script, woman. We're going to need some acting skills. I don't mind getting all that money, I just don't want to look like the geek of all time on national television."

Coby did as he instructed, her giggles mingling with his laughter. She heard her father's footsteps coming down the stairs of their small apartment and glanced up at Devin. He'd heard, too. She grinned at the almost comical way Devin's laughter ceased abruptly.

Waiting until Gil was just outside the kitchen doorway, she said, "Parent alert, parent alert! Quick, stop enjoying yourself or he'll think we're well adjusted."

Gil walked into the room, stopping to plant a kiss on Coby's upturned cheek. "You," he said, standing back and pointing a finger at her, "are a well-adjusted menace, Kidrock."

Then, to Devin, he said, "How're you doin', Michaels?"

"Great, Coach. You?"

"The same," he said over his shoulder as he made his way to the refrigerator. "Coby, where's the—"

"It's on the first shelf behind the catsup."

"Thanks." He closed the refrigerator, then placed the bottle of fruit juice he'd asked Coby about in the duffel slung over his arm.

"When will you be back from the gym?" Coby asked.

Gil checked his watch. "It's seven now, so count on me at about eight-thirty."

"Okay. See you then."

"Yeah," he said, striding out of the kitchen. "Get lots of *studying* done."

The sound of the front door closing signaled her father's departure, and Coby glanced up at Devin. His eyes crinkled at the corners and there was a grin on his lips.

"Kidrock?" he asked, like the cocky jock he was.

WHAT WAS HE so worried about? What could happen in an hour and a half?

Gil downshifted and took the corner at the end of his street, not liking how many things came to mind in answer to that question. Lots of things could happen, too many things, things he didn't want to think about.

He couldn't help himself. He thought about Coby mentioning that she noticed boys so much more these days. Boys in general, but Devin Michaels in particular, apparently. He thought about driving up last night and seeing them standing next to Michaels's car, not a good quarter inch of air separating them. What he thought about most was turning his car around and heading back to the apartment, skipping his every-other-night workout at the gym.

On the heels of that, he remembered telling Coby how important trust was between parents and kids. Whether he liked it or not, that was a two-way street.

No doubt about it, this being the parent of an almost-eighteen-year-old girl—and she was still just a girl—was a trickier proposition than he'd imagined it would be. The phrase "damned if you do, damned if you don't" came whizzing to mind.

Of course, he knew what he wanted to do. He wanted to go home and sit outside that kitchen with a drinking glass to the wall.

Intellectually he understood that she'd hit the age where all this noticing boys and raging hormones stuff was normal. Hell, he wasn't so old that he didn't remember what it was like to be eighteen years old. But still, protective instincts died hard. Especially when it was just as easy to remember Coby as a four-year-old who used to place her little feet on top of his and plead, "Dance me around Daddy, dance me around." He'd dubbed her Kid Rock and Roll, Kidrock for short.

She was too grown-up to be his Kidrock now. And just because he wanted to protect her didn't mean it was in his power to do so. He couldn't shove her into a convent any more than he could monitor her conversation through kitchen walls.

But she was a responsible teenager, Gil reminded himself. She'd given him and Ceil every reason to believe that she would handle any situation with the good sense she'd always exhibited. There was no reason to panic, or even worse, alienate her with parental strong-arm tactics.

Memories of his own adolescent years strengthened his resolve. His parents had tried to impose their will in large doses. Especially on the issue of career choice. He had resisted just as strongly as they had pushed.

Gil pulled his Mustang to a stop in the fitness center's parking lot. As always, when he thought about his family, it conjured up an image of his older brother, Greg. With the image came the pain of loss, still sharp after all this time.

His hand draped over the gearshift, Gil stared sightlessly ahead, remembering. Greg had a bright and shining future ahead of him. Every opportunity had been there simply for the taking. Even with their high expectations, their parents hadn't pressured Greg overtly; they hadn't needed to. A classic over-achiever, he had applied pressure to himself. The stress had been as self-inflicted as his death.

Gil's eyes stung with tears he refused to let form. He blinked them away and banished the memories, then got out of his car, locked it and pocketed the keys.

He walked to the health club's entrance, wondering how, even after twenty-odd years, thoughts of Greg's suicide could still manage to fill him with such a terrifying feeling of helplessness.

"THROUGH HERE is the ladies' locker room," the slender, leotard-clad fitness instructor said as she led the way into a room filled with showers, curtained dressing rooms and, of course, lockers. "Change into your tights and I'll meet you out at the front desk. We'll get you weighed and measured, then run through the ladies' weight and Nautilus machines."

"Fine. Thank you," Lesley said, and watched the girl—Tammy, or Tanya, no... Tawny—turn the corner leading out of the dressing room. She found an empty locker and placed her purse and duffel bag inside, then took her tights, leotard and shoes to a dressing stall.

The health club was certainly everything Stacey had said it would be, Lesley thought as she skimmed black stirrup-footed tights up her legs. Not only was it equipped with free weights and Nautilus machines, it boasted a walking track, aerobics center, olympic-size swimming pool, saunas, Jacuzzi and racquetball courts.

If the price was right, and Stacey had given every indication that it would be, then Lesley could mark finding a health club off her list. It was something she'd planned to get done last week. But then everything on last week's list had been pushed ahead to this week—partially because of unforeseen busywork at school, but if she were honest with herself, Lesley knew where the real blame could be placed. She knew what had kept her mind off her work and her imagination in the clouds for more than a week now.

She wouldn't rehash the situation again. She wouldn't allow herself to spend any more time thinking about Gil, about his visit that evening a week ago or his brief, albeit control-shattering, kiss. No more wondering if she should just throw common sense out the window and go with the attraction they both seemed to feel. She'd given the matter all the consideration she had time or energy for. Her mind was made up. She wouldn't speculate on the what-ifs or why-nots of an involvement with Gil Fielden, not for one second more.

And that *was* what he wanted, she thought as she adjusted the shoulder straps of her leotard. He wanted an involvement. His declaration that day in her office had meant exactly what she'd suspected. His kiss had brought that message home. The only question she'd been left with was exactly what the parameters of such a relationship would be. He could want a no-strings-attached, sex-on-every-other Tuesday sort of thing—something she'd be opposed to no matter how attracted she was to him. Or maybe he was in the market for something different. Something like love and commitment.

She was no different from any other normal human on the planet, Lesley thought as she wrestled with the shoelaces of one aerobic shoe. She'd welcome both of those things. But the few times she'd been intimately involved with men hadn't worked out because of the priorities in her life at the time. Her sisters, until now, had always come first. Until now. Now it seemed, would be the perfect time for a new relationship.

But the relationship had to be one that would work, not one that was doomed from the start. Assuming he did want more than an every-other-Tuesday affair, didn't Gil recognize conflict of interest when he saw it? Didn't he realize that her job as principal included the duty of regulating him and his coaching staff?

Lesley reached for the other shoe, recalling what her sister Kelly had advised when they'd discussed the situation over the phone two days ago. "You look at things so pragmatically, Lesley, which is fine for things such as buying a car or choosing a job,'' she'd said. ''But I wish you'd give your ironclad control a rest and go for it, for once. Think from the heart. Even better, get in tune with your hormones. You say you're attracted to this guy, so why not let that be your guide for the time being?''

Lesley sighed, leaving the curtained stall to put her street clothes in the locker.

Hormones, indeed. Just because hers had decided to make themselves known in such a deliberate fashion lately didn't mean she was going to ignore the fact that she had a brain. And what that brain told her was that this situation had all the earmarks of disaster.

Lesley checked her reflection in one of the full-length mirrors, tugged down the legs of her leotard, then exited the locker room. She was almost at the front desk when she stopped short, confronted with the knowledge that if she bought a membership to this club, she'd be seeing a lot of the man who was single-handedly responsible for her hormones' recent rebellion.

He was bent over a fountain, taking great gulps of water. The fountain, Lesley noted with no small amount of dread, was directly in line with the front desk, where she was to meet Tawny.

He'd obviously just finished working out. His blond hair was damp around the edges and his skin was ruddy from exertion. Even so, he looked wonderful. Too wonderful, Lesley decided as she swerved off her path and circled behind the desk. Spotting the doctor's office-type scales a few feet away, she hurried toward them, hoping she'd be able to catch Tawny's eye from there.

Okay, so she was being childish. She knew she couldn't go on ducking Gil forever, even if she had managed to do so for the past week at school. Still, she didn't want to talk to him here, not with him looking the way he did and her dressed in a snug, riding-up-in-back leotard.

Tawny looked her way and came striding over, tape measure in hand. "Well, here you are," the girl called out as she approached Lesley. "I was beginning to wonder where you'd gotten off to."

"I just thought I'd save some steps and come directly to the scale," Lesley said, her smile feeble.

"Okay, let's get started."

EVEN FROM THE BACK, Gil knew who those legs and long black braid belonged to. When he caught a glimpse of Lesley's profile he was not surprised. At last he had a chance to see the lady who'd been avoiding him for the past week.

After leaving her house the other night, he'd planned to give her a few days to mull things over. From what he knew of her, she was a by-the-book, look-at-things-from-every-angle sort, and he hadn't wanted to screw up by rushing her. A few days was one thing. An entire week was a whole different matter.

He had decided tomorrow would be the day he would call her, drop by her house or corner her in her office. Maybe they could go out to dinner, catch a movie, something like that. But he could alter his game plan. She was here, he was here. What better time than the present?

He took a step, then stopped, looking down at the sweatshirt and shorts he wore. It seemed the present wasn't the best time after all; he looked like hell. He should probably wait until tomorrow, or maybe call tonight after he got home.

No. He'd waited long enough. He didn't want to wait any longer.

"WAIT A MINUTE," Lesley said before Tawny could write down the weight registered on the scale. "That can't be right. Not three months ago I weighed twenty pounds less than this on my doctor's scale."

"Oh? Well, let's check it again." The girl slid the weight indicator over and inched it back again until the beam balanced. It rested on the same number as before. Tawny looked up with a shrug. "It's pretty accurate most of the time. Are you sure you haven't put on a little weight since then?"

"Yes, I'm sure." Lesley felt more than a little embarrassed. Tawny probably thought she was lying through her teeth. She wasn't. This scale was wrong. Lesley could have understood it if the scale were five or ten pounds off, but twenty? No way was she letting Tawny record that weight on her card. "That can't be what I weigh."

"I'm sure she's right, Tawny," said a familiar masculine voice just over her shoulder. Lesley closed her eyes. So much for waiting for a more appropriate time. She turned, coming face-to-face with Gil, his blue eyes twinkling and full of the devil. "This woman doesn't weigh—'' He peered over her shoulder, making a comic effort to see what the scale said.

Lesley clamped her hand over the weight indicator and sent it sliding down the beam. She folded her arms across her middle and raised an imperious, principal-like brow.

"Wait a minute, wait a minute. What do we have here?" He glanced down, and Lesley's gaze followed his. "Here's your problem. Someone's foot is pressing down the scale." He removed the toe of his gym shoe and looked up, his grin wicked, his wink mischievous.

Lesley tried but couldn't prevent the twitching of her lips.

Tawny giggled. "Come on, Coach," she said. "You're interfering with a weigh-in here."

"Yes, Coach. You're interfering," Lesley said, still struggling to keep a smile from forming.

"Gil," he said quietly and for Lesley's ears alone. "Remember?"

Lesley remembered all too well, but she kept her face impassive as Tawny readjusted the scale.

Speaking to both of them this time, Gil said, "I have to do something to make up for interrupting. How about if I finish giving Lesley the grand tour?"

"That would be great," Tawny said. "I'm the only one here to man the desk tonight, and—"

"Oh, no. That's not necessary," Lesley said quickly. "I've already had most of the grand tour. We were just going to go over the Nautilus equipment."

"On which I'm a pro," Gil put in.

"Yes," Tawny said. "Coach worked here for a while when we first opened."

"It's late. I think we can just skip the rest of the tour for tonight, Tawny," Lesley objected.

"Now, Lesley, you're not by any chance avoiding the Nautilus machines, are you?" Gil put an arm across her shoulders and propelled her in the direction of the machines, as Tawny stared after them. "We wouldn't want everyone to think that our new principal is into avoidance, would we?"

His meaning was clear. He was all too aware that she'd been evading him at every turn. And though his eyes still held a trace of amusement, she saw the other message they conveyed—he'd had enough of her runaround.

"No," she said with a sigh, "we certainly wouldn't want anyone to think that."

"Good."

Taking a look at all the Nautilus equipment spread out before her, thinking about the aerobics classes, pool and saunas, Lesley couldn't help feeling a little guilty. She realized that her job was one that required fairly long stretches of sedentary work and that she'd need some sort of exercise. She also realized that though monetary considerations had kept her from joining a health club like this one in the past, she could afford it now.

But membership to this club was a luxury. Her sister Linda, no matter how much she argued against Lesley's assistance, could use the money more. Lesley didn't want her suffering under the strain of medical school and a part-time job. Remembering the edge in

Linda's voice yesterday when she'd called to thank Lesley for the clothes she'd sent, she knew that giving her money was out; Linda's stubborn independence wouldn't allow it. But she could continue to get around that. Clothes, an occasional meal ticket at the—

"Okay, here we have a machine that works on the pulley theory." Gil squatted down and grasped a leather strap that was connected to weights by a thick steellike cord. "You strap it to your ankle and—come on, Lesley, step closer."

Step closer. All thoughts of Linda's finances fled. Gil, glancing up from the floor, his expression challenging, was all she could think about. His gym shorts were stretched tight across thighs that had obviously made good use of these bodybuilding machines.

"Come on now."

She did as he asked, wishing she'd never brought up the subject of health clubs with Stacey. Facing forward, Lesley clasped her hands tightly around the bar at chest level while he buckled her in. She watched their reflections in the mirror that went from floor to ceiling. She was acutely aware of his fingers brushing her ankle as their images converged.

"Kick backward. Yes, like that, but keep your back straight. You'll do a series of ten on each leg." He rose from the floor. "These develop this muscle here." His fingers made contact with the back of her thigh. She closed her eyes and nodded.

The scenario repeated itself as Gil explained each machine. He showed her which particular part of her anatomy would benefit from each exercise. His touches were fleeting, almost as impersonal as his explanations.

Lesley couldn't command the same level of calm. Her body heat seemed to escalate three or four degrees—partially because of physical exertion, partially because of his touch. She thought her nerves were on the verge of snapping. There were only a few more machines for him to show her. Just enough to do her in completely.

They approached the next apparatus. Gil circled around to the opposite side of a long padded bench. "Hop on," he said, patting its surface. "No, you'll need to lie facedown and hook your ankles around here." He helped her get into position, then stepped back. "Now lift with your feet, pulling toward the small of your back. Again, you'll do a series of ten."

Gil planted his hands on his hips and forced his gaze elsewhere. He wasn't going to show her what muscles would be developed from regular use of *this* piece of equipment. His heart, he decided, wasn't up to the strain. Each time he touched her, each time his fingers brushed across the shiny-soft fabric covering her legs, her waist, her back, he'd wanted to let them linger.

Damn, but he needed to hurry this thing along.

The weight bar clanged into place, and Lesley stood, her face flushed and framed in wisps of damp hair. He averted his gaze again.

"This one is for the biceps, triceps and pecs," he said, striding briskly toward yet another piece of equipment. "You sit here and position your forearms on either side of the padded flexor. Bring your arms to the center, then out again. Ten times.'' He rested his arm on the machine next to them and studied his shoes while waiting for her to finish.

"I'm, uh . . . having some trouble.''

Gil looked down at the weights. The level was set too high, something he would have noticed had he not been trying to speed things up. "There," he said after he'd inserted the pin at the correct weight for a beginner. "You . . . you'll also find it easier if you, uh, spread your knees apart. Yeah, like that.''

He'd come up with some great ideas in his time, but demonstrating exercise equipment to this woman wasn't one of them. Why the hell hadn't he waited until tomorrow? Why couldn't he get his mind off her . . . biceps, triceps and pecs. He could. He could invite her out to dinner as he'd planned. Dinner. It had a nice, safe ring to it.

"I'm ready for this one," she said, pulling Gil's gaze up from his shoes.

"Oh, yeah. Right." He moved his arm and motioned for her to take a seat on the bench. "It's a shoulder press. Just—"

"Push this handlebar thing up and down ten times?''

He grinned. "Yeah, the handlebar thing.''

"Is the weight set on the right level?''

He looked down, then back up. "Yes ma'am.''

"Okay, then.''

This one was a killer, Lesley thought. Toward the end of her ten pushes, the muscles in her arms felt as if they'd caught fire, and her breathing had accelerated for reasons that had nothing to do with Gil.

"Listen, Lesley. About last week..."

The handlebar came down with a clank. "Last week?"

"Yeah. Last week. I haven't had a chance to get back to you since then."

Lesley grasped the handgrips again, oblivious to the burning in her arms. She did five more lifts of the handlebar. "I've been terribly busy and—"

"Me, too."

"Oh." She'd rehearsed what needed to be said when this moment came, but her mental list was nowhere to be found now. Neither was her voice. She just sat on the bench doing God knows how many more shoulder presses.

Gil stopped the movement of the handlebar with his hand. His expression was serious. "You know next week is the Midland Lee game."

"Um, yes, I'm aware of that." What did the Midland Lee game have to do with last week at her house?

"I like to celebrate whipping the socks off them with a little obnoxious gloating. Sort of my own little tradition."

She grinned, her grip on the handlebar loosening.

"What I do is, I put on my Warren jacket and go over to Midland that Saturday night."

"I see. And do you just stand on a street corner waiting to be mugged by a Rebel fan or...?"

"Oh, no, that's small potatoes. I do it up big. I make reservations for dinner at either Luigi's or La Bodega, the two busiest restaurants in town. That way I can be obnoxious to even more of the fair citizens of Midland at one time."

Lesley shook her head. Her smile was impossible to contain. If she wasn't careful, he'd reel her in with his sense of humor alone.

"If I can find a jacket in your size, we could be obnoxious together. What do you say? Mexican or Italian?"

CHAPTER SIX

GIL WATCHED Lesley's grip on the handlebar loosen and her hands drop to her lap. "You're asking me out," she said. "A date."

"Yes, Lesley," he said dryly. "That's about the size of it." He grinned at her, hoping he might coax some lightness into her oh-so-serious expression, but there wasn't a chance. Not with her looking away, refusing to meet his gaze.

She nodded, took a deep breath, then said, "I see."

He frowned at the way she said it—carefully, like a psychologist talking to a patient on a couch. Her eyes were distant and trained on the stacked weight bars in front of her.

She bit her lip. "You know, ever since that night at my house when you and I . . . that is when you—"

"When I kissed you?"

She lifted her gaze, the distant look gone now. "Yes," she said, her voice a hoarse whisper. "When you kissed me." She brushed at the damp tendrils of hair on her forehead with her palms. "I have a little problem—no, a big problem—with . . . with—"

"With us?" he prompted.

She nodded again, and her brow wrinkled into a slight frown. Her eyes, Gil thought, watching the slow downward sweep of thick black lashes that framed them, were so green, so beautiful, frowning or otherwise. The urge to kiss her again hit him full force. But he wanted it to be long, drawn out, with both parties completely involved.

He settled for listening instead. It came in a poor second, but he had an idea he knew what this problem was. And would like to be done with it. Quickly.

"You know that as principal at Warren, I'm a member of the district executive body."

Ah, yes. The district executive body. He'd been right on track. For some reason she was still worried about no-pass, no-play. That shouldn't surprise him. Hadn't he told himself she was by the book? But if she thought the issue of no-pass, no-play should concern the two of them personally, she was completely wrong. "Don't tell me you guys have a meeting scheduled for this Saturday night," he said wryly.

If he'd hoped for a smile, he'd hoped in vain. "Are you ever serious?" she asked.

"Oh, sure I am. There are things I take very seriously." He looped an arm around the handlebar she'd released and leaned toward her, close enough to inhale the subtle perfume she wore, but not so close that she'd bolt from the bench. "Tell me, should I be more serious to get you to go out with me?"

"No. I mean, yes. Yes, I guess you should. Be serious for a moment. Do you know what being a member of that board means?"

"I know exactly what it means. You and all of your other principal buddies govern no-pass, no-play for this district. You're the people the state legislature put in charge to keep guys like me operating on the up-and-up.'' He couldn't resist adding, ''Don't suppose there are any openings on that board that I can apply for?''

''Be serious, Gil—''

''It was a joke, okay? Just a joke. I know what you're saying. You don't take your responsibility lightly. I respect that. But there's no reason you shouldn't be able to accept a date with me because of that.''

''Aren't you familiar with the phrase 'conflict of interest'?''

Conflict of interest? It was his turn to frown. ''Yes, I'm familiar with it.''

''Then you understand why anything between—'' She waved her hand to indicate the two of them. ''It would be a mistake, Gil.''

''Now wait a minute. Conflict of interest? That's nuts! You make it sound as if we're politicians voting on a bill that'll benefit us personally or something.''

''It's just like that, Gil. You know very well that in many parts of this state it is to the principal's benefit to have winning sports programs. It can mean increased interest from the private sector in the form of donations to the school. Haven't you been listening to the news? Reading the papers? Why, there's a principal right now up on charges for creative grading methods and other cases in which university presidents have changed athletes' grades. I won't have people thinking that I—''

''Since you don't go in for creative grading methods, what are you worried about?''

"I'm worried that if people were to see us out together, they might speculate. They might think that I was conveniently looking the other way so that you could—"

Annoyed, Gil leaned in close again. "Lesley, I've already told you: the law's the law. There's nothing I can do but obey it. Now, I'll admit that I took advantage of every bit of leniency the last principal at Warren gave me, but if you refuse to be lenient, then there's nothing I can do. Have I broken any of your precious rules so far?"

She shook her head.

"Then there's nothing wrong with us going out together, is there?"

She wished there wasn't anything wrong with it. She wanted to go out with him. At the moment, she wanted to do a whole lot more than that. The health club was virtually empty and he was very close. Close enough that only a few inches and her fear of losing control kept her from kissing him right then and there.

But that had always been her problem. She wasn't the courageous type, the type to take risks. "You make it sound so simple," she said finally.

"It is."

"No. No, it isn't, because..."

She started to look away again, but he captured her chin in his hand. "Why, Lesley? Because why?"

She would probably live to regret it, but for some strange reason she decided to be honest. "Because, given the... strong attraction between the two of us, I'm not so sure that couldn't happen, that I wouldn't turn my head and look the other way."

Gil smiled at that. And, as if her words gave him license to do so, he stroked her jaw with his thumb and lowered his mouth to hers.

Startled, Lesley shut her eyes and felt him brush her lips once, twice, before covering her mouth with the warmth of his. Then his hands moved from the nape of her neck to her arms and, without breaking the kiss, he drew her up from the bench and pulled her body against his.

The kiss took on a more serious tone when Gil traced the shape of her mouth with his tongue, then coaxed her lips to part for him. At the first touch of his tongue to hers, Lesley's pulse sped up and her hands clutched at his shoulders.

Somewhere in the far reaches of her brain, it occurred to Lesley that she should protest, pull away, tell him that she didn't want this. But that would have been a lie. And it appeared she was into honesty tonight.

Honesty. The word kept repeating in her head as he drew her away from the fine edge of reason and into the reality—the pure pleasure—of the moment.

She shivered, panicked for a moment at the realization this man was capable of undermining her rigid control. Then he slid his thumb down the scooped neckline of her leotard, stopping just above the rise of her breast. He broke the kiss and whispered her name.

Lesley's eyes opened and her gaze connected with his. She released her hold on his sweatshirt and looked away. Her breath coming unevenly, she attempted a rueful laugh. "Well, I... guess that just proved my point." Embarrassed, she took a step backward, but he grasped her arm.

"It proves mine, too."

She wet her lips and found that the taste of him lingered there. Raising her gaze, her voice unsteady, she said, "I don't understand."

"Yes, you do." He traced the curve of her cheek with his knuckle, and his words took on a gentle tone. "There's something happening between us, Lesley. You've admitted to the attraction, yourself. And it makes all that damned district executive body stuff trivial, doesn't it?"

The district executive body. He'd made her forget. No, she thought, remembering that honesty was her byword tonight. She'd let herself forget.

"I wouldn't call putting our careers on the line trivial stuff," she said softly. "As to the 'something' that's happening between us…we're adults, Gil." She lifted her gaze—and lifted her chin for good measure. "As adults we understand that we can't always have what we want. And despite this attraction between us, we have some measure of control over our hormonal urges, don't we?"

With that, she turned on her heel and left Gil staring after her.

He watched her turn the corner to the dressing rooms, then plopped down onto the bench where she'd sat, shaking his head. The woman was one contradiction after another. She was business suits and she was exercise clothes straight out of a man's fantasy. She was a stickler for the rules yet wore whimsical socks with little Scottie dogs on them. She was a woman who took pains to appear cool and dignified, yet had just shown him hints of a highly passionate nature beneath her poised surface.

She even spoke in contradictions. One moment she'd been telling him that she didn't know if she would be strong enough to be on that board and have a relationship with him at the same time. The next, she was telling him in no uncertain terms that she was adult enough to resist the attraction they felt for each other.

He picked himself up off the bench and made his weary way to the men's dressing room and showers. So she could control her "hormonal urges," he thought as he grabbed his duffel from the locker. Well, he could, too. He just didn't *want* to. He stripped down, found an empty shower stall and stepped inside. Turning on the taps, he braced his hands against the tile, ducked his head under the hot spray and decided something. The trick was in making her see that she didn't really want to control herself, either.

"I SWEAR," Stacey said, with her hand over her heart and her gaze directed heavenward, "it's true love this time. I mean it. He's the one."

"Oh, Stacey," several of the women gathered in the teacher's lounge groaned in chorus.

"No, really." She poured herself a cup of coffee then handed the pot to Lesley, who did the same. They found two empty seats on the sofa and took them. "I know I've only known him for a week, and I know that we've only had two dates, but there's just something about this one. He's so... different from all of the guys around here, you know?''

Martha Price, head of the mathematics department, grinned at what Stacey had said. She sent a wink Lesley's way.

Lesley grinned back. She had noticed that a subtle change in her relationship with the faculty had taken place. During her first weeks at Warren she'd felt they were keeping her at a friendly distance. They'd treated her more like the boss than one of the gang. But now that a month and a half had passed, everyone was more relaxed around her. Lesley was beginning to feel more like one of the family.

"So, Stacey," Lesley said, after taking a sip from her mug, "where did you happen to meet Mr. Right?"

"We met last week at—are you ready?—the comedy club on Bowie Street. You know where I mean—next to where the old mall used to be? Anyway, he was sitting one table away from me and I could see him really well. I glanced up from time to time and he was laughing at all the same things I was. So I could tell right off that he and I have the same sense of humor, right?''

Sadie Quinn—one of Warren's senior English teachers—looked up from her needlework. "A sense of humor is certainly important," she said.

"It's definitely at the top of my list," Stacey said, then hardly pausing to take a breath, she continued, "Anyway, when the first break between comedians came, Russell—isn't that a great name?—just waltzed right over. At first I thought he was going to talk to my friend, Rene, who is simply too gorgeous for words, but he didn't. He sat down right next to me and introduced himself."

"Sounds like a winner to me already," Jane Simpson, the home economics teacher, said dryly.

"Oh, he is."

"Has he told you what he does for a living, Stacey?" Lesley knew her sisters would have groaned at the question, saying she sounded like a parent. They were probably right. But she'd come to care for Stacey a great deal in the short time she'd worked with the girl. She only wanted the best for her.

"He most certainly has." Stacey's smile was smug as she pretended to give them all a haughty look. "He is employed by the one and only Wayne Thomas of W.T. Software, Inc. Russell is a computer programmer whom Mr. Thomas personally recruited from St. Louis, Missouri, thank you very much."

Lesley could see that that fact had elevated the young man in everyone's esteem. She understood why. One couldn't live in Warren, Texas, for longer than a day without hearing of W.T. Software, Inc. and its founder, Wayne Thomas. A native West Texan, he was a local hero because he'd based his now-successful software company in Warren. When he'd refused to move out at a time when many other employers in the area left because of the oil bust, he'd become more than a hero. His company, along with a few others, was responsible for keeping the town's economy stable. Several other area communities weren't doing nearly as well.

"Hmm," one of the women commented. "This is sounding better and better. Tell us more."

Stacey needed no encouragement. "Well, he's a gentleman through and through. And," she said, putting on an exaggerated drawl, "he thinks my accent's cute."

They all laughed, and when the laughter had faded, each had advice for Stacey on how to go about catching and keeping this new man.

"Now, Stacey, remember to play hard to get, but not *too* hard."

"Yes, and don't forget that you'll want to show off your culinary skills fairly soon," added Jane Simpson.

"Oh, no! What culinary skills?" Stacey said in dismay.

"The ones I'll teach you," Jane said calmly. "I don't like to brag, but I can have you speaking fluent cordon bleu in a New York minute."

"You'd do that for me? Really?"

Stacey's profound relief and excitement over the promise of cooking lessons had Lesley shaking her head. "Oh, Stacey, you have nothing to worry about," she said. "No man in his right mind could resist you, cordon bleu or no cordon bleu."

Stacey smiled widely. She looked at the other women in the room. "I think we can let her stay, huh?"

Lesley laughed along with the others. Jane, ever the homemaker's advocate, mumbled, "Still, there's nothing wrong with being well-rounded. A little gourmet cooking couldn't hurt."

The door to the lounge swung open, and Dwight Collins, the vice principal, walked in. "Good morning, ladies," he said, then, as was his habit, he whistled the entire way to the coffeepot.

"Morning, Dwight," Lesley said, taking note of the fact that some of the women in the room didn't return his greeting. Dwight wasn't the most well liked man on the faculty at Warren, Lesley supposed. He wasn't what one would call a "people" person.

A quick glance at her watch told Lesley that the pep rally would be starting in fifteen minutes. She was scheduled to say a few words during this morning's program, so she needed to get going. She took her coffee mug to the sink, rinsed it out and set it on the counter. Heading for the door, she noticed several of the others getting ready to leave as well, including Stacey, who squeezed in front of Lesley and grabbed for the door handle.

"Hey there, Stace, not so fast," Dwight called after her.

Stacey heaved a sigh. "What is it now, Mr. Collins?"

He poured himself a cup of coffee, then took a sip. "Did you get those letters typed for me?"

"They're on your desk," she answered, not bothering to mask her weary tone. "In triplicate, as instructed."

"One copy on Ms. Tyler's desk?" he asked.

"Yes, one copy is on Ms. Tyler's desk."

"Good, then. I wanted you to see that I'm on top of the situation with those defective typewriters we were sent for the typing lab," he said to Lesley.

"I never doubted it for a moment, Dwight." She nudged Stacey to open the door. "I've got to get to the pep rally, so I'll talk to you later," she told him before exiting the lounge.

When the door had closed behind them, Stacey shot Lesley a long-suffering look.

"What? Is Dwight piling too much work on you these days?"

"No," Stacey said. "Not any more than usual. It's just that he's such a . . . kiss-up."

Lesley chuckled. "Oh, Stacey. He may go a bit overboard sometimes, but he's just ambitious. There's nothing wrong with that."

"Maybe not, but you should have seen him last year when he knew that Mr. Moore was going to retire. He really laid it on thick, because he thought he was sure to be promoted to principal even though he's only been a vice principal for two years. And he's started it again because another principal's job is coming open next year here in the district."

Lesley knew there was some truth in what Stacey said. Dwight Collins was a bit of a yes-man. But she couldn't fault his work. Overly ambitious or not, he was an excellent vice principal. "Well, he may be obnoxious at times, Stacey, but give him a break, huh? You have to admire his devotion to his job."

"Okay, boss," Stacey said with a grudging smile. "Anything you say."

"And don't call me boss."

"Right," she said, then gave Lesley a little wave before turning in the direction of the office.

Lesley strode quickly toward the field house, seeing that she only had three minutes until the pep rally started. The hallway was full now, a virtual sea of students dressed in black and gold, noisily making their way to the pep rally.

Lesley thought about seeing Gil again. It had been two days since she'd seen him last and about a week and a half since that night at the health club. He'd been friendly, nothing more. She'd thought she still detected a flicker of interest in his eyes when he looked at her, but had decided it was a trick of her imagination. She'd told him where she stood and he had obviously taken her at her word. Which was good, because she didn't think she could deal with his interest and combat her own unreasonable attraction, as well.

"I see you're all decked out in the traditional game-day black and gold." Gil's voice came from behind her a moment before she felt his hand settle on her shoulder.

Lesley felt a jolt of something that was suspiciously close to pleasure when his fingers brushed the fabric of her black blazer. He was just being friendly, she reminded herself. Swinging an arm over someone's shoulder was the friendly, West Texas thing to do.

"Good morning, Coach," she said, keeping her voice even. "You're certainly in high spirits this morning. That must mean you predict a win for Warren in the Permian game tonight." She smiled at several students as they passed by and nodded hellos to teachers.

"I'd say this mini winning streak we've been on is responsible for that." He looked down with a grin, gave her shoulder a squeeze. "How about you? Ready for your speech?"

"Oh, yes. I'm ready."

They'd come to the field house door. Gil's arm dropped from her shoulder. He paused for a moment, looking at her, then pushed the door open. "Well, then. Let's get to it."

They walked past the band, seated at one end of the gymnasium floor, past cheerleaders doing stretching exercises in the center of the room, and came to a row of chairs for faculty, which was perpendicular to the football team's seats.

Gil sat down next to Lesley. He crossed an ankle over his knee and smiled at her. It was a friendly, cordial smile, and Lesley returned it. She glanced up at the bleachers filled with students as the band struck up the fight song. She stood along with the rest of the crowd and, as Gil rose beside her, she caught a faint whiff of the cologne he wore, clean and masculine.

After several cheers led by cheerleaders, a skit acted out by some of the football players and marches played by the band, it was Lesley's turn at the microphone that sat in the middle of the field house floor. One of the cheerleaders introduced her, and Lesley stood, smoothing her black-and-gold-plaid skirt. She walked to the mike.

"Thank you," she said when the students' applause had died down. "I consider myself lucky to have been chosen principal here at Warren. For the several weeks while I've been settling in, I've been pleased to find that we have one of the best faculties in the Texas school systems, a student body made up of bright, enthusiastic students—" she paused at the applause that comment brought "—and a school spirit among both faculty and students that rivals any I've seen in my experience in this state.''

Another round of clapping. Lesley smiled as she waited for it to fade. "I'd like to thank you all—students and faculty alike—for the warm welcome you've given me. I'd also like to wish the football team much success tonight in their game against Permian. Coach Fielden has assured me that the only thing that might hinder their chances is if their fans aren't there in droves to cheer them on. See you at the game," she said, then looked back and nodded toward Gil to indicate it was his turn at the microphone.

He made his way across the room slowly to the accompaniment of frenzied cheering from the students. Everyone loves a winner, Lesley thought. The Wildcats hadn't been expected to win as many games as they had so far. But slowly, surely, they were disproving everyone's expectations of failure.

And Gil was responsible for their success. His grin broadened as he looked up into the crowd on the bleachers. His stride was confident, and the wave he gave the students garnered even louder shouts.

When he reached the microphone, Lesley stepped aside and started to move back to her chair. He held her in place by looping his arm through hers square-dance-style. The students found it highly amusing. Lesley wondered what he was up to.

She plastered a polite smile on her face and watched him closely.

"Well," he said into the microphone, "we whipped Midland Lee soundly last week, didn't we?" His words brought the expected response from the crowd.

"What do you say we do the same to Permian tonight?"

Lesley clapped along with the students, still watching, still waiting.

"The team would like to remind you," he continued, "that their annual parking lot sale for charity is tomorrow. This year the profits go to benefit the women and children's shelter. Donations have been good, but not nearly good enough. We need some household items and more clothing, I'm told. Anything you can give will be appreciated, and the proceeds, as I said, will be going to a good cause.

"Now, our new principal, Ms. Tyler, here—" Lesley smiled politely when he turned his gaze her way "—told me earlier that she might be stopping by tomorrow with a donation or two." Lesley struggled to keep the surprise from her expression. "What were those donations you'd mentioned again, Ms. Tyler?"

She was going to kill him. They hadn't discussed the sale or donations earlier! "Well, I...um have some...dishes and other...odds and ends," she said, leaning toward the mike. She supposed she *could* use a new set of dishes.

"There, you see?" he said, looking back up into the bleachers and patting her on the back like a buddy. "Ms. Tyler's got the right spirit. Let's see some more of that from the rest of you. Remember, eight o'clock tomorrow morning. We want to see your shining faces—and your donations—in the parking lot outside this field house."

CHAPTER SEVEN

THE HOUSE WAS so damned quiet.

The late-October morning sun shone through the shuttered windows over Lesley's kitchen sink. Her coffee maker dripped its final drip, and she filled her cup. She took a sip then sighed wearily, tightening the belt of her long white terry robe as she walked to her dinette table. After adding dishwashing detergent to the bottom of her shopping list, she reached for her glasses and the morning paper. There was a sale at Dillard's, she noticed. She could check that out before shopping for groceries and after dropping off clothes at the cleaner's.

The house was too damned quiet.

Lesley wondered when she would ever get used to it. When she'd shared an apartment with her sisters in Austin, there had been noise—regardless of the time of day—every day of the week. Funny, but she had thought that she would welcome the moments of peace and quiet that living alone would bring. She hadn't imagined that she would come to miss the noise, to hate the silence.

Nor had she imagined that she would waste time on a Saturday morning instead of getting errands done, but that was exactly what she was doing. Her chair made a scraping sound on the linoleum when she quickly pushed it away from the table. A glance at her watch told her it was seven-thirty. If she wanted to get to the post office and dry cleaner's before the mall opened, then she needed to be dressed and on her way.

The phone rang, and aware that only three people in the world knew she got up before seven on the weekends, Lesley reached for it, a smile already in place. "I was just thinking about you," she said.

"Oh, you were, were you?" Kelly said with a laugh. "And how did you know this wasn't someone calling to sell you siding for your house?"

"Too early for that. It could have only been one of three people, and I had all bases covered since I was thinking about all of you."

"Oh, Lesley, you've been on our minds, too. We miss you so much! The other night Linda was saying that she didn't know if she could make it until Christmas before seeing you again."

Lesley twisted the phone cord with her fingers. "Me, either, Kell. Christmas seems so far away," she said in a hoarse voice. "So that settles it. I'm moving back."

"Get serious. A couple of weeks ago you loved the challenge of your new job, had exciting new decorating ideas for your house—and don't I recall your mentioning a certain football coach?"

Without warning, thoughts of Gil's kiss surfaced. She could almost feel the brush of his lips against hers, hear the sound of her whispered name. Unsettled, she closed her eyes. It was one thing when seeing him could do this to her, quite another when the mere mention of him made her giddy. "Um, everything is still going well, but the silence around here is getting to me."

"Oh? And here I was hoping the coach might take care of all your free time." Lesley waited for the grilling to begin and was surprised when it didn't. "But I won't go into that right now. Get out your pad and pencil so you can think better," Kelly teased. "I've called about something important."

Lesley's mind zeroed in on the words "something important."

"What is it, Kelly? Is something wrong?" She lowered herself to the chair, reaching for her yellow legal pad as instructed. Maybe Kelly's business was in trouble, Lesley worried. Maybe she needed money.

"No, no, no. Nothing is wrong. In fact, things couldn't possibly be better. I'm calling you with good news."

"Oh, thank goodness. Well, don't keep me in suspense. Tell me the good news."

"Oh, Lesley, I'm so happy. I wanted to call you last night when Stephen asked, but it was so late. Lesley... I'm getting married!"

Lesley's breath caught in her throat. Stunned, she was unable to think of a single response. "Married?" she parroted.

"Yes, married. Isn't it terrific?"

"I...well, I guess so. I...don't know what to say. Sweetheart, this is so...sudden, isn't it?"

"Lesley, please say that you're happy for me. You know how much it means to me that you approve.

And, yes, it is sudden, but not for the reason you might be imagining.''

Lesley blinked, not understanding at first, then realization dawned. "Oh...that. No, I hadn't...gotten around to imagining that yet.'' She took a deep breath, unable to imagine any of it. "What *is* the reason, Kell?"

"The reason is that we are totally, foolishly, obsessively, crazy in love. He's the most wonderful man on the planet, Lesley. And he makes me feel like I'm the most wonderful woman. How long we've known each other doesn't matter. We want to be together and don't see the need to wait.''

"And have you ... set a date?"

"Yes. December. We want a Christmas wedding.''

Lesley closed her eyes. *Foolishly* in love was a good way to describe it. Kelly had only known Stephen for what ... four months? On top of that, she'd just gone into partnership with another woman in a travel agency business. How could she think of jumping into marriage with someone she barely knew, especially now when so much was going on in her life? "Kelly, honey... have you thought about waiting until your new business is a little more stable?"

"There's no need to worry about that, Lesley. The agency may not be *Fortune* 500 material yet, but we're keeping our heads above water. I realize money may be tight for Stephen and me, but it'll only be for the first three years while he's in school.''

"School? I thought you told me that Stephen had a job as an auto mechanic.''

"Well, he did, but he's decided to go back to UT for his business degree."

"Business degree," Lesley echoed flatly. She scribbled the words "one income" on the side of a blank page. On the other side she wrote, "food," "rent," "utilities." In her head she could hear only one word. Disaster. It repeated itself over and over again.

"Yes," Kelly said. "Then he's going to take over the management of his father's auto shop here in Austin. In three years we'll both be big-shot business owners."

Yes, Lesley thought, in three years. But until then it would be Kelly supporting the two of them. Kelly paying all the bills. Kelly responsible for their financial security. Having had experience as a young woman responsible for the welfare of four, Lesley knew how heavy a burden that could be. She could also foresee the problems it would create in a new marriage, and she didn't want that for Kelly.

"Kelly, I know what you're wanting to hear from me is that I'm overjoyed for you. But I can't be completely happy until I know that you've considered some things before taking such a big step."

"What things?"

Lesley opened her mouth to reply, but her words were interrupted by the ringing of her doorbell. She sighed. "Kelly, hold on, there's someone at my door."

"Should I . . . call back?" Kelly's voice was quieter now, edged in disappointment. Lesley didn't want the conversation to end on that note.

"No, I'll only be a second."

Lesley walked quickly to the door, her mind clamoring for ways to set Kelly straight. There had to be something she could say to convince her sister of the folly of this situation. *Love,* she thought, shaking her head.

She pulled open the door. Gil Fielden raised his hand in a little wave.

"Hi there. Like the outfit," he said, nodding toward her robe with a smile much too cheerful for either this time of morning or her current mood. "I'm here to pick up your donation and—"

"My donation?"

"To the parking lot sale, remember? I also need to ask—"

"Come on in," she said. "It's on the kitchen counter." She held the door open for him, then hurriedly led the way through the living room. "I was going to bring it by myself. I didn't realize you'd be coming to pick it up."

Well, Gil thought, aren't we brisk this morning? Then he realized why. Her phone was off the hook, lying on the dining room table. "Right there," she said, pointing to a box sitting on the counter. "I'm, uh, on the phone, so..."

So he should pick up the donation and leave? He silently damned his poor timing. "Something's come up concerning the parking lot sale and I need to ask a favor of you. I hate to be rude, but do you mind if I wait around until you finish your call?"

Oh, great, Lesley thought with a sigh. What a perfect time for school problems to arise. "Uh, okay. Just give me a minute."

"Oh, hey, take your time." He spotted the pot of coffee. "Don't mind me. I'll just help myself to a cup of coffee."

"I'm back," he heard her say into the phone. "Honey, are you there?"

Gil busied himself opening cabinets, searching for a cup and wondering who the hell "honey" was. It was, of course, the height of bad taste to eavesdrop, but that didn't stop him. He opened another cabinet and spotted a row of mugs. Curiously they were lined up next to an empty space on the bottom shelf. He looked over his shoulder with a frown at the box of dishes she'd donated to the sale.

"No, no. I'm not angry with you, Kelly," Lesley said.

Kelly, Gil thought, closing the cabinet and forcing himself to concentrate on pouring his coffee. "Honey's" name was Kelly.

"It's just that this has come out of left field and...yes, I understand...I want you to think about some important things before taking such a big step...I don't want you hurt...but going into a marriage with so many strikes against the two of you..."

Gil took his cup to the sink, opened the shutters and looked out into Lesley's backyard. He felt guilty for having listened in on her private conversation, even more guilty that it was relief that had put a stop to his eavesdropping. Kelly, it seemed, wasn't competition; Kelly was a friend of hers.

He sipped at his coffee, listening again—not to the words she was saying, but to the tone of Lesley's voice. She was clearly distressed. And the longer she spoke with Kelly, the more distressed she sounded. When he heard her hang up the phone, he closed the shutters and turned around.

She stood, ran a hand through her hair and stared down at the table she'd been writing on. Her eyes were troubled.

"I'm sorry about the interruption," he said, putting his cup down on the counter.

Her gaze lifted. "What? Oh...oh, no. That was...my sister. She's getting married." She looked more than merely troubled, Gil thought. She looked as if she were about to cry. "You'll, um, have to excuse me. I'm not dressed." She turned to leave the dining area.

Concerned, Gil moved forward, stopping her with a touch on her arm. "Lesley? Are you okay?"

She lowered her gaze. "No," she answered, her voice rusty, her hands nervously toying with the belt to her robe. "I don't think so." Then she turned and walked out of the dining room.

He heard her bedroom door close, then there was silence.

She was in the bedroom crying. He'd bet the district championship on it. He took two steps in that direction, then stopped, raking a hand through his hair.

He couldn't just barge right in and force her to use his shoulder to cry on. On the other hand, an inexplicable protectiveness had his conscience demanding that he do something. He went into the kitchen for his coffee, then paced back to the table. Picking up her list of errands, he marveled over the fact that one portion of the list included Christmas presents, sizes and col-

ors. Christmas presents! he thought. She had made a
list of Christmas presents in October! The people on
his list were lucky if he got out to buy before Christmas Eve.

He glanced at her bedroom door and took another
sip of his coffee. On the surface she was so...together.
Organized, and on top of it all. It was strange seeing
her otherwise. Her bedroom door opened, and Gil
hastily dropped the list onto the table.

Lesley walked into the room. Jeans and a lilac-
colored button-down shirt had replaced the robe. Her
hair was under the collar of the shirt until, with an ec-
onomic flip of her wrist, she pulled it out and let it fall
over her back. It was in a low ponytail, tied with a
purple satin ribbon.

Gil set down his cup on the table, watching as she
buttoned the cuffs of her shirt. Her eyes were slightly
red but dry.

"You look...very nice," he said.

"Thank you." She picked up a purse that sat on the
table, then reached for the list next to his hand. "You
said a problem's come up with the parking lot sale?"

Brisk again, Gil thought. Brisk and businesslike.
She'd cried her tears without the need of his or anyone else's shoulder.

"Well, yes. Three of the adult volunteers we had
signed up to help in the booths aren't able to make it.
I was going to ask if you'd consider donating some
time today, but I understand now if you don't want
to—"

"From what time to what time?" she asked.

That she would actually consider it now surprised him. "From now until about six this evening, but, hey, I know you have a lot on your mind. And it looks as though you've got a long list of errands there."

She folded it in half, then slipped it into her purse. "No. I can help out. It'll keep my mind off my problems for a while until I can think things out more clearly."

"But—"

"I can do my errands after school next week. You need more manpower, I need...something to occupy my mind." She swiveled and headed for the front door, stopping to switch off a lamp on the way. "Don't forget the box of dishes," she said, then held open her screen door for him.

He automatically reached for the box, then stopped, remembering the empty shelf in her cabinet. "About those dishes. I should probably mention that sometimes I tend to get carried away. I've even been known to bulldoze people into doing things they might not really want to do. Sort of goes along with the whole "coach" thing. Of course, it's usually for a good cause, but I—"

"You?" she said, her lips twitching. "Bulldoze?"

The twitch became a smile. Until now he hadn't realized how much he would welcome seeing one.

"I needed a new set anyway," she said.

"Well, only since you're insisting," he said, grabbing up the box. He walked through the door she held and carried the dishes to the trunk of his car. After he'd closed the lid, he came around and unlocked the passenger door for her. She murmured a quiet thank-you and got in.

It seemed to take an eternity for his car to warm up. An eternity filled with silences. He took a quick sideways glance at her, then looked forward again. Small talk. He'd never been good at it, but he felt the need to try. "You, uh, think you'll need a jacket? Might get a little nippy."

"No." She was staring at her hands. "I rarely feel the cold."

Well, that had taken up a whole three seconds. He put the car into gear and wondered if he should bring up the subject of her sister. She was probably thinking about her anyway. Maybe he could be of help in the listening department, at least.

Before he could decide whether or not to mention Kelly, Lesley broke the silence.

"I, um, hope you don't mind giving me a ride," she said. "I could take my car if it's an imposition."

Gil smiled and turned his car off Lesley's street onto a main thoroughfare. "It *is* quite an imposition. Frankly, I was surprised when you sashayed right up to the door, expecting a ride just because we happen to be going the same way." He heaved a put-upon sigh. "And God knows, if there's one person I don't particularly want to spend time with, it's you. But what can I say? It's a curse—I just can't seem to say no when a beautiful woman's involved."

She grinned, knowing full well she shouldn't allow herself to feel so pleased about his remarks. The man knew how to flirt so well, and she hadn't changed her mind about becoming involved with him. But what was the harm in simply enjoying an attractive man's attention? Today of all days, she decided, she needed to feel better about herself.

Now that was a curious thought. Lesley glanced out the car window. She understood why she was so upset about Kelly's hasty plans, but why should the situation make Lesley feel down about herself? She realized that she was a parental figure to the girls and that parents often suffered self-doubts when their children took wrong turns. But was that why Kelly's announcement had made her so emotional? Or was there more?

The separation from her sisters was becoming more and more difficult to handle. And it wasn't merely on an I-miss-you-so-much, this-quiet-house-is-driving-me-nuts basis. Other, more subtle forms of the separation were getting to Lesley. Linda's adamant refusal to accept financial assistance and her constant reminders that she was now an adult, for instance. Gayle's determination to rely less and less on advice from Lesley on matters such as taxes or car insurance. And, of course, there was Kelly's call this morning. What hurt most of all, Lesley thought, was that she'd had no idea how serious things were between Kelly and Stephen. Kelly had never told her.

She reminded herself it was only natural that the girls were growing up and handling things on their own, becoming more independent. But it didn't feel natural. It felt as if they were moving on...without her.

Lesley stole a glance at Gil. He was a parent. A parent who knew about separation from his child.

Though she was aware of the differences in their situations, she wondered if he'd ever felt the way she was feeling today.

It seemed impossible. He was so easygoing, flirtatious and fun. Not to mention self-assured. Still, how could he not have been affected by the outcome of his divorce? How could anyone remain untouched by such a difficult situation? Fingering the strap of her purse, she cleared her throat. "Your, uh, divorce must have been very hard on you. I mean, I remember you telling me that you and your ex-wife parted on friendly terms, but I can't help wondering about Coby. It must have been heartbreaking to know that you wouldn't be as involved in her life as you would have if you'd remained married to her mother."

Gil was surprised. Surprised that she was the one to initiate conversation, and even more surprised at her choice of subjects. Though he'd been trying to come up with a topic of conversation that might prod Lesley from her introspective mood, his divorce hadn't been a subject he'd considered.

"Well, yes. That was the worst part. I was lucky, though. Ceil felt strongly about including me in as much of Coby's life as possible after we split up. She let me see Coby even past the limitations of the custody agreement." He chuckled, remembering just how adamant Ceil had been about his role as Coby's father—part-time or otherwise. "Once," he said, "when Coby was about six or seven, she wanted more than anything to sit on the bench at football games when I was coaching. I thought it was no place for a little girl to be. Well, when Ceil got wind of it, she was hot. She lectured me on what a disservice I was doing to both Coby and myself by not including her in that part of my life. She also asked if my decision might have been different if Coby had been a boy."

Lesley smiled, liking the woman even though she'd never met her. "And did Coby get to sit on the bench after that?"

"Are you kidding me?" He looked over at her, managing his best cocky expression. "Do I look like a man who could be swayed that easily? A man who would capitulate to the combined pressure of an ex-wife and a seven-year-old girl?"

"Yes."

The cocky look was replaced by a sheepish grin that was no less appealing. "She was there every Friday night after that," he said. "Ceil brought her there herself."

Lesley chuckled. "Ceil sounds like a wonderful mother."

"She is," he stated simply. "She's also the one behind our new living arrangements. Part of the reason is that she and Coby were having some mother-daughter clashes, but mostly it's because Ceil wanted me to have this time with Coby. She says Coby will be an adult before we know it, and things will never be the same again."

"That's so true," Lesley said. *So true.* But she wondered if he knew what was in store for him when Coby left. "It'll be hard to let her go once you've gotten used to having her there all the time. Have you thought that maybe it would have been better to keep things on a visitation basis, so when Coby leaves it won't be so... difficult?''

Gil frowned. He'd never thought about it that way. Oh, he'd known he would miss Coby once she was gone. But would he have refused to let her live with him in order to avoid the pain of missing her once she left? No. Unequivocably, no.

He stopped the car at a red light. He shifted his eyes to look at her and saw that the remark she'd made hadn't been a mere casual observation. She knew about missing someone; he could see it in her eyes. He suspected that someone might be the sister with marriage plans. "No matter how much I'll miss her," he said, "I'm grateful for the chance to have her with me. Yes, it'll be lonely around my place once she's not there. No, I wouldn't give up this opportunity because of that."

The car behind them honked, and Gil forced his gaze frontward. He drove through the intersection. "What about you, Lesley? Moving away from your family must be difficult, too."

"I...only have my three sisters left now," she said. "My parents died more than ten years ago."

"I'm sorry."

"Thank you. But it was a long time ago. It's just been my sisters and me since I graduated from UT."

"And your sisters are what? Older or younger than you?"

"Younger. Kelly is twenty-five, Gayle is twenty-three. Linda, the baby, is twenty-one."

Several questions occurred to him. As a UT graduate, Lesley would have been about twenty-one. Her sisters had been eleven, thirteen and fifteen. Had a relative taken them in? He wanted to discuss it with Lesley, but discussion would have to come later. He signaled for a turn, then pulled his car into the school parking lot. There would be plenty of time for discussion this evening, he thought. He had plans for tonight. Plans that included Lesley.

"Well, are you ready for all of this?" He draped a wrist across the steering wheel and nodded toward the sale that was already in progress.

"They come out in droves for this, don't they?" The lot was already teeming with people. If the number of people here at eight o'clock in the morning was any indication, the women and children's shelter would be blessed with a sizable donation.

"This is nothing, wait until about ten o'clock." Gil turned to look at her. "Lesley, are you sure you're up to this?"

His concern was sweet but totally unnecessary, Lesley decided. Working the sale today would be a good diversion. It would keep her mind off December weddings, sisters and homesickness. "I'll be fine, really. I'm glad you needed me to help out," she said.

"Well, let's go to it, then."

He got out of the car and swung around to the trunk for the dishes. Lesley did the same. Rolling up her sleeves, she asked, "So, where do I go?"

Gil closed the trunk. "Oh, I have the perfect place for you." He steered her in the direction of the booths. "The absolute perfect place."

They shouldered their way through the masses of sale goers, finally coming to a stop in front of a booth that had Lesley a bit puzzled. Workshop tools, lawn mowers, rakes and hoes—it had everything the handyman and/or gardener might need. Everything she knew nothing about. And furthermore, Lesley thought, Gil was more than aware of that, since he'd helped her with the bookcase.

"David, Kent," Gil called out. "Front and center." He placed the box of dishes on the ground. Two high school football players stopped setting up the various lawn equipment and tools and came forward. "Ms. Tyler is going to be helping you today."

"Hey, Ms. Tyler," the taller boy said. The other—was he David or Kent?—handed her a black baseball cap with a gold *W* on the front. Gil took it from her and set it on her head, threading her ponytail through the hole in back.

Lesley gave Gil a sideways frown. "Can I ask why you'd put me in a booth filled with items I don't even know the names of?" She remembered some of the other booths they'd passed on the way. Several of them seemed much more perfect for her than this one. "Why can't I be in the toys and games booth? Or what about housewares or clothes? I don't even know what this is," she said, picking up a strange piece of wood with glass tubes in the middle.

"That's called a level."

"I don't do levels, Gil," she said.

He tugged on the brim of her cap. "There's a method to my madness," he said. "Why do you suppose I put the best-looking woman in town here in the booth where all the men will be coming? I call that good sales sense."

Lesley scowled. "I call that sexism alive and well in West Texas."

Gil winked. "It's all a part of the coach thing I keep telling you about."

"The coach thing," Lesley muttered, continuing to scowl at him as he walked away. "Ten bucks says he'll get to be in the sporting goods booth." But that wasn't the direction he took. Her hands went to her hips as she watched him saunter away, not toward bowling balls and golf clubs, but to can openers and tea sets. He no more than got the cap on his head before he was approached by a woman with an item in her hands. He looked up, waggling his brows at Lesley. She rolled her eyes.

Once David and Kent had given her a basic run-down on pricing and had told her how much she was allowed to let the customers bargain her down, she began to feel a bit more secure. The men buying these items, they told her, would know enough about the tools they wanted to buy. She didn't necessarily need to know how they worked to sell them.

Her first customer was an overall-clad gentleman who appeared to be in his fifties. Lesley squared her hat and got down to business. She approached the man. "You, sir, look like a man who knows the value of an excellent level when you see one."

"HEY," DEVIN SAID, giving Coby a mock glare. "You gonna sell that Barbie junk or just play with it all day?"

"Oh, like you've got room to complain," she said, placing Barbie in her red Corvette and parking it inside Barbie's Italian villa. "I noticed you didn't exactly want to part with old Teddy Ruxpin a few minutes ago. Don't deny it."

Devin reached down a hand to help Coby up. "What can I say? Ted's a great conversationalist."

She laughed, dropping his hand to brush off the seat of her jeans. "Dad created a monster by putting you in the toy booth."

"Me? What about you? You've paid more attention to Barbie and her friends than to me ever since you got here."

"Aw," she said sympathetically. "Does the big strong football jock feel left out?"

"Maybe so." He shoved his hands into the pockets of his letter jacket and looked away. "Maybe I'd like a lot more attention from you than I'm getting lately."

Coby glanced away, busying herself with a row of stuffed animals. She knew what was on Devin's mind, but she didn't want to discuss it, didn't know *how* to discuss it.

"So, are we just not going to talk about it?"

"Talk about what, Devin?" she hedged, retying an oversize giraffe's satin bow. She wished business hadn't slowed down so much at their booth in the past few minutes. She also wished their adult helper hadn't chosen this particular time to take a coffee break.

Devin's sigh was audible. Coby didn't need to see his expression to visualize his impatience. He moved closer to her side. "Talk about us," he said. "Talk about something other than schoolwork or the drama club."

"We do talk about things other than school and drama, Devin. We discuss people we know and your games and—"

"Coby." He grasped her hands, stilling them on the miniature tea set she was rearranging. "Us. I want to talk about us."

"Okay. What about us?"

"Look at me, come on." He tilted her chin with a finger. Her gaze lifted to his. "We've been going out together, on more than a just-friends basis for two weeks now, and I get the feeling that things were better between us when we *were* just friends. Does what I'm saying make sense?"

Yes, it made sense, Coby thought. They'd been a couple ever since the Get Acquainted dance. They went out on dates together, walked to classes together, sat together at lunch. But Devin was right, things had been better when they'd been just friends.

She didn't know what to say to him. In fact, that pretty much summed up the problem. As Devin's friend she'd felt comfortable saying anything to him, acting any way she pleased. Now things were different. He wasn't just a buddy anymore. He was her boyfriend.

"I, uh, understand what you mean, Devin, but—"

"But what?"

Yeah, Coby thought, but what? Her friend Susan thought Coby was crazy. "What do you mean you don't know if you want to be going with Devin?" she'd asked. "He is so popular, so good-looking. Are you totally nuts?"

Totally scared was what she was. She had no experience with boys whatsoever. Until this year she'd never even gone out on a date. She was nervous about how to dress, act, talk... More than anything she was nervous about the emotional stuff, nervous about...intimacy. Hadn't she proved it last night by freezing up?

She pulled her hands from his. "Oh, Devin, it's just that this is all new to me. I mean, we've only been going out for two weeks now. And...and I'm sorry about last night, but..."

"No, Coby," he said in a lowered voice. "You don't have to be sorry about last night. Okay? Last night was my fault. You told me you wanted to take things slow. I shouldn't have rushed you.

"But look, Coby," he said, his eyes diverted, his hands back in the pockets of his jacket, "it's different between us than between most people who go together, because we were friends first. So I...know things about you. One thing I think I know is that you've never...I mean, you haven't ever come right out and told me, but you've never actually...done anything with a guy before, have you?"

Coby wanted to die. "Devin! Do we have to go over this right now? I said I was sorry about last night." Why had she ever thought going out with Devin would be a good idea? She was crazy, all right. Crazy to have chosen someone as a boyfriend who knew her so well.

"Will you stop being embarrassed about it? The only reason I brought it up is to reassure you that you were right to put a stop to Mr. Hands here before anything happened."

A grin pulled at the corners of Coby's mouth. *Mr. Hands*. Devin's sense of humor was one of her favorite things about him.

"Good, you're smiling." He linked their hands together, rubbed his thumb over hers in a gentle caress. "That's what I want again, to see you smile a lot. Like you used to before things...changed between us.

"I really like you, Coby. And I want more than just friendship, more than just a mutual interest in drama and school. But I won't rush you, you can count on that. If that's what's causing you to be...different around me now, then you don't have to worry, okay?"

She nodded, hoping that her shyness and lack of experience really *was* the whole problem. What else could it be? She didn't want to lose Devin as a friend. She *wouldn't* lose Devin, she vowed. She would give the relationship time, take things slowly and...it would work out. "I'm not worried, Devin," she told him.

"Good." He squeezed her hand. "I'm glad."

"Me, too." She smiled, then caught sight of their helper coming back from his coffee break.

Devin spotted him, too. He let go of her hand. Before he moved away from her, he bumped Coby's hip with his. "Get back to work, woman," he growled.

Several customers and sold toys later, Devin strolled back to Coby's side of the booth. "Hey," he said, "is Coach dating the principal now?"

Coby gave him a surprised look. "Ms. Tyler?"

"Yeah." He motioned across the lot with a jerk of his head.

Coby lifted a brow, then looked in the direction that Devin had indicated. She saw her dad standing next to the principal. While that might not be enough to suspect that they were dating, or even interested in each other, the way he smiled down at Ms. Tyler and playfully tugged on the cap she wore might be. Her dad and Ms. Tyler?

"Well," Coby said. "What do you know about that?"

CHAPTER EIGHT

"EXCUSE ME, lady, but do you think we can get some help over here with these tools?"

Lesley swiveled then smiled. "Hi, Stacey," she called. She set down the pocket set of metric sockets—after a full three-quarters of a day selling, Lesley had found she'd become familiar with some of the names—and made her way over to Stacey. The girl's arm was looped through that of a young man standing next to her. Russell, Lesley thought, anxious to meet him.

"What can I show you and your friend? I've got your screwdrivers, I've got your wrenches, I've got your handy-dandy auto-repair kits. Just tell me what you need, I've probably got it. We don't like to think of our items as used," she drawled, "we like to think of them as merely broken in a bit."

Stacey giggled. "I think you missed your calling," she said. "I didn't know you'd be working here today."

"Neither did I. A couple of the volunteers couldn't make it, so I got volunteered to take up the slack."

"I see." Stacey tugged her companion closer. "Russell, I'd like you to meet Lesley Tyler, Warren's principal. Lesley, Russell Compton."

"Nice to meet you, Russell," Lesley said, shaking his hand. He was quite attractive, with dark auburn hair and brown eyes. And he had a nice smile, she thought. Warm, like his eyes.

"You, too."

"Russell and I were just going to stop by for a minute, but we've been here nearly an hour now," Stacey told her. "We didn't intend to buy anything, either, but Russell's trunk is full of all kinds of broken-in treasures. Right, Russ?" She smiled up at him, her heart in her eyes. He nodded, his answering smile filled with affection.

"Anyway," Stacey chattered on, "can you believe this crowd? I've talked to people I haven't seen in ages. There were three cousins, my Great-Aunt Maxie, and two girls I went to high school with. Oh, and look, Russ, there's your boss, Mr. Thomas. He must be a friend of Coach Fielden's."

Lesley glanced where Stacey was pointing, and spotted a man at the housewares booth who was talking to Gil. So that was the esteemed Wayne Thomas, Warren's hometown hero. He was distinguished looking in a West Texas sort of way. Somewhere in his late forties, he had black hair that had silvered at the temples and was as neatly styled as any executive's. It was the Western-cut shirt, blue jeans and hand-tooled belt with the initials W.T. stamped on the back that gave the software entrepreneur the look of a gentleman rancher.

At that moment he and Gil broke into laughter, and Gil slapped the man on the back in a manner that had Lesley wondering if the two were more than just acquaintances. It wouldn't surprise her if they were. With Gil, it would be difficult to remain a mere acquaintance for long, she thought.

"I think I'll go over and say hello," Russell said. "Do you mind, Stacey?"

"Of course not. Go ahead."

He leaned down, giving Stacey a kiss on the cheek before leaving.

"Well? Was I right? Is he not the most gorgeous man?" Stacey enthused once Russell was out of earshot.

"I think you've found a winner."

"So do I. Two weeks may not be long enough to judge, but I've never felt this happy before." Stacey needn't have spoken aloud. Her expression said it all. Her eyes glowed with happiness, and her mouth was stretched in the broadest of smiles. Lesley thought about Kelly, remembering that her sister had spoken of Stephen in those very terms. She wished she could feel as good about them as she did about Stacey and Russell.

"Listen, I'm going to go over and join Russell, okay? I'd like to meet his boss."

"Sure, I'll see you later," Lesley said, then watched as Stacey joined the three men. Russell's arm automatically went around Stacey's shoulder when she stepped up beside him; hers slid around his waist. Lesley tried to form an image of Kelly and Stephen— a young man she'd met only once—in that same pose, but the image wouldn't come.

She forced her gaze away from the couple and her thoughts away from Kelly. Today, she reminded herself, she wanted mindless activity.

"David," she said, and her helper looked up from the small hand tools he was rearranging. "Is there something that needs doing?"

"Sure, Ms. Tyler. I noticed those rakes and hoes and stuff need to be straightened again. Need me to help?"

"No, that's okay. I'll get it." She had to stop to assist two customers on the way but finally made it to the garden section. When she'd almost completed the straightening and was looking around for another chore, she saw Gil's daughter inspecting one of the lawn movers with great interest. The breeze had ruffled her straight blond hair, and the girl finger-combed it away from her face.

"Can I make you deal on that mower?" Lesley asked, approaching her.

"Oh, hi, Ms. Tyler." She rose from a crouching position. "It wouldn't get much use, since we live in an apartment. I was just kind of looking around," she said. "Well, actually, that's not completely true. I saw you here and thought I'd come over to say hi."

"I'm glad you did," Lesley said, smiling. "I guess congratulations are in order for you and Devin."

"They are?"

"Yes. I heard that the two of you landed the lead roles in *Arsenic and Old Lace*."

"Oh, yeah," she said, grinning. "We're pretty excited about that."

"You should be. I also understand that Devin decided to keep both football *and* drama on his schedule. How is he doing?"

"He's keeping up pretty well, I guess. Gradewise he could be doing better, but he's not failing or anything. And he's doing great in drama. Mrs. Higgins says he's a natural actor."

Lesley remembered how worried Coby had been the first day about being responsible for nudging Devin into taking the class. "See? Now aren't you glad you introduced him to acting?"

"Yeah. I guess so."

The resemblance between father and daughter was evident when Coby grinned. They had the same mouth, Lesley noted, the same captivating expression when pleased about something.

"The only problem is with Devin's parents," Coby said. "They're not real thrilled about him being in drama. They're afraid it'll interfere with the football."

"Oh, that's too bad. Maybe when they see him in the play they'll change their minds."

"Yeah. Maybe." Coby wondered if she should just come right out and ask Ms. Tyler what was on her mind. She hadn't planned to at first, she'd merely been curious about the woman. That curiosity satisfied, she found she was anxious to know more. "I, uh, heard that you rode to the sale with Dad this morning," she said. "Will he be giving you a ride home, too?"

"Yes, I suppose so. Why do you ask?"

"I was just…I mean, I was wanting to know in case I needed to find a ride with someone else." Coby felt funny lying about it that way. But she couldn't just come right out and ask if Ms. Tyler and her dad had something going on.

"Oh. Well, I'm sure I could find a ride somewhere else if it's going to be a problem," Lesley said.

"No, no. That's all right. I don't want you guys to change your plans for me," Coby said. "Devin's right over there and I can ride with him. I was, you know, just wondering."

"Change our plans?" Lesley asked, her voice puzzled.

"Yeah. If you two are going to go out tonight after the sale—"

"Why, no," Lesley said. "Why would you think that your father and I have plans, Coby?"

"He said he'd be out tonight, so I thought maybe since you had ridden with him to the sale this morning... well, I thought that meant he'd be doing something with you."

"Um, no. No, we're not doing anything together."

"Oh," the girl said, and Lesley could've sworn she heard disappointment in the single syllable. "But, you know, I think it would be pretty cool if you guys did want to go out together."

Lesley's eyes widened in surprise.

"You probably have lots in common," his daughter went on. "Both of you are teachers. That is, he's a coach and you're a principal, but still... And he hasn't dated at all since I've been living with him." Coby frowned, noticing that Ms. Tyler looked uncomfortable with what she was saying. "Oh, you're probably going with someone else right now, huh?"

"What? Oh, I...no, but—"

"Oh, really? You're not?" Coby's frown lifted. "Well, then, since both of you are single and have so much in common and all..." Coby rolled her eyes, then gazed down at the pavement, realizing how stupid this was sounding. "It's just that Dad always worries whether I'll approve, you know, of his dates. And so I—" she exhaled "—I just thought I'd say that I do."

Lesley didn't know what to say. This was such an awkward situation. She was pleased, moved in fact, by Coby's approval, but... as a candidate to date her father?

"I'm very touched that you feel that way, Coby. And I know that your father considers your opinion valuable. But, um, like I said, we...have no plans for this evening... or any other evening for that matter."

Lesley waited for a reaction, hoping she'd handled the situation with the proper amount of tact, and at the same time hoping she'd gotten her point across.

Coby nodded. "Okay. Listen, you probably think I was being too nosy...."

"No. I think it's fine that you're curious, Coby. He's your father."

"Oh, good, then. Well, I...guess I'd better get back to the toy booth. It was... great talking to you."

"Yes. It was good talking to you, too."

"See ya," Coby said, then left Lesley to wonder if she'd imagined the conversation that had just taken place.

A few hours later, Lesley had slipped the talk with Coby to the back of her mind. The sale was winding down, and, from all appearances, it had been a big success. The tool booth alone had taken in more than two hundred dollars. The weary grins wreathing other volunteers' faces told Lesley their booths had done well, too.

The cleanup went quickly. Lesley helped David and Kent haul leftover items to a storeroom in the school. They would be added to next year's donations, she was told.

Once their booth had been cleaned up and dismantled, Lesley looked around the lot for Gil. His booth had been cleared away, too, and neither he nor his student helpers were anywhere to be found.

It was he who finally found her. He came up behind her, startling her by placing his hand on her shoulder. There were two people, a man and a woman, with him.

"Here she is," he said, dropping his arm across both of her shoulders. He smiled down at her. "I thought you might want to meet two colleagues of ours from Andrews," he said.

"Oh. Why, yes, of course." She made an attempt at pulling off the cap, which immediately became entangled with her ponytail. Gil untangled hat and hair with his free hand. His other hand never moved from its proprietary position on her shoulder. "You say you, uh...teach in the Andrews schools?" Lesley asked.

"They certainly do," Gil said, handing her the cap. "Jeannie and A. J. Graves, meet Lesley Tyler, our new principal here at Warren."

"So nice to meet you," Jeannie said, and A.J. seconded it, shaking her hand vigorously.

"We've been listening to your coach brag for the past half hour about his come-from-behind team," A.J. said. "As always, we're glad that our school is small enough to be in a different division."

"Yes," Lesley said, giving "her" coach a caustic look. He ignored it. He also kept his hand on her shoulder. "I...um, noticed you have the same last names. You're married?" she asked distractedly.

"Yes," Jeannie said. "In fact, we just celebrated our six-month anniversary."

"Newlyweds," Lesley said, beginning to get an inkling as to why Gil had introduced them. She gave Gil another look, which he again ignored. "Congratulations."

Before a thank-you could be issued, Gil chimed in again. "Yeah, great, isn't it? And you know, it's the strangest coincidence." He squeezed her shoulder. "A.J., like you, is the principal at their school. And Jeannie here is a coach, like me. She heads up the girls' sports program."

"YOU KNOW, you never did tell me your favorite food. Mexican or Italian?"

Lesley stared at Gil in the dusk-darkened interior of his car. She'd seen that expression before. Somewhere between amused and smug, it was one she'd grown more and more familiar with the longer she knew him. He thought he'd made a point by introducing her to his married friends from Andrews, but he was mistaken.

"Since we ended up not going out to eat together that night, and since we won't be going to eat together in the future, why do you need to know?'' She looked straight ahead, realizing she sounded petulant, even sulky, but not particularly caring. She hated the feeling of being railroaded.

"Just giving you the chance to choose what you'd like to eat," he said mildly. "You should have taken me up on my offer of Luigi's or La Bodega's, though. Now your only choice is Taco Villa or Sam's Spaghetti Emporium. They both have takeout."

"Gil," she said with a sigh, "I haven't changed my mind about us."

"I know that." His words were matter-of-fact as he checked over his shoulder for cars, then changed lanes. He flashed her a grin. "That's why I'll have to work on you some more."

Lesley shook her head. The man was too used to winning. He didn't seem to be able to grasp the concept of giving up. "And what if I say that I don't want takeout food, Mexican or Italian? Or that, more specifically, I don't want to be 'worked on'?"

"To the first I'd say that you've gotta eat. You're probably too tired to cook, which is entirely my fault. And you have no dishes. I take the blame for that, too. Since you won't be seen with me in public, I'm forced to resort to takeout. If Mexican or Italian isn't to your liking, then—"

"It's not the food I object to, and you know it. It's the fact that you feel there's a chance for the two of us to...to..."

"Get to know one another better," he supplied easily. "That's all I'm asking for at this point, Lesley.

Some of that was happening this morning when I brought you to the sale. It wasn't so bad, was it?"

"No, but—"

"And what about this business with Kelly? Wouldn't it be nice to have someone to discuss it with tonight before you call her back? I'm the perfect someone, Lesley. I already know all the details. We can go from there. I could help you figure out what you're going to say—what?" he said, seeing her shake her head.

"I *would* like someone to talk it over with, but I'm not so sure you're that perfect someone. Things could...get out of hand," she said, thinking about the night at the health club. It had been all too easy to forget herself in a public place. What would happen in the privacy of her own living room?

"You're gonna get mad if I say I certainly hope so, aren't you?"

"Gil—"

"Okay, okay. If I promise to keep the subject on Kelly, will you let me buy you a taco, and will you let me eat one with you at your house?"

It was tempting. As she'd said, it would be good to talk it over with someone before she called Kelly again. Stacey would be out with Russell tonight, so there was no point calling her. And Gil *did* know the details. She wouldn't even mind sharing a taco with him.

"I'm taking you at your word on this, Coach. No 'working on me,' okay?" she said finally.

He smiled, not bothering to correct her on the "Coach" business this time. "Great," he said, pulling his Mustang up to the Taco Villa drive-through and cranking down the window. "I've been craving a burrito with red sauce all day long."

Forty-five minutes later, seated at her kitchen table, Lesley watched in amazement as Gil finished his third burrito, then wadded up the wrapping.

"How do you keep from gaining weight when you eat like that?" she asked.

"The health club," he said, swallowing his last bite. "And the fact that I don't always eat like that."

"I see. It's burritos with red sauce that bring out the glutton in you." Lesley folded her lone taco wrapper neatly and took a sip of her soft drink, glad she'd given in to Gil's request for Mexican food and conversation. True to his word, he'd kept the subject off them, listening instead to details about her background as they related to Kelly and her sisters and the upcoming wedding. Maybe she should have been surprised at how easy it had been to confide in Gil, but she wasn't. Though few people knew about her mother's breakdown, Gil was now one of them.

"I eat more when I'm nervous," he said, breaking into her thoughts as he strode back to the table after depositing trash in the bin.

Lesley looked up with a short laugh. "You've never been nervous in your life," she scoffed.

"You don't think so?" He slid into his chair with a casual ease that belied his suddenly serious expression. His eyes darkening to a steely gray, he said, "I do get nervous. I'm nervous now."

"I find that hard to believe."

"You shouldn't. It has to do with making promises that are damned hard to keep."

Gil sensed her uneasiness even before she rose from her chair and headed for the trash with the meticulously creased and folded paper that had been her taco wrapper. "I'll put on some coffee," she said.

"Sure. Sounds good." Gil moved to the living room, taking a seat on the couch and vowing to tread in safer waters.

"So," he said, raising his voice so she could hear him in the kitchen, "getting back to the wedding. You feel that Kelly and Stephen's major stumbling block is going to be the money?"

"Well, yes. And I think it could be a big enough stumbling block to cause some significant problems for them." She came around the corner, leaning one hip against a wall, the empty coffeepot in her hand. "I'll use me as an example."

"You?"

"Yes. As I told you, after Mother's breakdown I ended up feeling more or less responsible for the girls. We had a sitter, of course—I was only ten years old at the time—but certain things naturally fell to me, being the oldest."

"What kind of things?" Gil asked. Though she'd mentioned that her mother's illness had meant added responsibilities for her, he still had a hard time imagining what those responsibilities could have been. Ten years old was too young, he thought.

"Well, Dad was a terrible cook," she said with a wry smile. "And an even worse housekeeper."

Gil was careful to keep his expression bland. Good Lord, he thought, her father had let her cook and clean for them at that age?

"Anyway, as I was saying, I've always felt as if I should take care of the girls. After Mother and Dad died I became financially responsible as well." She headed back for the kitchen and filled the coffee maker with water. "I had just graduated from college when Dad died. I got a teaching job and an apartment big enough for four." The light in the kitchen went out, and Gil watched Lesley walk back into the living room. She settled on the opposite end of the couch.

"As you well know," she continued, "a teacher's salary isn't always enough to support four people. It was awfully tough at times. In fact," she said, her voice growing more somber, "sometimes I didn't know how we'd make it." She shook her head. "Kelly doesn't understand. She doesn't remember how rough it can be. I know she's twenty-five, not an unreasonably young age to be considering marriage, but they have some major strikes against them right now."

Gil nodded in agreement. "So you're going to try to convince her to wait?"

"What else can I do? He's going back to school, she would be supporting the both of them on a salary from a company that's just barely opened its doors, and they've only known each other for four months."

Gil took a sip of his coffee, knowing that, under the circumstances, his reaction would be similar to Lesley's if Coby was involved, no matter how old she was. He also remembered being on the other side of the argument. He and Ceil had been young and equally headstrong when they'd approached both sets of families. "I hate to be the voice of doom, but you realize how difficult it's going to be convincing them to wait, don't you? That first-love stuff is pretty potent.''

"You don't think it would be possible for me to talk to them? Maybe if I got together with the two of them ... if I just sat them down and discussed it with them. I could fly to Austin next weekend and—''

"Risk alienating her."

Lesley sighed. "I know. But how do I go about helping her without taking that risk?" Frustrated, she said, "Oh, I don't seem to know how to handle my relationships with the girls at all anymore. Since the move I ... well, the distance seems to have changed everything. They've put everything into perspective just fine. Now they see me as their big sister, nothing more. I just don't seem to have adjusted quite as well."

"And you think you should have?"

"Yes. They're right, after all. That was then, this is now. Though they may have needed more from me once, they don't anymore. My problem is that I think I still need to be their parent as well."

"Sounds normal to me."

"Normal? It's not normal. I'm just their sister. And we're half a state away from each other now. Never mind the fact that they're all in their twenties and—''

Gil reached for the hand she'd draped across the back of the sofa, effectively halting her words. "You know what it sounds like to me? It sounds like the empty-nest syndrome in reverse. They didn't move out, you did."

"It does, doesn't it?" A smile slowly edged its way across her lips. "I never thought about it that way before."

"And you wouldn't tell a parent who had sent their last child off to college that what they were feeling was abnormal, would you?"

"No," she said, the smile still hovering. "No, I wouldn't." She rose from the couch and made her way to the kitchen for the coffee. "You know, you're pretty smart for a—"

"Don't say it," he warned.

"What?" she asked, poking her head around the corner.

"You were going to say pretty smart for a jock, weren't you?"

"I was not. I was going to say for a man."

A grin played at the corners of her lips as she came back with two cups of steaming coffee. "Thanks," he said when she handed him a cup.

"You're welcome."

Lesley folded one knee beneath her when she sat, reminding Gil of the day her foot had fallen asleep. Suddenly he thought of massaging that foot, kissing her.... He pushed the image aside, wondering how he'd get through this evening without kissing her again.

"I take it the decision to move away from your sisters wasn't an easy one," he said.

"Hmm. You're right." She set her cup down on an end table, twisting slightly at the waist to do so. Gil's gaze went to the purple satin ribbon that held back her hair. The day's exertions had tugged several wisps of hair free of the ponytail, and they lay now across the soft ivory skin of her neck. He forced himself to concentrate on her words when she turned back to him.

"I'd always seen myself more as an administrator than as a teacher, and the girls knew that. They pushed, prodded and generally drove me crazy until they'd convinced me that it was an ideal career move I couldn't afford to pass up."

"I'm glad they were pushers and prodders."

"Oh, right. Sure," she said, her tone light. "You were just thrilled when I became principal at Warren. Thrilled with all the changes I made."

He smiled. "Well, yeah... at first I wasn't. But do you want to know what I thought the very first time we met?"

"I think I already do."

"Oh, I don't know about that." He captured her hand and ran his thumb over hers. "I thought you were going to be a major pain."

"And you were right," Lesley said, her manner flip.

"Yeah. I was right."

Surprised, Lesley gave him a look of pretended outrage. "Oh, you were, were you?"

He laughed and stubbornly held fast to her hand when she tried to pull away. He laced their fingers together. "Yep."

"Well..." She stared down at their hands, noticing the patterns of blond-brown hair that swirled at his wrist. "That was in the beginning. Do you... still think of me as a pain?"

He moved closer to her on the couch, until his knees were almost touching hers. "Yeah, you're a pain, all right. But only because you're still so hesitant about us."

It had happened. Her prediction about tonight. And so easily. She cleared her throat. "I seem to remember something about a promise you made earlier."

"The one where I said I'd keep the subject on Kelly?" he asked, studying their clasped hands. "Am I to be held solely responsible for the change of subject?"

"No," she said slowly. Not for the change of subject or for the attraction she tried to hide from both herself and him.

His lips curved in one of his oh-so-appealing grins, and he moved closer. His fingers dipped inside the collar of her shirt, sending showers of warmth outward from the place on her neck he was touching, caressing.

An objection formed in her mind, but it never found voice. It was tripped up, sabotaged by the memory of sensations she suddenly longed to feel again.

His mouth met hers. The kiss seemed to take up where the last one had left off, sparking newer sensations. The feel of his fingers, warm and firm, through the fabric of her shirt. The pleasure of whisper-soft murmurs he made against her lips when her hands explored his strong arms, his shoulders, the light stubble of his jaw.

Good sense took over for a moment and Lesley's hands stilled. She murmured his name, making a token protest.

"Shh," he whispered back, clearly recognizing the objection for what it was. Then he kissed her again.

And again. She parted her lips for him, for herself. Arguments be damned, good sense be damned, everything be damned! She was doing as Kelly had once instructed. Thinking with her hormones. And it felt good. Too good.

Gil knew he had to stop. It was crazy. Lesley was in his arms, exactly where he wanted her to be. But he had to stop. For her.

He pulled away, watching confusion replace the desire in her eyes.

"Gil, I—"

He put a finger to her lips to forestall any comments or protests. "No. Don't say anything." He took a deep breath, wondering if such valiant restraint might find him a place in heaven one day. He placed a kiss on her brow, then rested his forehead against hers.

"I don't want you to let what happened here make you crazy," he said. "You've got other things on your mind right now. Deal with them first." He lifted his head and looked deeply into her eyes. "Just know that I'm here, that the situation between you and me is here and that one day you're going to have to face it."

He got up and walked to the closet in the entryway to retrieve his jacket. She following him, her arms hugging her middle.

"Will you do me one favor?" he asked, sliding his arms into the sleeves, then snapping three bottom snaps. "Give yourself a break with your sisters. There's no handbook on how quickly you're supposed to adjust to this situation. Protective instincts don't go away just because you change your mailing address.''

"You're probably right.''

"Yeah," he said. "Pretty smart for a man, huh?''

She laughed, then gasped when he stole another quick, heated kiss. When he pulled back, she looked away and Gil turned her face toward him with a finger at her chin. His tone quite serious, he told her, "Though I'm not expecting you to dwell on the matter, fantasizing is allowed.''

He left her with a smile on her face. She locked the door behind her, then leaned back against it, sighing. What in the world did she think she was doing falling in love with a man like Gil Fielden!

CHAPTER NINE

THE APARTMENT WAS QUIET when Gil returned home, except for the noise from the television in Coby's room. She must have forgotten to turn it off before leaving with Devin, he thought as he hung up his jacket, dropping his car keys on a nearby table.

He whistled on his way to the stairs. Tonight had gone pretty well, he thought. There might have been doubts and caution in Lesley's eyes, but there'd also been passion. In her eyes *and* in her kiss. He thought of what she'd once said about hormonal control, and smiled. He liked Lesley out of control. He'd like to see a lot more of it.

Turning at the top of the stairs, he nudged open Coby's door and was surprised to find her there. She was lying across the bed with the phone at her ear.

"Oops. Sorry," he whispered, already backing out the door. "Didn't expect to find you home this early."

She rolled her eyes and mouthed, "I'm talking to Mother."

"Oh. Okay." He pulled her door closed and walked down the hall to his room, not thrilled with the hassled expression on his daughter's face. He'd been under the impression that Coby and her mother had been getting along better. What could have happened? he wondered as he shut his door and discarded his jeans and shirt in favor of a worn but comfortable set of sweats.

Moments later, Coby's knock sounded on his door, signaling that he was about to find out. "Come on in."

Coby did just that, then dropped to the edge of the bed and leaned back on her elbows. She watched him sort laundry for a minute or two. "Thought you'd be out late tonight, too," she finally said. "Did you have this dying urge to wash clothes, or what?"

"Nope. I just decided to make it an early evening," he answered, pitching a pair of jeans on the jeans pile. He thought for a moment about saying something to Coby about Lesley, then decided against it. After all, there wasn't much to say. Yet. "What about you?"

"I was too tired to go out. And Devin has relatives in town he needs to visit with, so we decided not to go anywhere."

"I see. Throw me those two shirts by your arm, will you?" He caught them and added them to his other colored shirts. "You and your mom arguing again?" he asked.

"Of course," she said with a harassed look. "You didn't think she could actually let more than two months go by without throwing one of her famous fits, did you?"

"Coby, there's no need to be sarcastic."

Coby expelled a long-suffering sigh. "Right. I should be the model of patience. After all, I had such a good role model in her."

Gil frowned. "Coby—"

"All right, all right. It's just that she makes me so mad sometimes. She's on her soapbox about grades again."

"Grades?" Why was Ceil worried about Coby's grades? The most recent update he'd received on Coby's grades had been last Friday, when the weekly reports had come out. The reports had been Lesley's idea; they were her way to make sure extracurricular-activity teachers were kept abreast of their students' averages before there was cause to worry. Coby's grades, as he recalled, had been fine.

"Yeah. Remember my grade in English that dropped from an A to a low B? Well, Mom is a friend of my English teacher, and that teacher told her about the B. And of course Mom had to make a federal deal out of it."

"I see."

"Why should she have a say, Dad? You're the parent I'm living with now, and you didn't get upset about the grade."

"She's just concerned, Coby."

"Obsessed, you mean."

"Concerned." But he was inclined to agree with Coby if Ceil was having fits over B's. Good grief, this was their daughter's senior year; she deserved to be cut some slack after twelve years of perfect performance. Ceil needed to lighten up a bit. Maybe she'd forgotten what had happened to Greg, he thought. Maybe it was time he had a talk with his ex-wife to remind her of what pushing a teenager could do.

"I know that your mother gets on your nerves about the grades," he said, "but try to remember that I always wanted to know how you were doing when you lived with her. It's the same thing."

"Yeah, but you wouldn't have overreacted if I'd ever brought home a grade that was less than perfect. I'm tired of having to be perfect for her. At least you understand that I can have other interests besides my studies and still get by just fine."

"That's not to say that I don't want you to do the best you can. But, yes, I do think you can be interested in drama as well as all of your other classes. Look, I'll make you a deal. You be sure those grades don't slip any more and I'll talk to your mom. Deal?"

Coby smiled. "Deal."

"Good. Grab that pile of shirts and bring it down to the washer for me, huh?"

"Sure." She picked up the clothes and followed him down the stairs. "By the way, Dad, just where were you before you cut your evening short?"

Gil paused on the bottom step and looked up. He guessed there was no harm in telling her where he'd been. "I took Ms. Tyler home from the sale, then we ate some takeout at her house."

Coby grinned. "Now isn't that strange."

"What do you mean, 'strange'?"

"Oh, just that I asked her today if the two of you were going out tonight, and she said no."

"You *asked* her?" That must have gone over like a lead balloon, he thought.

"Uh-huh. I hope you don't mind," she said, nudging him in the back to move off the stairs. "I mean, you're always wondering whether I approve of your dates or not, so I wanted to find out if she was...one of 'em."

"I don't mind," he said, continuing on his way to the utility room. "I guess I'm wondering where you would get the idea that the two of us were dating."

"You were giving her some pretty intense looks at the sale today, Dad."

Pretty intense looks? He hadn't realized he'd made things so obvious. Flipping up the washer lid and turning it to the permanent press cycle, he filled the machine with the first load. "And you say that she said no, huh?"

"Right." Coby deposited her armful of clothes on the floor next to the apartment-sized washer and dryer. She leaned her elbows on top of the dryer and gave her father a mischievous grin. "What do *you* say, Coach?"

The kid was too smart for her own good, Gil thought, giving her a sideways glance. "I say that she's not really convinced that it's a good idea for us to date, but that I'd like to change her mind."

"What do you mean she doesn't think going out with you is a good idea? What's wrong with you, I'd like to know! Oh, let me guess. She's probably got you figured for a typical jock, right?"

Gil smiled at the way Coby immediately jumped to his defense, even when no defense was needed. He leaned back against the washer and folded his arms across his middle. "She's worried about conflict of interest because of the no-pass, no-play thing. You know she's the one who has to oversee it, and I'm one of the ones she has to oversee. That kind of thing. But," he said, winking at Coby, "between you and me, I think I'm wearing her down."

"All right! Go for it, Dad."

"Go for it?" He laughed, swung an arm around Coby's neck and walked her out of the utility room and toward the refrigerator, stopping there for two colas. He handed one to Coby, then popped the top on his. "You weren't this gung ho about the last woman I dated. Seems to me I remember you going through a why-can't-you-and-Mom-get-back-together routine."

"It was just a stage, Dad. Besides, Ms. Tyler is pretty together. I like her."

"You wouldn't have a problem with the two of us dating?"

"Nah." Coby took a sip of her drink. "Oh, I almost forgot. *Saturday Night Live* is on. Want to watch it with me?"

"I wouldn't miss it," he said, scrambling to his favorite chair in the living room before Coby could get there. He answered her scowl with a smug look.

LESLEY TRACED a fingertip over the edge of the elegant crystal champagne flute. It was beautiful, so beautiful. And expensive. But not so expensive that it was completely out of her price range. She could keep the purchase to only four pieces of the imported crystal and still be within her allotted wedding present budget.

She glanced across the department store aisle to the stoneware dishes that Kelly had mentioned needing and sighed. She liked the popular Southwestern-styled pattern that Kelly had picked out. And it was a more practical gift—for the price of four of the flutes she could buy the whole set of stoneware.

She bit her lip and stared again at the lovely creation in her hand. It caught the light in the room, making it its own. Holding it up, Lesley turned it this way and that. Beautiful, she thought again, utterly exquisite. And a luxury item, pure and simple, she told herself.

The stoneware was what she'd buy, of course. Practicality demanded it. Just as practicality demanded she set down the crystal and find a saleslady before her entire lunch hour was gone. She'd already been in this store, grappling with the same decision, two other times this week. She wasn't about to leave here a third time without making up her mind. Giving the crystal one last wistful look, she headed for the stoneware.

"That's one of our most popular patterns of stoneware," an approaching saleswoman said. She peered through half glasses at Lesley's selection and smiled. "Is your kitchen and dining room done in the Southwestern style?"

"No. It's not for me. My sister is getting married. She's registered at your store in Austin."

"Ah, yes. Right this way." The woman led her to a computer that held the information they needed. "Your sister's name?"

"Kelly Tyler."

"Yes. Here she is. And what pieces would you like to order?"

Lesley's thoughts flew to the crystal. She imagined the pleasure in Kelly's eyes when she opened such a gift, imagined the pleasure she would feel giving such a gift. Taking a deep breath, she made one last attempt at recovering her usual practicality but didn't quite manage it. At least, not entirely.

"I'd like two place settings of the stoneware," she said. "And I'd like two of your crystal champagne flutes in the Eternity pattern."

"Oh, the Eternity," the woman said, her eyes lighting up. "Your sister will be thrilled, I'm sure."

Walking out of the store moments later, Lesley had to smile at how purchasing the crystal had made her feel reckless. She shook her head. Yes, she was a regular daredevil, all right. Her sisters would get quite a kick out of it when she told them. But when their laughter died down, she thought, they would understand. Making a decision such as the one she'd just made hadn't come easy for her. It was a new feeling, this recklessness, but a good one.

Kelly would definitely approve of her behavior once she laid eyes on those flutes, Lesley thought. Just as she was now more approving of Kelly and Stephen's plans. The difference that two weeks could make was amazing. She'd even discussed the wedding with Kelly, both over the phone and in person last weekend when Kelly and Stephen had driven to Warren—at Kelly's insistence.

It had reassured Lesley to see how much Stephen truly cared for her sister. Even more reassuring was the fact that he cared enough to want Lesley's blessing. He'd taken her aside, talked to her about finances, told her of the modest savings account he had set aside and assured her that he was ready to carry his load by working weekends at his father's shop if necessary. He hadn't realized how much of a burden he'd lifted from her shoulders.

And now that the load was lifted...

Unlocking her car and starting it up, Lesley switched her thoughts to Gil. He'd told her not to dwell on their relationship as long as things hadn't been resolved with her and Kelly.

Fantasizing is allowed. Who had he been kidding? Allowed? It had become damn impossible to prevent it! Was it the same for him? she wondered. Had he thought of her, too? She'd seen very little of him since the night at her house—just a few times in passing, at school and from the stands at the last two football games she'd attended. Maybe absence, in his case, hadn't made the heart grow fonder. Maybe he hadn't spent time imagining, fantasizing.

She had.

Often.

"STACEY," LESLEY SAID, watching the secretary collate the weekly grade reports. "Do you mind if I distribute those today? I'd like to get out of the office for a few minutes."

"I don't mind. But why don't you just go to the teachers' lounge for a break. You haven't had one all day."

"No, I need to check on something while I'm out."

"Okay." Stacey handed Lesley the stack. "Hey, by the way, did you finally make a decision on those dishes? Or did you come back empty-handed again?"

"Yes," Lesley said with a smile as she opened the outer office door. "I made a decision."

Twenty minutes later she'd delivered all but two of the reports; only the drama and football departments remained. Opening one of the double doors at the back of the auditorium, Lesley slipped inside and made her way down the large center aisle. It was dark except for the lights on stage, quiet except for the lines being read by the actors. She found the drama coach sitting about halfway down, intent on the scene being rehearsed. Lesley knelt beside Mrs. Higgins's chair. "I have your weekly grade reports, Genevieve," she whispered, handing them to her.

"Thank you, Lesley." The woman never took her eyes off the stage.

"Do you mind if I watch for a few moments?"

"Not at all. I'm awfully proud of this production." Her gaze finally moved to Lesley. "I think you'll agree that I've been blessed with some of the most dedicated and talented young people this year."

"So I'd heard," Lesley commented, then focused her attention on the scene. Coby had the part of one of the aunts in *Arsenic and Old Lace*. And from what Lesley could see, she was doing an excellent job of bringing the dotty old woman to life. Devin's role was that of the nephew Cary Grant had played in the movie version. And it was apparent to Lesley that Coby hadn't been exaggerating the boy's talent. If anything, she'd understated his ability.

He was wonderful. Though Lesley was no expert, she knew talent when she saw it. His portrayal of the beleaguered nephew at wits' end over his aunt's unorthodox solution to loneliness was as charming as Grant's. Lesley smiled as she watched, totally drawn in. Devin had his character's frustration and disbelief pinned down, she thought. And his timing was right on the mark. No doubt about it, Devin was a natural actor.

Mrs. Higgins called for a break, and Lesley thought about what Coby had said at the sale. Devin's parents weren't pleased with his interest in drama. It was understandable, considering all the football scholarship offers he'd received. She shook her head, hoping their displeasure wouldn't result in a demand for him to give up acting. It would be a shame for his talent to go to waste.

A glance at her watch told her there was only a half hour left of school. She turned to go just as the scene on stage was beginning again.

When she got to the door, it swung open and Gil entered the auditorium, almost colliding with Lesley head-on. He grasped her upper arms in an effort to steady her. "Hey, there," was his soft, whispered greeting.

"Hello." Lesley's heart beat faster, and not because of the near collision. "I was . . . just coming to see you."

"You were?"

"I . . . had to deliver these grade reports."

"Oh. Yes, the reports." His hands fell away. There had been a distinct note of disappointment in his voice that was somewhat encouraging, Lesley thought. "I came down to catch Coby in action before afternoon practice starts," he said, glancing over Lesley's shoulder at the stage.

Lesley turned, watching with him. "She's terrific. They all are. I stopped in to see a bit of rehearsal myself."

Gil concentrated on the scene, his smile growing as the action progressed. He laughed softly at one of Coby's lines.

"See what I mean?" Lesley said.

"Yeah. She's something, isn't she?"

"Yes." Lesley looked up at him. "So is Devin, don't you think?"

But his eyes were on Coby and Coby alone. He looked down at her with a grin. "Devin who?" Then he took her arm. "Let's go," he said, leading her out of the auditorium.

He let go of her arm once they were in the hall, and glanced pointedly at the slips of paper she still held. "You said you wanted to give me those reports?"

"Uh . . . yes. And I'd like to talk to you in your office if you don't mind. It's about no-pass, no-play."

"Okay," he said as he began to walk in that direction. "So, how are things on the sister front? Have you had a chance to talk to Kelly?"

"As a matter of fact, things are much better with Kelly. She and Stephen came to visit me last weekend."

"They came to Warren?"

"Yes, they did."

There was a smile in her eyes, a welcome sight after the tension Gil had witnessed two weeks ago. It occurred to him that this was the way he always wanted to see her, happy.

"It may surprise you to know that I'm almost looking forward to the wedding now," she told him.

"Is that right?"

"Yes, it is. Stephen seems to be quite a responsible young man, and it's apparent how much in love they are. I'm actually glad they found one another."

"And how about you and Kelly?" he asked. "Does she understand now how difficult the situation's been for you since the move?"

His concern touched Lesley. "Yes. We talked about that, too. You know, it's amazing what one weekend of conversation can do. We discussed all of it—how the girls feel about their independence, my need to still be involved to a certain point."

As they continued down the hallway toward Gil's office, the details of Lesley and Kelly's discussions came tumbling out. "And so I think the conversations we had led to better understanding of each other. I realize now that my protective instincts toward the girls were blocking my ability to see them as adults. And Kelly said she'd never considered that I might be experiencing 'reverse empty-nest syndrome,' as you called it."

Gil was glad that Lesley and Kelly had resolved things. For more reasons than one. "I'll bet that takes a load off your mind," he said.

"Oh, yes." She was careful to keep her gaze directed forward, knowing exactly what he meant. If the situation with Kelly was no longer something to dwell on... Trying to keep the mood light, she quipped, "And I was able to put the ways-I-can-convince-Kelly-to-change-her-mind list aside."

Gil chuckled, but he was silent the rest of the way down the hall. Lesley's mind filled the void with doubts and insecurities.

How could a relationship between them work? Aside from her fear of conflict over the no-pass, no-play issue, they had such different personalities. Gil was the very definition of cocky self-assurance. He was aggressive, a winner, someone who by his own admission had bent the rules to serve his purpose in the past.

Lesley on the other hand had never met a rule she didn't like. And while she supposed people might consider her self-assured, they had no idea that her way of maintaining that was to arm herself with lists. Lists that told her what to do, when to do it, even how to do it. Impulsiveness, to her, was as difficult to fathom as the Chinese alphabet.

As usual where Gil was concerned, her hormones jumped into the fray, reminding her that their attraction was real. Very real. Though there was a respectable two to three feet between them as they walked, Lesley's physical reaction to him was undeniable. Of course, the fact that he was dressed in a sweatshirt and shorts didn't help matters. That particular outfit had had top billing in two full weeks of fantasies.

"Here we are," he said suddenly, putting an end to reverie. He unlocked his office door, motioned her in, then closed the door behind them. She took the chair he offered, looking around the room while he sat behind his desk. Great, she thought, no real privacy here. One wall was half glass and looked out into a small gymnasium where a P.E. class was being held.

The room, she thought, was an organizer's nightmare. A huge bulletin board on the wall behind him had five years' worth of messages and memos pinned to it, leaving absolutely no space for more. The desk itself was a catastrophe. Books on sports, more paper, even a basketball littered its surface. Lesley bent over, picking up several stray sheets of paper that had spilled onto the floor. She handed them to him.

"Thanks," he said, adding them to one of the piles. He gave her a self-deprecatory grin. "It's the maid's day off."

"So I see." The maid, she decided, hadn't been in for quite some time. All along the floor next to the half-glass wall lay various pieces of sports equipment. Footballs, a baseball bat or two, even a tennis racket that needed restringing. If it weren't for the desk, the office would look more like an equipment room.

Gil's phone rang, and Lesley busied herself watching the P.E. class in the gym. Maybe she'd picked a good time to tell him, she thought, what with all those boys and coaches so close and visible. With her and Gil so visible to the boys, she amended.

He hung up the phone, then leaned back in his chair. "No-pass, no-play, huh? What wonderful new restrictions are in store for me today?"

His voice held a teasing note, but it wasn't enough to soothe the sudden attack of nerves she was experiencing. "No new restrictions," she said. "But I do have a...change."

He gave her a suspicious look. "What kind of change are we talking here?"

"I...don't think you'll be opposed to it. Keep in mind that I *do* want to hear your opinion, pro or con. If you object for any reason—"

"Lesley. Tell me your change."

Yes. The time for hemming and hawing was over. She turned a deep breath and dove right in. "I've decided to turn everything dealing with no-pass, no-play over to Dwight Collins. He's expressed a definite interest in overseeing the programs I've initiated, and I feel confident that he can handle the extra duty. And it will free up my time to—"

"Hold it," Gil cut in. He sat up straight. "Why, Lesley?"

"I was...telling you why. Now that my programs are all in place and Dwight is anxious to take on more responsibility, I see no reason not to give it to him."

Her explanation was all very well and good, Gil thought, but that wasn't her entire reason. Or at least he hoped it wasn't. He hoped her decision to distance herself from no-pass, no-play had something to do with eliminating conflict of interest, with taking steps toward a possible relationship with him. Of course, she'd still be on the district executive board, he mused. Would she consider that a barrier to becoming involved with him?

The past two weeks had been a true test of his patience. Though he'd told himself he could wait even longer if need be, Gil knew now that he couldn't. He rose from his chair, planted both palms on the cluttered desktop and leaned forward. "I'm not asking about Collins's abilities or his interest in no-pass, no-play. I want to know if this means what I think it means. Are you here to talk to me about school policies or are you here to talk about us?"

This was it. She'd brought herself to the edge of a cliff and it was time to either back away or find the courage to jump. In the past she'd always chosen safety over adventure, caution over risk. That, however, was before Gil. He made her want adventure, made her... want. "I'm here to talk about us."

His expression was unreadable. For several seconds he simply stared at her as the whistle around his neck swung in tiny pendulumlike arcs with each breath he took.

Seconds, Lesley thought, had never felt so long.

Then he stood straight, lifting his hands from the desk. His expression calm and his voice mild, he said, "So Dwight Collins will be the head watchdog now."

"Yes. He'll oversee everything. Grade reports, study halls for extracurricular students who need them, everything."

She cleared her throat. "I'll still be on the district board, but this is a solution to our... conflict-of-interest problem." Her gaze met his and she took the final step off the cliff. "I... wanted that barrier gone, Gil, and this is the way I've gotten rid of it. I've decided the, um... time for fantasizing is over."

Gil's heart slammed in his chest. This was exactly what he'd been wanting to hear her say for two weeks now. No, he'd wanted it since the night at the health club. Even before. How, he wondered, could one brief statement, one moment in time, make such a difference? Because everything *was* different now. Better. The best.

He stood, a smile curving his lips as he started around the desk. Then he noticed the blur of bodies on the other side of the glass. He pulled up short, remembering that he and Lesley were in full view of about fifty gym students. Frustration dampened his jubilation. "You had to pick now to tell me this, didn't you?"

"I—"

"Hey, Coach, what do you want me to do with these—"

"Out!" Gil's eyes never left Lesley's face as he boomed out the order to a teenage boy who'd stuck his head in the office door.

"Uh, yeah. Sure, Coach . . . I'll come back later."

The door closed quietly.

Gil pushed papers aside and propped one hip against the edge of the desk. "You know that I want to touch you right now. Kiss you," he whispered. "But I can't."

"I . . ." Lesley ducked her head, wondering how shyness could surface when she'd all but told him she wanted him. A matter of mere inches separated them. "I want that, too."

He shook his head and gave a wry chuckle. "We're something, huh? We choose the most public places. . . ."

"Yes."

He looked up, his eyes seemed intent on consuming her whole. For a moment she was almost fearful. She might have stepped off the cliff, but it didn't mean she'd abandoned her instincts for survival. She wondered if it was possible to be with Gil and not lose some of herself in the bargain. Right now it seemed impossible. Highly traitorous feelings were swamping her good sense. For the first time in her life, self-control seemed out of reach, even undesirable. She still had enough common sense, however, to make her get out of her chair and move to the door.

Gil followed. He grasped her arm before she turned the knob. "Come here," he said, and jellyfish that she'd become, she allowed him to walk her to a closet. He opened the door and held it wide, effectively blocking them from view of the class.

"Am I to assume this is your way of saying public places be damned?" she asked, hoping she assumed correctly.

"Yeah," he said, swooping down to deliver a breathtaking kiss.

CHAPTER TEN

BALANCING TWO BOXES, her purse, and the plastic-sheathed dress she'd bought for tonight, Lesley turned her key in the lock and gave the stubborn front door a little kick at the bottom to unstick it. She raced inside the house, dropped her packages, draped the dress over a chair and sped to answer the phone before it stopped ringing.

"Hello."

"Lesley? Dwight."

"Oh, hello, Dwight."

"You sound as if you've been running a race. Hope I haven't called at a bad time."

"You haven't. I'd just come home and heard the phone as I was unlocking the door."

"Should I call back later?"

"No, of course not. What's up?"

"It's nothing major. I just thought you might want to be advised of something. You'll be hearing about it soon enough, but I thought I'd tell you now and get it out of the way."

Lesley eased into one of her dining room chairs. "Has something happened?"

"Well, Mr. Sibley and I had a few words at the football game last night."

She frowned. "Go on."

"Seems that several of his band booster members have expressed their extreme displeasure over one of your policy changes. You know, the one affecting the band's trip to play for the Cowboys' halftime show later this month?"

"Yes." She knew the policy, all right. It had been one of the most glaring examples of rule bending she'd seen since coming to Warren. She'd reworded the penalty unequivocally. Now that the time for the band's trip was getting closer, she wasn't surprised that there were complaints.

"Sibley and his bands' parents feel that since they busted their rear ends raising the money for that trip, all of their little Johns and Janies should be allowed to go, good grades or bad. They think that the students with bad grades shouldn't get to perform in the halftime festivities, but that should be punishment enough. Sibley says *they're* the ones paying for those kids to be on the buses, *not* the school system. Money, not grades, is the issue."

Lesley sighed, propping her chin in her palm. It had been a mere two days since she'd made the decision to give Dwight no-pass, no-play, and already there was a problem. For a moment, anxiety surfaced. What if she'd jumped the gun on this? What if her desire to minimize conflict of interest between Gil and herself had pushed her to decide too hastily? "What did you tell him, Dwight?"

"Oh, probably the same thing you would have. I told him that I didn't care if they'd busted their rear ends or not, the policy change will remain in effect. If those students don't measure up, they won't get to perform during the halftime show, and they won't get to go to Dallas, either. As you said, there's no deterrent to bad grades if a student is allowed to go along for the ride and enjoy the weekend with the rest of the band members."

Lesley smiled. "That's exactly how I would have handled it, Dwight."

"Well, as I told you, this is nothing major. But you can be sure that Sibley will try to go over my head with this. I thought you might like to be warned in advance."

"Yes, thank you."

"I'd thought about waiting until tonight at the faculty dinner, but I didn't know if you'd be coming or not."

"I wouldn't miss it." She glanced at the dress she'd placed on the chair. It had taken her all day to find it, but it was worth the effort. The dress-shop owner, in typical dress-shop-owner style, had called her "a vision in black velvet." She didn't know about that, but she did know the *dress* was beautiful. Would Gil think so? she wondered for the hundredth time.

"Oh, well, I'm glad I called. Tonight probably wouldn't have been the best time to discuss school business anyway," Dwight said.

Lesley smiled at Dwight's obvious eagerness to please. The episode she'd witnessed that day in the teacher's lounge between him and Stacey might not have left a good impression, but she knew him to be a demon when it came to his job. "Dwight, stop worrying. It's reassuring to know that I made the right choice.''

"Why, thank you, Lesley.'' There was a pause, then he added, "Listen, I won't beat around the bush about this. You know that there's a principal's position in the area coming open next week. I've applied for the job. A recommendation from you will go a long way for me with the superintendent. I just want to make sure that you have plenty of reasons to recommend me.''

"Yes, I know about it. And I think you have a good chance for the job. You don't have to worry about my recommendation, Dwight. Your overall job performance is impressive. I wouldn't have given you the extra responsibility if I hadn't thought so.''

"Good." He sounded relieved. "That's good to know."

"Listen, I've got to start getting ready, so—"

"Oh, sure. I'll let you go. Listen, thanks Lesley.''

"You're welcome. Goodbye, Dwight.''

"Bye.''

Lesley cradled the receiver, thankful for Dwight's ambition. There truly was no reason for concern about the way he would be handling things. She was convinced of that now.

She was also convinced that she had to get moving if she was going to become a "vision in black velvet'' in a mere hour and a half.

She filled the tub full of hot water and scented bubbles and admired her new hairdresser's handiwork in the mirror. The woman definitely knew her way around a brush and curling iron. And Lesley agreed with her, the style was . . . sexy. It made her feel sexy.

Pulled up in a sleek French twist, it would do provocative things to the low-cut back of that dress.

Sexy. Provocative.

She'd certainly come a long way since she first met Gil. She had felt schoolmarmish that day. Plain and practical in contrast with his vibrant physicality. But she didn't feel that way now. All day, thoughts of the coming evening had filled her with a new awareness of herself, of her sexuality.

Looking down, Lesley unfastened the buttons on the shirt she'd worn to avoid messing up her new hairstyle. Practical Lesley. Sensible, organized Lesley.

She took the shirt off and glanced up, catching her reflection in the mirror, watching the rise and fall of her breasts with each breath as she wondered about the changes Gil had effected in her. She no longer wanted to be simply practical, sensible Lesley. As Gil had so succinctly put it, she wanted more. She was ready for more.

It had been a gradual change, she realized, starting with that first day in the field house. By slow, steady degrees it had gathered force, fueled by kisses that inspired urgency, touches that had left her with a feeling of longing.

She shed the rest of her clothes and immersed herself in the warm bubble bath, her mind pleasantly occupied with fantasies of the evening to come.

Pleasant.

Somehow the word didn't fit when she thought of making love with Gil. With a smile, she closed her eyes and sank lower in the water. Intense. Exciting. Passionate. Now, those were words....

GIL APPROACHED Lesley's front door, tugging at the new gray-and-red silk tie Coby had selected for him earlier today. He'd wanted the blue one. To match his eyes, he'd explained. To match that tired blue suit of his, she'd countered. And she'd been absolutely right. He'd owned that suit for years because he'd hated shopping.

Coby had taken him in hand. "You want to look sharp, Dad," she'd said, dragging him to the suit racks. "Jeez, you'd think you'd never heard of ZZ Top."

He'd bitched and moaned through the entire shopping spree, but in the end he'd had to agree with her. The black suit, white shirt and silk tie looked good, even if it had set him back the price of a weekend at the Superbowl.

He lifted his hand to his hair, then remembered not to touch. Troy, the hairstylist with the earring whom Coby had chosen, would undoubtedly hunt him down for that. Mousse, he thought with disgust. He'd actually let the guy put mousse in his hair. It looked nice, he supposed, it was just that he'd always had his hair *cut,* not styled. At least he hadn't let Troy give him that perm he'd been so enthusiastic about.

He unbuttoned his jacket and slid his hands into his pants pockets, affecting a casual pose. It wasn't going to work. No matter how hard he might try, there was no way he could feel casual tonight.

He couldn't remember a first date ever being this important. The devastation to his checking account today alone was proof of that. He didn't know how he'd manage it, but he intended to take things slow. No more pushing. No more rushing. He'd learned a lot about Lesley since the day of the parking lot sale, and he'd be smart to put some of that knowledge to work for him. Give her time, give her room. That would be his new motto.

He rang the doorbell.

Long moments passed before she finally opened the door. When she did, she completely dashed his hopes for ever living up to that new motto. She looked beautiful, so beautiful. The dress she wore was black velvet and covered much too much skin to look that seductive, but it did. She did.

"Hi," she said breathlessly, ushering him in.

"Hi." His gaze flicked downward to her stocking feet.

"I sort of . . . fell asleep in the bathtub. I only need a few more seconds."

"Oh, sure. Go ahead."

She turned to leave for her bedroom, and Gil caught his breath. The back of her dress was . . . well, there was no back. "Oh, Lord," he murmured. The new motto didn't stand a chance.

"Ready," she said when she reappeared, this time in black heels.

"You look beautiful, Lesley. That dress is something else."

"Thank you, sir." She smiled, walking closer to him. Her hand went to his sleeve. "But look at you.

This suit," she said with awe in her voice, "is very sharp."

Gil grinned. "What? This old thing?"

"And is that a new haircut?"

"Style. It's a new hair *style*."

"I like it. A lot."

"I'll be sure to tell Troy."

"Troy?"

"Yeah, Coby found him. You'd love his earring."

She laughed, turning to reach for a small black purse that lay on the coffee table. Gil couldn't take his eyes off the silky length of her back.

"Well, I'm ready if you are," she said brightly, turning back to him.

"Okay." He crooked his arm, trying, but not quite managing, a light tone. "Let's go then."

She took the arm he offered.

"Won't you need a coat?" he asked as they stepped out into the cold night air.

"Not if you park close. Besides, we wouldn't want to ruin the effect of my new dress, would we?"

Gil pasted on a smile for that, then opened the passenger door of his car, closing it when she'd settled in. Oh, no, we wouldn't want to ruin the effect of the dress, he thought to himself as he swung around the car to his side. She couldn't ruin the effect of that dress if she wore iron plating over it. Because *I'd* still know what was underneath. *I'd* still be going crazy knowing how much skin was exposed. *I'd* still be thinking...

HE'D LIED when he'd said he wasn't much of a dancer. He danced, Lesley thought with a sigh, divinely. Of course, it could all be a trick of the mind. Maybe it was the combination of the wonderfully masculine cologne he wore, the fact that she'd just begun to get a bit of a rush from the wine and the heavenly feel of his arms around her, one hand warm against the skin her dress exposed. Maybe all that led her to believe he danced so well. Whatever it was, she didn't want the song or the evening or the sensation to end.

They swayed in time to a Glenn Miller song, "Moonlight Serenade." Which was appropriate, since the hour neared midnight. Forever, she thought, leaning deeper into his embrace. She wanted the night to go on forever.

She hadn't felt that way at the beginning of the evening. When they'd arrived at the country club, her arm looped through Gil's, conversation in the room had stopped. Their fellow teachers had reacted much as Lesley had expected, quite surprised to see the two of them together. Even so, she hadn't expected to feel quite so uncomfortable. Her steps had faltered, and she'd wanted to find an exit.

Gil hadn't missed a beat, however. He'd greeted the faculty members with his usual winning smile and hellos all around. He'd given her arm a squeeze, winked at her reassuringly, then gone about finding them seats at one of the long tables as if nothing was amiss. That shouldn't have surprised her, though. He'd never had a problem with the two of them being seen together.

The shock had worn off some throughout the meal, but Lesley had still sensed a cloud of uneasiness that hovered until dessert. That had been when one of their more blunt co-workers had decided to speak up. "So, Coach," he'd said in a voice loud enough for everyone at their table to hear, "just how long has this thing between you and our new principal been going on? I feel like a wife, the last one to know."

Lesley's spoonful of strawberry mousse had stopped midway to her mouth. Color flooded her cheeks, and her gaze darted to Gil's. She hadn't been the only one set back by the question; Gil was disconcerted, too. But only for a second.

"Actually, Willard, it's only just beginning," he'd answered blithely. Then he took her hand in his and smiled into her eyes before speaking to Willard again. "So, if you could put in a good word for me with her every now and then..."

The tension had evaporated like magic. Several of the teachers around them had smiled, some had laughed. Lesley had squeezed his hand in silent thanks, answering his smile with one of her own.

Too soon, the final bars of the song played out, and Lesley lifted her head. Propriety demanded that they step apart. Neither wanted to.

Gil removed his hand from her back, letting it fall to his side. He couldn't pull his gaze away from her face. Her lips were curved in the hint of a smile, her eyes heavy lidded and slumberous. Damn! he thought, wanting to kiss them closed again, wanting to drag her back into his arms, simply... wanting.

Where the hell had his brains been when he'd picked the dinner dance for this first date? A restaurant and movie would have served his new resolve much better.

He placed his hand on her shoulder, turning her in the direction of their table. Hearing her heavy sigh, he looked down at her. "Something wrong?"

"Not really. I was just enjoying myself so much I hated for it to end."

He'd also been enjoying himself. Too much. "So you're a sucker for a Glenn Miller song, too, huh?"

They'd come to the table, and Gil held out Lesley's chair. She looked up at him as she sat. "Oh, no. I mean, I love to listen to dance-band music, but what I enjoyed so much was dancing—" she paused "—with you."

He was certain she had no idea what she was doing to his control. If she did, she'd never have worn such a torturously seductive dress. She wouldn't have danced so closely, either, pressing the elegant contours of her body against his. And she wouldn't have said what she'd just said. This business of taking things slow must be an acquired skill, he thought. He was having trouble getting the hang of it.

But he would master it. The stakes were too high not to. He sat next to her, nodding to a waitress who offered to refill his coffee. "I think you're a pretty nifty dancer yourself, Ms. Tyler."

Lesley shook her head no when the waitress offered her a refill. She picked up her wineglass, taking a healthy swallow. "You know what I think? I think you were being much too modest when you said you couldn't dance." She slanted a smile in his direction, circling the rim of her glass with a fingertip. "And here I thought you didn't know the meaning of the word."

"What, modesty? Sure I do. I can be as modest as the next guy."

Her look was skeptical.

"Well, if I absolutely had to be, I could."

Uncharacteristically Lesley giggled and lifted her wineglass again. Gil watched her take a long swallow. Unless he was mistaken, that wasn't her first glass of wine tonight. He'd been too preoccupied to notice how many times the glass had been filled, but judging from the telltale flush on her face, the unusually bright green eyes, he'd guess it to be more than once. A grin tugged at his mouth.

"And what about you?" he asked, nodding toward the glass. "You're letting the old principal image slip a bit tonight, aren't you?"

"You think so?" Her quick frown was replaced by a thoughtful look. "Maybe I am. Maybe it's high time."

"There's nothing wrong with your image."

"No? Well, I think my sisters might be right. I should lighten up a bit. Stop being so serious all the time."

"Is this you or the wine talking?"

"It's me. This is only my third glass this evening, Gil. But that just goes to prove my point, doesn't it? How many people do you know who can get so . . . relaxed on such a small amount of wine?"

"Tolerance to alcohol has little to do with one's personality, Lesley."

"Oh, no? That's where I have to disagree. When a person is always conscious of the need to maintain a 'serious' image, they usually steer clear of alcohol, don't they? That leads to a lower tolerance."

Gil nodded. "I suppose you're right."

"Course I am."

He reached for her hand on the table, lacing his fingers through hers. "And that's always been important to you, keeping up a serious image?"

"Not so much the image part. But being serious? I guess so. There's little room for mistakes when other people depend on you. And I was always afraid I'd mess up somehow, that if I didn't pay strict attention at all times, my sisters might have had to pay the price."

Again Gil pictured her as an adolescent, much too young to have been saddled with cooking and cleaning and looking after small children. In his opinion, those three young women owed Lesley a great debt. She'd been the one to pay the price. "You wouldn't have messed up, Lesley."

"I made sure of it. I was constantly on guard against any pitfalls. I made sure to look ahead, and I was scrupulously aware of schedules and the like." She chuckled. "You wouldn't believe what a list maker I became. There were grocery lists, lists of things to do, activities that the girls were involved in—"

"Christmas lists," he added.

"Oh, yes. Christmas lists, of course."

"So what you're saying is that you're through with all that now."

She seemed to consider what he'd said. "I don't know. I'd like to be. But saying it is one thing, the actual doing is another. Those lists are my security blanket, in a way. It'll probably be difficult to change that aspect of my personality, don't you think?"

What he thought was that he found her personality charming. He didn't see the need to change one single thing. Unless, of course, something was making her unhappy. "My opinion is, 'If it ain't broke, don't fix it.'"

She smiled flirtatiously. "You feel it ain't broke, then?"

"I feel it ain't broke."

They left the dance thirty minutes later, Gil teasing her about needing him as a designated driver. "I'm not tipsy," she insisted, "merely relaxed." He knew that. It was just that she was so fun to tease. Fun to be with, to talk with. More than fun to dance with, he thought as he pulled his car up behind hers in the driveway.

He left the car running, telling himself it was because they needed the heater, not that he might need to make a fast getaway. She reached for the shoes she'd slipped off, putting them on, then grasped the door handle. She paused, her gaze connecting with his then sliding to the keys still in the ignition. "You're coming in, aren't you?"

"It's getting late. I wouldn't want to put you out."

"Nonsense," she said, turning off the car and handing him the keys. "I found the most marvelous shop in the mall today. It had all these gourmet-flavored coffee blends. I bought four different kinds.

And," she added magnanimously, "I'll even let you pick your favorite flavor."

He opened his mouth to protest, but she was already out of the car and walking to her door. He closed his eyes briefly. Trouble, he predicted. This could be trouble.

He got out of the car and caught up to her on the porch. She was fumbling with her key in the lock. She shivered, glancing up at him with a wry grin. "I know, I know. I should have worn a coat."

"Hey, I tried to tell you."

She gave the bottom of the door a kick, and it opened. He closed it behind them, watching as she slipped out of her shoes again. "Feet hurt?" he asked.

"Outrageously so," she answered on her way to the kitchen. "Must have been all that dancing. Have a seat."

Gil thought about taking off his jacket, then decided against it. He did loosen his tie. He'd only just sat down on the sofa when Lesley came back into the room carrying four small sacks in her hands. She stood in front of him, holding them up for his inspection.

"Now, I don't want to influence your decision," she said, setting three of the sacks aside on the coffee table and handing the remaining sack to him, "but... choose this one."

He couldn't help but grin at the appealing picture she made. He'd seen that look before. It was the same look that his daughter got when she'd say, "Please, Daddy, please." He was a sucker for that look.

He held up the bag. "Hmm, chocolate orange, huh? I don't know."

Her face fell. "Oh. You don't like chocolate?"

"No, no. I love chocolate. And I love oranges. I was just saying 'Hmm, chocolate orange.'"

"Give me that," she said with a laugh, grabbing the sack. She turned on her heel and headed back to the kitchen, giving him another tantalizing glimpse of the back of her dress.

It had been designed, he decided, with the intention of destroying a man's sanity. Of course, he was finding it more and more difficult to maintain his sanity around Lesley no matter what she was wearing. Exercise clothes, jeans and tennies. He'd even been seeing those suits she wore to school in a different light these days.

With damning evidence like that, he knew he'd gone past simple attraction and was heading for a full-blown case of lust. No, not merely lust. Something much deeper, much more substantial. Something that felt a hell of a lot like love.

The realization doubled his resolve. It might be acceptable in these modern times to explore one's uncertain feelings through intimacy, but it wasn't acceptable in this situation.

"You take yours black, right?" she asked, reentering the room carrying a small tray with two mugs.

"Right." He reached for his coffee, his eyes widening at the aroma. "This smells great."

"I know." She sat next to him on the sofa, pulling her knees under her and reaching for her coffee.

"When I smelled it in the coffee shop, I thought I was in heaven. Wait till you taste it."

He did. "Oh, that's good stuff."

She smiled over the top of her mug, then brought it to her lips, sipping delicately. She closed her eyes, savoring the taste of the coffee. "Heaven," she whispered when her eyes opened. She set her mug on the table, then settled back again, propping her arm on the back of the sofa and her chin in her palm. "Did you notice who Mr. Moore was with tonight?" she asked.

He tried to remember, tried to get his mind off the fact that her arm was only inches from his shoulder. "Oh, you mean the redhead? I figured that was his daughter."

"That's what I thought, too, but I overheard a conversation in the ladies' room. She is no daughter, I'll have you know. She is a twenty-two-year-old golf caddy he met at the country club not two weeks ago. Is that something?"

"Sure is. I didn't know Moore played golf."

Laughing, she punched his shoulder. "Gil! You're supposed to be shocked at the age difference. Mr. Moore has to be at least twenty-five years older than that girl."

"What I'm shocked at," he said with a smile, "is how far that image of yours has slipped tonight. Gossip, Ms. Tyler? Are you sure you only had three glasses of wine?"

"Yes, I'm sure," she insisted with a hurt look. "The wine might have helped relax me, but that's all it did."

She looked away then, and Gil worried that he'd said the wrong thing. "Lesley, I'm kidding." He set his coffee on the table and crooked a finger under her chin, turning her face toward him. "You understand that's all I was doing, don't you?"

"I guess so." Her voice was quiet. "It's just that...I don't know. I don't want you to think that the only reason I was enjoying myself tonight was because of what I'd had to drink."

"I don't."

"Are you sure?"

"Of course I am. But you know me, sometimes I don't know when to stop kidding."

She covered his hand with hers and brought it up to rest on her cheek. "Tonight was wonderful because I was with you."

He closed his eyes briefly, then opened them, his breath catching at the serene but compelling look in her eyes. He traced his thumb over her cheekbone, then trailed it to the corner of her mouth, stopping just short of brushing it over her full lower lip. "I thought it was wonderful, too."

"Did you, Gil? There were moments when I had the strangest feeling that you weren't having a good time."

"No. Nothing could be further from the truth."

Her gaze fell away from his. "I felt as if I were dragging you in here against your will. For me, tonight was like something out of a fairy tale. The country club with all of its glittery decorations, you looking so handsome in your new suit—"

"You so beautiful in this dress," he added, coaxing a soft smile from her lips. "Lesley, I'm sorry if I led you to believe that I wasn't enjoying myself. I was. I am. I'm also...worried."

"Worried?"

"I don't want to screw things up, you know? You're important to me. And I guess that made me a bit more cautious than usual. But that's all it was, caution."

Her smile grew. "You sound like me now, Gil."

He chuckled. "Yeah, I guess I do."

"Will you do me a favor?"

Anything, he thought, this time not curbing the urge to edge his thumb across her lip. "Name it."

"Will you kiss me?"

His startled gaze flew to hers.

"There are no glass walls with teenage boys on the other side here," she said, her voice low. "And we're not in a public place like the health club. Imagine it. Privacy for once. Just you and me...alone."

His heart beating a frantic rhythm and his thoughts tangled in indecision, Gil simply stared. He stared at her hair, pulled up in an elegant style that left her neck bare and accessible. He stared at her eyes, darkened with emotion, with invitation. He stared at her lips. They too invited, beckoned. "Yes," he groaned, pulling her to him. "Yes, I'll do that."

He'd been naive, incredibly naive, to believe for a single moment that he could call a halt to the more elemental feelings he had for her. At the mere touch of her mouth to his, his blood heated with the need he'd been downplaying all night. Her faint murmur of pleasure was all it took to send that need rocketing through his body.

Deepening the kiss, he pulled her closer. Her breasts strained against his chest, and her mouth opened under the insistent pressure of his. His hands slid from her neck to her back. Forbidden territory, he'd thought earlier. His to touch, to explore, he told himself now.

His hands roamed the satiny texture of her skin; hers went to the buttons of his shirt above his loosened tie. She unfastened the buttons and her fingers slipped inside. Her touch was hesitant at first, then gathered urgency that threatened to send his desire out of control.

Out of control. Oh yes, he was about two days past control. He pulled her down with him to lie face-to-face on the sofa. Face-to-face, mouth to mouth, heart to thundering heart.

She murmured his name against his mouth when he slid his hand to her breast, then she looped her arms around his neck, straining upward.

She broke the kiss with a soft moan, burying her face in his shoulder. Her breath was quick and hot against his skin. His own came just as fast. "Lesley," he whispered between soft kisses he placed near her ear.

"Um?" She arched her neck, slid one gloriously long leg between his.

"I loved being with you tonight. Believe me, I did."

Her thick black lashes fluttered open, and her lips curved in the most delicious of smiles. She twined her fingers through the hair at his nape. "You do have a convincing way about you, Coach."

Reluctantly he moved his hand, tilted her chin and took another sweet kiss from her lips. The words "I want you" were on the tip of his tongue. So was a declaration that common sense warned him against: "I love you."

"Lesley..." He levered himself up on his elbow and brought her hand to his mouth, depositing a kiss in the center of her palm. "We have to stop. I..."

Her smile dimmed and she trailed her index finger along his jaw. "You're kidding again, right?"

Wishing to hell he was, he shook his head. "I should have never started something that...well, that we can't finish tonight."

She lowered her gaze, a slight frown marring her brow.

"I didn't bring...that is, I'm not exactly prepared for certain things tonight."

Lesley looked up at him, confused for a moment, then realization dawned. Precautions. "Oh," she groaned, covering her face with her hand.

"Hey, what's this about?"

She peeked through her fingers. "I'm embarrassed. I didn't even stop to think about...about that."

He chuckled softly, pulling her to a sitting position and straightening her dress where it had slipped off her shoulder. His hand lingered. "You see? You need a cautious guy like me to offset all that reckless behavior of yours."

"Mr. Caution, that's you."

"Yep." He stood, grasping her hand to help her up from the sofa. At the door, he pulled her into his arms and kissed her again. He rested his forehead against hers and exhaled a sigh. "Caution can be good. Anticipation's half the fun, right?"

Yeah, right, she thought after sending him on his way. Caution can be good. Anticipation is half the fun. She was just going to repeat that over and over to herself until she believed it.

CHAPTER ELEVEN

THE CALENDAR SAID it was November, making spring
fever an impossibility. Lesley had it, nevertheless. She
suffered all the classic symptoms. Constantly gazing
out her office window, daydreaming in lieu of working; forgetting about appointments until ten minutes
before they were to take place; making up lists then
losing them. November or not, she had spring fever.
And it was Gil Fielden's fault.

He was the star of her daydreams. He intruded on
her thoughts several times a day just to rattle her
composure and wreak havoc on her normally consci-
entious manner. She thought of him when she should
have been remembering dentist appointments or calls
to her sisters. And what disconcerted her even more
than the fact that he had her so scrambled was the R-
rated content of those daydreams. Invariably she
would imagine him standing before her in some stage
of undress, his shirt half off or all the way off, reveal-
ing the broad chest and muscled arms she'd touched
fleetingly on the night of the dinner dance. His slacks
or jeans—whichever he was wearing—were taunt-
ingly unbuttoned. The look in his eyes was electric,
silently telling her all the things he was longing to do.

Lesley dropped the pen she'd been drumming against the desk and jerked her gaze away from the window. Good grief, it wasn't as if she never got the chance to spend time with the man, never talked to him or touched him or even kissed him. In the two weeks since their first date, they'd been together every possible moment. After his football practices in the evenings, on the weekends, whenever their respective schedules permitted. They were…getting to know each other better.

Two weeks ago she wouldn't have thought that was something she'd have complaints about. But she'd found out that Gil's idea of getting to know one another was a bit different than hers. He favored public places for their outings—picnics in parks, window shopping at the mall. He also favored double-dating with friends or Coby and Devin. Lesley had enjoyed meeting his buddies and their wives or girlfriends, and she'd loved becoming better acquainted with Coby and Devin, but she wanted Gil to herself some of the time. Even more, she wanted him to want her to himself, as well.

It was odd that his newfound caution was having such a crazy effect on her libido. She'd been the one who, although attracted to him from the start, had been careful to keep her feelings in check. She'd been afraid of losing control of her emotions, afraid that loss would affect both her job and his. Remembering how she'd once informed him that she wasn't one to give in to hormonal urges, Lesley shook her head. How the tables had turned.

There was a soft rap on her door, and Lesley pushed her errant thoughts aside. "Come in."

Stacey, her arms laden with files, strode in. She set the stack on Lesley's desk, then extracted two folders from the top, handing them to Lesley.

"Here are the reports you asked for, and I wanted to remind you of the meeting you have with Melanie Thornton's parents after school."

"Thank you, Stacey," she said, opening the first folder.

"Is there anything else,?" Stacey asked, her tone brisk.

Lesley glanced up, surprised to find Stacey regarding her with an expression that was cool and businesslike.

"Stacey, is anything wrong?"

"No. Why should anything be wrong?"

"You sound put out about something. Is everything okay with you?"

"Who, me? I'm fine. Everything's fine. Russell and I are fine, the new puppy that Russell surprised me with is fine, though she hasn't quite mastered the art of paper training yet. But wait a minute, I forgot. You know all of that, because friends share what's going on in their lives and keep each other informed."

Lesley frowned. "What's this all about?"

"Oh, nothing. I just happened to hear the news that you and Coach Fielden are dating, not firsthand from you, but in the teachers' lounge. But, hey, I'm obviously just the office secretary and not the good friend I thought I was."

"Oh, Stacey, you are a good friend. I'm sorry. I should have told you myself, but—"

"No problem."

But Lesley could see that it *was* a problem. The hurt look was still there in Stacey's eyes even though Lesley had apologized. She felt terrible that Stacey had had to hear of this new development from the other teachers. Stacey had been the first person in Warren to reach out to her in friendship, and she deserved better than being relegated to acquaintance status. "I simply wasn't thinking. For obvious reasons my head has been in the clouds for the past couple of weeks."

"It has?" Lesley could tell Stacey wanted to know more but was struggling valiantly to hold on to her hurt pride.

"Mmm-hmm. But you know all about that. Remember how distracted you were when you and Russell first started dating?"

"Yes."

Lesley gave her a beseeching look. "Well, are you going to let me redeem myself or not? Don't just stand there. Pull up a chair and ask me what you want to know."

Stacey laughed and relented, doing as Lesley instructed. Her laughter fading, she said, "You don't have to tell me anything you don't want—"

"Stacey. Ask."

"Well, okay. You thought he was killer from the very first time you saw him, didn't you? I mean, just like the rest of us, you were immediately knocked out, right?"

Lesley smiled, remembering that was very close to what she'd thought. She also remembered how she'd tried to deny her reaction. "Yes. I thought he was very good-looking."

"I knew it! I just knew I detected an interest there. Oh, this is too good. All this time you were both attracted to each other. But here you were the new principal, making up all these new rules, and there he was the one who had to follow them. That had to have interfered with the course of true love."

Lesley laughed. "I don't know about true love, Stacey. We've only been dating a short while." But saying it aloud made her face facts. Weeks ago she'd worried that she was falling in love with Gil. Her heart told her now that she should stop worrying and admit that she had.

"Oh, but it will be. I know it will. That's just a detail. I talked to Coby about it, and she says you guys have been seeing a lot of each other since the dinner dance. Like every night." Stacey wriggled her brows.

"We have." What Lesley didn't tell her was that the frequency of their dates didn't necessarily rate raised eyebrows. She guided the conversation down a different path. "Stacey, you told me that you and Coby became pretty close last year when she was an office aide. Do you still talk to each other?" At Stacey's nod, Lesley asked, "Has she said how she feels about her father and me seeing each other?"

"Oh, you mean the whole my-dad's-date-could-become-my-new-stepmom thing? I'd thought about that," she said conspiratorially. "You have nothing to worry about. Coby and I still do talk, and she says she likes you a lot.''

"No, no," Lesley said with a sigh. "It's much too soon for talk about marriage or stepparenting. I was just curious to know what Coby thought.''

"Her mind's more on her grades these days than anything else. You know, with the big play coming up, she's worried she might miss out being in it.''

"She's worried about her grades?'' That was news to Lesley. She'd been under the impression that Coby's grades were excellent.

"Yeah. She's been spending so much time in rehearsals lately that she hasn't been able to devote herself to her studies as much as she'd like. I think it's her English grade that has her worried the most.''

"What is her English grade?''

"She said it's a low B right now. But that's only until she finds out what she made on the paper she just handed in. It's on Shakespeare's Globe Theatre. She was going to research it by visiting the replica of the Globe in Odessa, but she didn't have the time because of rehearsals. She says she knows that paper isn't up to par, and she's afraid it might lower her average.''

"Oh, no.''

"Yeah. It'll break her heart if she can't be in the play. Especially if it's true that a Hollywood agent is supposed to come see it.''

"A Hollywood agent is coming to Warren to see the play?''

"Sounds kind of bizarre, huh? But he's a relative of one of the kids in the play. The word's out that he'll be visiting during the holidays, so he's going to come to one of the performances. It's got all the kids in a frazzle like you wouldn't believe. Besides the regular practices Mrs. Higgins has them go through, they've been calling extra ones on the weekends on their own."

"Extra practices? But they're getting together twice a day as it is."

"I know. Is that dedication or what?"

"I don't know, Stacey, it sounds a bit foolish to me. Don't get me wrong—I'm always thrilled to see students so motivated. But what good will all those extra rehearsals do if their grades drop and the students aren't permitted to participate?"

Lesley had learned a lot about Coby since she and Gil had started seeing each other, including the fact that the girl was serious about becoming an actress. Coby had shown her college catalogs from universities known for their excellent drama departments, and she'd discussed with excitement her plans to pursue acting as a career. Stacey was right, Coby's heart would be broken if she wasn't allowed to perform in *Arsenic and Old Lace*.

"I hadn't thought about that," Stacey said. "Should I say something to Coby?"

Lesley considered it for a moment. "There's no need for a warning. As you said, Coby's aware of the consequences. But still, I'd hate to see her stretch herself too thin because of all those rehearsals."

"Maybe you should be the one to talk to her," Stacey suggested.

"Or I could say something to Genevieve about it."

"Don't know how much good talking to the drama coach will do, since the kids practice on their own time, but I guess it wouldn't hurt to try."

Stacey rose from her chair and shoved it back into place. "I've got to get back to my desk," she said, then gave Lesley a smile. "I think it's terrific about you and Coach."

Lesley returned the smile. "Thanks. Me, too."

Lesley got down to work, the conversation with Stacey about Coby hovering on the fringes of her concentration. The situation disturbed her. She and Gil had basically agreed to disagree about no-pass, no-play, but how would that be affected if Coby were concerned? Surely he wouldn't hold it against her personally. Would he?

Thirty minutes and three reports later, Gil showed up at her office door. As always when she saw him, her heart beat faster and a smile came to her lips.

"Got a minute?" he asked as he shut the door, then strode forward.

"Of course."

He pushed up the brim of his baseball cap and circled around to her side of the desk. He leaned against the edge of her desk and reached for her hands, pulling her up to stand in the V of his legs. Her hands went to his shoulders; his linked behind her back.

"What's with your secretary? She's out there grinning like she knows a secret."

Lesley toyed with the leather thong that held the whistle around his neck. She looked into his eyes, falling in love with them again, as she did at least once a day. "She's a sucker for romance."

"Oh, yeah?" He stroked the small of her back with his thumbs, and Lesley's stomach fluttered in response. "Well, so am I." He leaned forward, placing soft kisses at the base of her neck. "I'm also becoming a big fan of this hairdo. I think I like it up almost as much as when it's down."

"I wasn't...aware you had a preference. Why didn't you tell me?"

"Haven't had the chance." He kissed the ivory column of her throat. "Been too busy just looking at it all the time."

"Gil..." Her palms flattened on his shoulders.

"It's sexy like this. Makes your neck more accessible."

She closed her eyes, tilting her head to allow him all the accessibility he wanted. "I'll be sure to buy more hair pins."

He smiled against her skin, placing one last kiss just below her ear, before holding her away from him. "Are you coming over tonight after the game?"

"The game?"

"Yeah, you know, the district game? This one will determine whether or not we advance toward state playoffs."

"And if I know you, you're planning a victory celebration for tonight at your apartment."

He winked. "I'm much too modest to say that it'll be a victory celebration."

"Yeah, right," she scoffed. She smoothed the fabric of his sweatshirt with her fingertips, wondering if she was the only one invited to his house this evening.

"Would I be too forward if I asked if this was going to be a private celebration?"

"You're not being forward. But I'm afraid privacy is out for tonight. Coby and Devin will be there. I hope you don't mind."

"No. No, of course not," she fibbed. "And I wouldn't think of missing the celebration."

"Great." He brushed a kiss on her lips, then rose from the desk. "I'll pick you up at your house right after the game. Sound okay?"

She nodded. "Sounds good."

Lesley watched him leave, then sat back down with a sigh. She picked up her pen, drumming it on the desk as she gazed out the window for the millionth time that day. Caution is good, she reminded herself, grinding her teeth. Anticipation is half the fun.

"RUSSELL AND I ARE GOING to go for some Cokes and popcorn. Want some?" Stacey asked.

"I wouldn't mind some hot chocolate," Lesley said, reaching for her purse.

"Put your money away." Stacey looped her arm through Russell's. "This one's on us."

"Are you sure?"

"Sure she's sure," Russell spoke up. "She's trying to bankrupt me."

Stacey rolled her eyes and dragged him down the aisle.

Lesley buried her hands in her coat pocket and turned her attention back to the halftime show Mr. Sibley's band was putting on.

The stadium was packed, as it was every Friday night. The only thing different about tonight was the heightened tension in the air. This game, as Gil had said, would decide which team would advance toward the state championship. As it stood right now, it didn't look good for Gil's Wildcats. They were down fourteen to nothing.

But they would come back, Lesley reassured herself. They would listen to Gil's halftime talk and get fired up again. Local sportswriters hadn't labeled them the come-from-behind team for nothing.

"Hi."

Lesley pulled her gaze from the field. Coby was standing at her side. "Hi there. Have a seat," she said.

Coby dropped to Stacey's now-unoccupied place. "I don't like the looks of this," she said, a grim look on her face.

Lesley nodded, knowing Coby meant the football score. "Neither do I."

"You noticed it was Devin who fumbled the ball in the second quarter, didn't you?"

"Mmm-hmm."

"I hope Dad's not putting him through the wringer right now."

"Devin's not the only one making mistakes. If your father's putting him through the wringer, he's doing the same with the rest of them."

"I know. I just feel sort of protective."

"I think that's only natural," Lesley said with a grin.

"Yeah, I guess so." Coby dug her hands deep into the pockets of Devin's letter jacket. "Hey, did you hear the news about the agent who's coming to the play?''

"I did. You must be very excited."

Coby's eyes fairly glowed. "Oh, we all are. I mean, I know it's a long shot that any of us would actually be 'discovered' or anything, but it's neat to think about."

"You never know. I've been slipping into the auditorium from time to time. And I happen to think there's quite a bit of talent in the drama club. Maybe I'm a little prejudiced, but you and Devin are great."

"You mean it?"

"I most certainly do."

"Thanks. We've been killing ourselves getting ready for this. You wouldn't believe the number of rehearsals we've been having."

"Yes, I'd heard." Lesley pondered the need to say something to Coby about her English grade. She'd found out from Coby's teacher that the grade was indeed going to slip more due to the paper Stacey had mentioned. It worried Lesley. Coby was still within the limits of no-pass, no-play but not by much. Lesley made her decision. She didn't want Coby upset with her, but she didn't want her paying the consequences for a low grade, either. And Lesley had spoken with Mrs. Higgins about trying to get the kids to reduce the number of rehearsals. The drama coach wouldn't promise that she could influence the group but had said she would try.

"Coby, I hope you won't think I'm nosing in where it's none of my business, but are you keeping a close eye on your grades?"

Coby's excitement faded. "Well . . . sure."

"I'm only asking because I know how much you love drama. I don't want you to miss out on performing in that play."

"I understand. But there's nothing to worry about. Really. I've got everything under control."

Lesley could tell she hit a nerve. "It's understandable that all those rehearsals would take away from time you normally devote to studies and—"

"My grades are okay," Coby stated in a voice that indicated she wanted to drop the subject.

Realizing that harping wouldn't do a bit of good, Lesley decided to back off. "Good. I just wanted you to know that if you need any help. . ."

Coby nodded, giving Lesley a distracted smile. "Oh, listen, I almost forgot. Could you give my dad a message for me?"

"Sure." Along with the message, Lesley thought, she'd talk to Gil about Coby's grade. "What is it?"

"Tell him I'm sorry, but Devin and I aren't going to be at his celebration thing tonight. My mom's been wanting Devin and me to come over and I've been putting her off so much because of play practice that I feel sort of guilty. So we're going over there after the game. Oh, and tell Dad that she wants me to spend the weekend there and will bring me back Sunday night."

GIL SLAM-DUNKED an orange Nerf ball into the Nerf hoop anchored above the dining room door.

"Two points," Lesley said with a smile as she hung her jacket in the closet. She'd barely closed the closet door when Gil came up behind her, swept her high into his arms and twirled her in circles.

"Twenty-eight points, woman. The score was twenty-eight to fourteen!" He set her feet on the floor and delivered a quick, smacking kiss to her lips.

Lesley giggled. "You really must do something about these depressions of yours, Gil."

"I know, cheer up, right?"

"Right." She smoothed the collar of his polo shirt. "I'm happy you won."

He gave her another kiss, then raised his head, breathing an exaggerated sigh of relief. "I had my doubts we'd be able to pull it off at first."

"Oh, not me. I knew you'd win it all along."

"Yeah, I'll bet," he said, tightening his arms around her waist.

"I did," she insisted. "Just as I know you'll win all the games up to and including the state championship."

"That sounds like a terrific toast. You ready for some champagne?"

She gave him a mischievous grin. "Oh? Do you have some?"

"Wait here. I'll be right back with it."

In his absence, Lesley wandered to a bookshelf on one wall, inspecting the framed photographs while she waited. She'd noticed the pictures before but hadn't had the chance to really look at them yet. Most were of Coby, from infancy through her senior picture.

Lesley smiled when she discovered a photograph near the back of the shelf. It was a picture of Gil, a very young Gil, in a football uniform. His eyes were squinted, and he was posed as if he were just about to deliver a pass with the football he held in one hand. Lord, the girls in high school must have been as impressed with him then as women were now. A good-looking blond-haired, blue-eyed football star was always a sure bet as a heartthrob.

Spotting another high school picture of him, Lesley replaced the football photo. She picked up the one with Gil dressed in a cap and gown. But she noticed it wasn't a picture of Gil, after all. The boy looked quite a bit like him, but the similarity didn't extend to physiques. Gil had had a larger build even in high school, according to the photo she'd just put down. And this boy's expression was much more serious. Curious, she strolled into the kitchen, picture in hand.

Gil looked up with a smile. When he saw the frame in her hand, he grimaced. "Don't tell me you found that old football picture."

"What's wrong with that picture? I think you looked cute in your uniform."

Gil groaned. "I don't know about cute," he said, opening a cabinet and taking out champagne glasses. "But I do know why I keep it hidden at the back of the shelf. I don't want to be reminded on a daily basis of how many years ago it was taken."

Lesley chuckled. "But this one isn't one of you," she said, holding up the picture. "Is he your brother?"

Gil looked up. His hands stilled on the champagne bottle. "Yes. My older brother, Greg."

Lesley noticed the momentary sadness that shadowed his eyes. "I've never heard you talk about him before."

"I don't talk about it a lot. He died...committed suicide, actually, when he was in college."

"Oh, Gil, I'm so sorry. I didn't know."

"Of course you didn't," he said gently. He set down the champagne bottle and walked over to her. Lifting the picture from her hands, he stared down at it. "It was a crying shame, you know? He had so much going for him."

"I...Gil, I..." Lesley grasped for words. She couldn't begin to imagine Gil's loss.

"Oh, hey, listen. I know. It's tough finding the right thing to say to someone when they've lost a family member to suicide."

"Yes, it is. Do you...know why he did it?'

His expression grim, he nodded. "He left a note. It was short, but in effect it said that he just couldn't hold up under the pressures of college."

"Oh, my."

"I couldn't understand that at the time. I was in high school, and as I've told you, I wasn't the most motivated student as far as grades were concerned. But I've come to realize that school was Greg's life. He was on a full academic scholarship at Baylor, intending to follow in my parents' footsteps and become a college professor."

"Your parents were professors?"

Gil nodded, a grin forming. "Hard to believe that I came from that background, is it?"

Despite the seriousness of the conversation, Lesley couldn't help smiling, too. "I guess I just supposed that your parents were more of the athletic persuasion."

Gil chuckled at that. "Oh, no. In fact, they were none too pleased with their youngest son's career choice. But after giving me a few lectures on the matter, they backed off. I think they were content with Greg wanting a master's degree and doctorate. Enough so, that my being a black sheep wasn't quite so intolerable."

"But you say Greg buckled under the pressure?"

"Yeah." He looked down at the picture again, a faraway expression in his eyes. "Everybody's expectations of Greg were high. I think that caused him to take on more than he could handle." He heaved a sigh and looked up. "Enough of that. Tonight's for celebrating, remember?"

"I know, but—"

"Hey, it's okay." He gave her a hug. "It was a long time ago. We'll talk about it again sometime. Just... not tonight. Okay?"

"If that's what you want." She slipped her arms around him, returning the hug.

"It is."

He went back to his task, and Lesley took the picture to the living room, placing it next to his football picture on the bookshelf. When she returned to the kitchen, Gil was struggling with the cork on the champagne bottle.

"Hey, did Coby tell you about the agent who's coming to see their play? She's over the moon about it," he said.

The agent. This would be a good time to bring up Coby's English grade to Gil, Lesley thought. "Yes, she did. And there's something—"

The cork made a loud pop and Gil rushed the bottle to the sink. "I guess I didn't get it chilled enough. Hope you don't mind it a bit warm," he said apologetically as he began pouring the champagne. He glanced at his watch. "The kids should be here soon."

"The kids! Oh, Gil, I forgot to tell you."

"Forgot to tell me what?" he asked, his back to her as he put the wine in the refrigerator.

"I saw Coby at the game. She wanted me to give you the message that she and Devin won't be here tonight."

The refrigerator door closed slowly and Gil's gaze came around to hers. "What do you mean they won't be here?"

"It completely slipped my mind. She told me that her mother asked her and Devin to go over to her house."

"No. Coby specifically told me that she and Devin would be *here*. I talked with her this afternoon and she told me that."

The look in his eyes was more than one of simple irritation, Lesley noticed. And there was an edge, a worried edge, in his voice all of a sudden. "I think her mother has been asking Coby to bring Devin by to visit for quite a while now," she explained. "Coby said she'd put her mom off so many times because of play practices that she'd begun to feel guilty about it."

He ran a hand through his hair, clearly no less agitated after Lesley's explanation. "Well, I certainly like Coby's idea of advance warning. She's done this to me before, you know. I thought I'd gotten through to her that I don't appreciate last-minute—"

"Gil, I feel terrible. Don't be mad at Coby. This is my fault." Lesley crossed the room and laid a hand on his arm. "I should have remembered to tell you about it when you picked me up, but we were so busy talking about the game that it completely—"

"It's not your fault." A frown etched deep between his brows, he turned away from her, bracing his arms against the countertop. Lesley felt she had enough experience with teenagers to know when to become concerned over their behavior. And she felt Gil was overreacting to this situation. If, in fact, it really was Coby's failure to notify him of the change in plans that had him so upset, and not simply the fact that he didn't want to be alone with her. Again.

"For all that Coby is a bright kid," he continued, "sometimes she just doesn't think. She doesn't think that someone might worry about her, that someone—"

"If you're worried, why not call Ceil?"

"No, I'm sure she's where she told you she would be. I'm not concerned about that in particular—"

"What is it, in particular, that has you so concerned, Gil?" she asked quietly.

Something in her soft tone, in the precise phrasing of her question, made Gil drop his hands from the counter and turn to face her. Her stance was no-nonsense, arms folded across her middle; her gaze was level, unwavering . . . knowing.

She was on to him, he thought. And why shouldn't she be? It didn't take a rocket scientist to figure out that he was more upset about Coby and Devin's absence that he was about not being told. Tonight wouldn't have been the first time he'd relied on having other people around as insurance against getting...carried away.

"Is there another reason why you want them to be here?"

He nodded, clearing his throat. "Yes, there's another reason. I think you know what it is."

She walked toward him. "I know what it is. I just don't understand why. Will you tell me?"

Gil put his hands on her shoulders, wanting to draw her near but needing the distance, as well. "I'm not very good at talking. I'm better at issuing orders, telling people what to do—"

"Talk. I need to know why you seem to think chaperons are necessary when you're with me."

He sighed heavily. "It's not that I don't want to be alone with you. I do. But something's happened that I'm not quite sure how to handle."

"What's happened?"

"I found out what I'd meant by wanting 'more.'" The puzzled look in her eyes prompted him to explain. "Don't you remember that day in your office? I had it in my head that I was going to find out why you wouldn't give me the time of day when I was so knocked out by you that I couldn't think straight. I barged in after the faculty meeting, wanting to know why the hell you never smiled at me."

Lesley grinned, nodding. "I remember. It was the day that Sibley interrupted."

"Yeah. He came in right after I told you I wanted more than just a working relationship between the two of us."

"And you say you know what the 'more' is now?"

"Yes, I do. At least, I know what I want it to be." Gil took a deep breath, eyeing her carefully. "I want long-term, Lesley. I didn't know that then, but I do now." She started to say something, but Gil held her off. "No, no. Let me finish. I came away from my divorce having learned that infatuation or lust simply isn't the real thing. Neither one can be the basis for a long-term commitment. For several years I thought I wasn't cut out for long-term commitments, because I kept stumbling upon those very situations with women.

"With you I know what I'm experiencing isn't simply a case of the hots for your bod—" he grinned, sweeping her with a wicked look "—though there is that, too. But that's not all I'm feeling. Lesley, I'm not just infatuated or in love with the thought of being in love." As he had earlier that day, he pulled Lesley closer, standing her in the V of his legs. He clasped her upper arms in his hands. "I think I'm smack in the middle of it."

Lesley's breath caught in her throat. "Oh, Gil, I—"

"No. You don't have to say anything," he said, putting a finger to her lips. "I realize that I'm springing this on you a bit soon. We've only been dating for two weeks, and that's hardly enough time for you to be considering commitment. I just want you to understand why I've felt the need for chaperons, for taking things slowly, carefully," he said.

Lesley's heart threatened to burst with emotion. She laid her head against his chest, wrapped her arms around him and gave grave consideration to never, ever leaving the warm haven of his embrace.

It was so amazing. Amazingly wonderful to think that his feelings mirrored hers. He'd shown her that he was attracted to her, that he wanted her—at least she'd thought so until these past two weeks. But she hadn't dared to imagine that he had fallen in love with her.

"Lesley, you're not saying anything."

She smiled against his shirt, supremely happy. "You told me not to."

"And you do everything you're told without questioning it? Come on, I'm getting worried here. At least tell me there might be a chance for me if I give you some more time...."

She raised her head, smiling into his eyes. "Gil," she whispered, reaching up to touch his face, brushing his jaw with her fingertips. "I don't need more time."

Hope flared in his eyes, but it was tempered by that damnable caution she'd been seeing there for two frustratingly long weeks.

"I'm already in love with you. I don't just *think* I'm smack dab in the middle of it, I know I am."

His eyes widened, then the hope she'd seen became less cautious and a slow smile spread across his face. "And...long-term is what you want, as well?"

"Yes," she said.

All caution was abandoned with the kiss he gave her, the kiss she returned. Her hands were still on his jaw, stroking, caressing; his were tangled in her hair. Their caresses became more urgent, but Gil slowed the tempo, breaking the kiss to whisper in her ear. "I'm having a real good day, you know?"

Lesley's laugh was muffled against his shirt. "Me, too," she said, her heart reveling in the moment. She leaned back to look at him. "I want to make that toast now," she told him.

"Now?" he asked, comically astounded as he tried to recapture her lips with his.

"Yes, now." She held him off and reached for the glasses on the counter next to him. She handed him a glass and took one for herself, then raised it. "To your win."

"You want to toast the football game?" he said dryly.

She nodded, trying with great difficulty to maintain the serious expression she'd adopted. The smile in her heart kept threatening to break through. She clinked her glass to his, then eyed him over the rim as she took a swallow. "This is a three-part toast, so pay attention," she told him after he'd taken a drink.

"Okay."

"The second part is, to winning the state championship—your fifth if I recall correctly."

"You do," he said with a nod as he touched his glass to hers. He swirled the champagne over his tongue, knowing that from tonight forward he would associate its taste not with winning football games, as he always had in the past, but with Lesley...and with love.

"And thirdly, to Coby—"

"To Coby?" Gil had thought the third part would be related to them, not his daughter.

"Let me finish," she said. "To Coby, who has decided to spend not only this evening, but the entire weekend with her mom."

CHAPTER TWELVE

"THE ENTIRE WEEKEND?"

"Yes. The entire weekend. She'll be coming home Sunday night." Lesley arched a brow, giving him a challenging look. "What do you think about that?"

The prospect of spending the next two days and nights alone with her brought erotic images speeding to his mind. Thoughts of that evening at her house after the dance—the feel of her bare back beneath his hands, her long, slender body pressed to his, her fingers undoing the buttons of his shirt, then slipping inside...

That night he'd corraled his desire; tonight he wouldn't have to.

He raised his glass. "To throwing caution to the wind," he said.

"To throwing caution to the wind," she repeated, a smile lighting her eyes. She touched her glass to his, then sipped the wine.

Gil slipped the glass from her fingers, placing it next to his on the counter behind him. He curved his hand around the back of her neck, then turned her to walk with him out of the kitchen. He made a stop at the front door to lock it and turn off the porch light. Still unspeaking, he led her up the stairs to his bedroom.

With each step, Lesley felt a strange combination of anticipation and apprehension. She wanted to make love with him, but she couldn't seem to shake the sudden case of jitters that was accompanying her desire. Becoming intimate with Gil hadn't been a problem two weeks ago, she reminded herself. Then she remembered that two weeks ago she'd consumed three glasses of wine.

Apprehension grew into a small wave of panic when they finally reached the bed, calmed only when Gil whispered her name, gathering her to him. He brought his mouth to hers, holding her in a long, steady kiss.

"I couldn't have taken it much longer, you know. All that restraint," he said, his breath warm on her lips. He smoothed a stray strand of hair from her cheek, then brushed a kiss across the skin where it had lain. "Starting Monday, I was going full steam ahead with my plan to make you fall in love with me."

Lesley's nerves surrendered to a smile. She couldn't get over it. She had wondered and worried about that restraint when all along it had been because she'd found a man who, when he spoke of physical longing entwined it with words of love.

"What? Why are you smiling at me like that?"

"Because. Because you're so... you're..." She shook her head, dropping her hands to his shoulders, resting her forehead on his chest.

Gil tilted her chin up with a finger. "What am I, Lesley?"

"On the outside, you're this... this football coach. Big and tough and aggressive. But on the inside you're... caring, sensitive."

He gave a wry chuckle, sitting on the edge of the bed and tugging her down next to him. "Let me get this straight. I'm sensitive because I was going to steam-roller you into coming around to my way of think-ing?"

She brought his hand to her cheek, covering it with hers. "No. Because you were going to steamroller me into *loving* you, not into bed. It was the caring part of you that pulled back the night of the dinner dance, Gil."

"I thought that was the stupid part of me."

She laughed, then rose to her knees on the bed and faced him. She traced a gentle finger over his brow. "You were thinking of me. I didn't realize that then," she said. A smile tugged at the corners of her mouth. "I wanted to choke you, in fact." Her hands went to his throat, her smile becoming mischievous.

He grinned. "Are you going to choke me now?"

"Should I? Are you going to stop tonight?"

The grin left his face, and he pulled her onto his lap, wrapping her legs around him. Watching her eyes, he encircled her knees with his hands, stroking slowly upward over the snug denim jeans she wore. Lesley's stomach tightened when his fingers slipped under the hem of her sweater and caressed the skin just above her waistband. He inched her forward on his lap, nuzzled her neck with slow, open kisses. "If you knew the path my thoughts were taking right now, you'd have every right to strangle me."

She closed her eyes, her breath catching when his fingers dipped inside the waistband of her jeans in back, then made a maddeningly unhurried circle around to the snap. Quick shivers of excitement swept through her as she waited, feeling the snap give way first and his warm hand ease under the fabric. The hand drifted downward, eliciting a million delicious tingles along her skin. He stopped just short of the edge of her panties, making enticing circles with his thumb.

"I...wouldn't strangle you. My thoughts are on the same path," she said, reaching down to tug his polo shirt from his slacks. She wanted to touch him, too, wanted to finally feel the masculine chest and muscled arms that she'd been watching, dying over, for weeks now. His hands were on an upward climb again, the heels of his palms pressing breathtakingly close to the underside of her breasts. They presented an awkward predicament, those hands. She wanted to feel them on her, but she also wanted his shirt off...badly.

She pulled back slightly and his hands went still. His gaze darted to hers.

"Excuse me," she said politely, before pulling the shirt over his head. He released his hold, abandoning the satiny warmth of her skin so the shirt could come all the way off. He was smiling when she turned back from tossing it aside. "What? Why are you smiling at me like that?" she asked, mimicking his earlier question. Her hands went to his shoulders, sifted downward through the crisp whorls of hair on his chest.

He drew in a sharp breath at her touch. "You're...this principal on the outside. Efficient, professional and always extremely polite." He reached for the clasp of her bra, watching her eyes darken then close when he undid it and slid his hands under the lacy fabric to cup her naked breasts.

His own eyes closed, his pulse sprinting. "On the...the inside—" He leaned forward, suddenly craving her taste. She met him halfway, joining her mouth with his in a kiss that pushed all thoughts of conversation from his mind. Needs swiftly engulfed him, and, never breaking the kiss, he shifted her off his lap, then rolled with her to lie face-to-face with him on the bed.

Lesley smiled into his eyes, stroking his jaw. "What am I, Gil?"

His hands busy beneath the sweater again, he gave a self-deprecating chuckle. "I forgot."

She pinched him on the arm.

"Ow! It's your fault that I forgot," he said.

She grinned, leaning forward to apply a forgiving kiss to the spot she'd pinched. Anyway, she didn't need to hear what she was at the moment, she already knew. It had nothing to do with being an extremely polite principal and everything to do with being stirred up, aroused, excited...in love.

He found the hem of her sweater again, this time working it up and off her, the bra following quickly. Pale streams of moonlight provided the only illumination in the room and, as if exhibiting particularly good taste, blanketed Lesley's torso with shimmering light. Her breasts were full and round, their centers a delicate shade of rose. His breathing shallow, Gil lowered his head.

Lesley shuddered at the feel of his mouth on her breast. Sensation, half pleasure, half ache, spiraled through her as he caressed her with his lips and tongue. Instinctively she arched upward, giving a soft gasp when he drew her deeper into his mouth. She'd once imagined that making love with him would far surpass "pleasant." Her imagination, she thought now, had been right on target.

He murmured her name against her skin, moving to her other breast and favoring it with the same delightful torment. His hands were accomplices in the process, touching, stroking, gently kneading.

Then he came back to her mouth, initiating a kiss that he intended to be a gentle, tender demonstration of how beautiful he found her. But Lesley tunneled her fingers in his hair, deepening, darkening the kiss. He groaned, sweeping her mouth with his tongue and urging her bare warmth against his chest.

"You feel so good," he whispered, his hands moving over her back as he strung kisses along her throat to the velvety soft skin of her shoulder. It boggled the mind, he thought. He'd wanted her, wanted this for so long that he'd imagined a different scenario for this first time. He'd figured restraint and frustration would have made for a quick, frantic journey toward satisfaction, but that wasn't the case. He found that, more than anything, he wanted to savor, to linger, to stretch the seconds into minutes and the minutes into hours.

"You feel good, too," she said, a low moan issuing from her throat when his head dipped and his mouth claimed her breast again. The pleasure ache curled through her once more, and she shifted restlessly, bringing her hips into contact with his, feeling the urgent pressure of his arousal. Her breath caught; the ache intensified.

She heard two muffled thuds on the carpeted floor—Gil's shoes—then felt his fingers at the zipper of her jeans. Her heart pounding a furious rhythm, she urged him back up to cover his jaw, his throat, his shoulders with heated kisses.

"I thought I wanted...slow," he said, his voice halting as her mouth on his skin intensified his desire. He helped her remove her jeans and underpants, then glided a hand over her bare hip, his eyes connecting with hers when his fingers slipped between her thighs on the most intimate of quests. Her arousal apparent, he drew a ragged breath. "I don't think I want slow anymore."

"You don't," she told him, the erotic movements of his fingers quickening her pulse and blurring her thoughts. She had just enough concentration left to know that she wanted him completely unclothed, too, wanted to feel him against her, inside her, so she reached for the waist of his slacks and helped him take them off as he'd helped her.

Control. She'd once bragged that she had enough to ward off hormonal urges. Now she could hardly conjure up enough to wait the seconds it took for him to open the nightstand drawer for protection.

She would remember always that when he settled over her, it wasn't the alignment of body parts or fevered sensations she was most aware of. It was the strong, steady beat of his heart next to hers. How that was possible when he'd lifted her to such a plateau of sexual urgency, she didn't know. She only knew that it was so. And she sensed it was the same for him. Felt it in the gentle way he framed her face with his hands, the loving look in his eyes, the tender kiss he placed on her lips.

Then he was inside her, filling her with heat, with love, meshing emotion with the fevered sensations she'd anticipated moments ago. She wrapped herself around him, clung to him as he began to move within her, and answered his heady rhythm when passion demanded a faster pace. Her breath coming in quick gasps, Lesley lost coherent thought, her mind filled with nothing save the pleasure of Gil loving her, of her loving Gil. Then the pleasure peaked and burst over her in hot shimmery waves that went on and on. She whispered his name, heard hers torn from his throat when he found release.

Inexplicably a sliver of fear intruded. Losing control, a voice in her head told her, meant losing herself.

But Gil was there, pushing aside the intrusion by tightening his hold on her, resting his cheek next to her heart, and glancing up with an expression of love and a twinkle of humor. "Definitely smack dab in the middle of it," he said with an expansive sigh.

LESLEY STIRRED, drifting upward from the light sleep she'd fallen into. She blinked, confused at her surroundings for a moment, then, feeling the warmth of Gil's body behind hers, the weight of one leg pinning hers, her mind cleared. She turned a bit to look at him.

His hair was appealingly mussed, his features relaxed, his breathing deep and even. Smiling, she turned in his arms and reached up to brush back the silvery-blond lock of hair that had fallen onto his forehead.

I want long-term, Lesley.

She wanted it, too. So much.

She snuggled closer to him, thinking it was frightening how much she wanted it. Almost as frightening as how many changes had occurred in her life and how fast those changes had come. One moment, she'd been a vice principal in Austin, living with her three sisters. The next, she was in Warren with the new job, adjusting to being on her own, and no longer responsible for her sisters, as much as she'd wanted to be. Then, Gil breezed in, knocking her senses for a loop and forcing her to face the fact that she wasn't immune to the chemistry between them.

Thank goodness he hadn't allowed her to shout that chemistry down with logic, she thought, rubbing her cheek against the crinkly hair on his chest, then testing its texture with her fingertips. Thank goodness for his steamroller instincts.

"Are you warm enough?" His voice was low, husky with sleep.

She looked up. "I thought you were asleep," she whispered.

"I was." He took her hand from his chest and brought it to his lips, placing soft nibbling kisses on her fingers. "And I was having the best dream. I dreamed that the team had just won district and that I was alone with you because Coby was spending the weekend with her mother." He draped Lesley's arm across his shoulder and scooted her flush against him.

He buried his face in her hair, close to her ear. His voice as sexy as the feel of him stretched out next to her, he said, "I dreamed that you told me you loved me and that we made love."

"It wasn't a dream," she said, her body slowly awakening in response to his wandering hands. When they cupped the backs of her thighs, Lesley's eyes shuttered closed. "All that really happened. We did make love."

"Mmm. I know." His hands were moving again, his lips bestowing breathy kisses on her ear. "Can we do it again?"

She smiled, her hands moving to the backs of his thighs to reciprocate his action. "I thought we already were."

He chuckled, insinuating one of his legs between hers. "Can't put one past you, can I?"

"No!" GIL SHOUTED. "I said go out long."

Lesley frowned, waving her hand to indicate the distance she'd gone out. "This isn't long?" she shouted back. "How much longer is there?"

"To that elm tree."

She glanced back over her shoulder at the elm, noting that it was another fifty yards behind her. "You just want to wear me out so I'll be easy to tackle," she accused loudly. "This is far enough."

He laughed. "Oh, stop whining and go on. I'm not throwing the pass until you do."

She glared at him then swiveled, electing to walk the distance instead of sprinting as she'd been doing all morning. There was such a thing as too much exercise, she decided. Gil had proved it by running her ragged all morning, even though he hadn't so much as broken into a sweat.

Once she was beside the tree, Lesley turned, and the ball came hurtling toward her. She shuffled to the side, reaching up in what she figured would be yet another futile attempt, then, amazingly, she caught the damned thing.

"I caught it," she said in amazement, then held the football up, yelling. "I can't believe it! I caught it!"

"All right! Now run with it."

She did, this time deciding he wasn't going to tackle her. No way, no how. Oh, he had never actually hurt her all those times he'd pulled her to the ground just as she'd thought she'd gotten past him. But Gil needed a lesson in humility. And she was going to be the one to teach it.

"You're not going to get me this time, Fielden," she promised when she was several feet in front of him. She was proud of herself; she was panting, but not heavily.

"Oh, I'm not, Tyler?" He watched her like a hawk eyeing a defenseless fieldmouse. His feet were spread slightly, and he was poised for the attack.

But Lesley wasn't letting him intimidate her this time. She faked to her right, then to her left. Gil stood absolutely still, damn him. Lesley glanced past his right shoulder. "Oh, look over there, isn't that Tom Landry?"

He grinned, his hands going to his hips. "Won't work, Lesley."

"Okay, okay. I give up." She stopped jogging in place and slumped her shoulders. "It's not fair, anyway," she said poutily. "I never get past you—you're too good."

"Aw, poor baby," he said, chuckling. "Have I been too rough on you?" His guard down, he started walking toward her.

That's when she made her move. Tucking the ball at her waist, she sped past him, neatly sidestepping when he lurched for her, then spiking the ball on the ground when she made it to the imaginary end zone. She held up her arms referee-style. "Touchdown!" she informed him gleefully.

His hands on his hips again, he shook his head and started toward her. "Do you really want those six points when you had to cheat to get them?"

"You wish," she said, loving it that she finally had the chance to act cocky. "I didn't cheat. I outsmarted you."

He grinned, still advancing on her. "Think so, huh?"

"I know so," she said, but for all her confidence she was a bit leery of the rascally look in Gil's eyes. She backed up a few paces. "I don't have the football. You can't tackle me."

"I can't?"

"No." She continued backing up, glancing behind her to see how much of the apartment courtyard was left before she got to the fenced-in pool. Not a whole lot, she discovered. "Gil…" she warned. "That would be a foul or something."

"Unsportsmanlike conduct," he corrected, "or unnecessary roughness. Carries a fifteen-yard penalty." He quickened his walk to a jog, forcing Lesley to take action. Knowing she had little room for escape by moving backward, she shot forward, hoping for success a second time.

No such luck. Lesley squealed when he caught her easily and tackled her to the ground. Brushing her hair out of her face, she pushed up from his chest to look into his smug, triumphant eyes.

"We're going to have to have a talk about this competitive streak of yours, Gil," she said dryly.

"Yeah, I know. It's a curse." His arms tightened when she started to get up. "Where do you think you're going?" Scooting her within kissing range, he covered her mouth with his.

As always, Lesley's body went liquid inside. As always, she felt the world melt away until there was only her and Gil and the breathlessness he could create merely by kissing her. She closed her eyes and let the excitement spiral through her.

When the kiss was over, she laid her head on his chest and toyed with the scooped neck of his football jersey. "We're in an apartment courtyard, Gil," she felt obliged to remind him, even though the thought of moving was one she'd like to ignore. Every muscle in her body was in favor of remaining in a prone position, and though she knew she should be worried about someone spotting them in the deserted courtyard, she liked the solid feel of Gil's body beneath hers.

"Yeah, I know," he said with a heavy sigh as his fingers stroked through her hair. Getting to his feet, he grasped her hand and tugged her up. He plucked at the dried grass that had tangled in her hair. "How about that lunch I promised?"

She eyed him with the same skepticism she'd felt when he'd coerced her into playing football this morning with the promise of homemade lasagna for lunch. "You really made this lasagna yourself? It's not a frozen entrée?"

"I swear it."

He picked up the ball, and they headed back to his apartment, where he went to work on warming up a large glass casserole of lasagna. It certainly looked homemade, Lesley noted from her place at the kitchen table, and the aroma, she thought several minutes later, was marvelous.

Her first taste confirmed that Gil was telling the truth. This was no frozen grocery store offering, it was the real thing, made from scratch. She closed her eyes, savoring her first bite, then swallowed. "Gil, this is wonderful!"

He grinned, smugly of course. "You shouldn't be so surprised that I can cook. I may have been a bachelor all these years, but I also had a daughter with me every other weekend and two months in the summer.

"We ate out on some of the weekends, but you can't feed a kid fast food every night. So I learned how to cook—pretty well, if I do say so myself." He brought a forkful of the lasagna to his mouth.

"Not just *pretty* well," she said, an image of Gil in an apron and wielding a spatula bringing a smile to her lips. "You're an excellent cook."

"Thanks."

He was also an excellent father. Of course, she'd already discovered that from being around Gil and Coby so much lately. It was just that the little tidbit of father-daughter history he'd dropped served to remind Lesley that everything Gil did, he did with his daughter's welfare in mind. He would want to know of anything that might affect Coby's well-being.

"About Coby, Gil..."

He looked up as he reached for a slice of garlic bread. "You worried about how she'll react to our relationship? You don't need to, you know. Several times over the past few weeks she's let it slip that she approves of the two of us together."

"No, no. I'm not worried about that. But there is something else. It's...her grades."

He looked up with a slight frown. "What about her grades?"

Lesley filled him in on the situation, beginning with what Stacey had told her and ending with the information she'd confirmed with Coby's English teacher. Though concern had been evident in Gil's eyes at first, amazingly enough, his worry seemed to have vanished by the time she'd finished.

"There's nothing to worry about. Coby wants to be in the play too badly. She'll bring the grades up."

"Gil, I know that Coby is an excellent student, certainly capable of doing just that, but I'm afraid all those rehearsals will come into conflict with her schoolwork. Look what they've done to her English grade.''

He was quiet for a moment. "So what is it that you think she should do, drop the play?''

"No, of course not," she answered. "I thought maybe you could talk to her and, you know, remind her that she'll be losing the chance to be in the play if she doesn't take the time for her schoolwork.''

"She already knows that. You've made sure that all the extracurricular activity students know that, Lesley.''

Was she mistaken or had Gil's tone become just a shade frosty? His jaw had seemed to tense a bit, also. She ignored the tiny sliver of hurt his words had brought. "Gil, I know this is a subject you and I would probably be wise to avoid, but I'm concerned for Coby.''

"You're right. We should avoid talking about it.'' With those words, he pushed away from the table and took his empty plate and silverware to the sink.

Lesley stared down at her unfinished lunch, her appetite gone. She hadn't imagined that Gil would react to the news about Coby so...so apathetically. She knew he viewed no-pass, no-play in a different light than she did, but this was his daughter she was talking about. She picked up her plate and silverware and went to the sink with them.

"You're not going to finish that?'' he asked, all signs of frostiness replaced with his former good humor as he squirted dishwashing liquid into the rapidly filling sink.

She gave him a quizzical look. "Gil, I don't understand how you can be so indifferent to Coby's problem."

"There's not really a problem as far as I can see."

"Not really a...?" Lesley's amazement grew. "Gil, her teacher told me that she's gone from a solid A to a high C in a very short period of time. And with her wanting to perform in the play..."

"A C was average the last time I looked."

His cool tone was back, and Lesley set down her plate and forced him to face her. "With no-pass, no-play, a C is dangerously close to Coby not being allowed to participate in something she's got her heart set on."

"Oh, that's right, I almost forgot. With the law, average students are no longer average, they're dangerously close to having privileges ripped away from them."

His sarcastic manner had Lesley biting back an equally sarcastic reply. Instead she strove for a calm voice. "The law has changed things. Whether we happen to agree with those changes or not, we have to live with them."

"Yeah, I know." He turned back to the sink, reaching for her dish. "Look, it's not that I haven't accepted the law. I have. But I don't have to like what it does to kids who aren't as capable as Coby."

Lesley nodded. "Granted, it puts some extra pressure on the student, but—"

"*Some* extra pressure? You yourself told me Coby is on edge. I've noticed it, too. If Coby, who has never had a problem with grades, is stressed out over it, then just think what the other, more 'average' students are going through.''

Lesley sighed. "Gil, I won't deny there are problems with the law. And I don't want to rehash our differences. I'm merely suggesting that you talk to Coby. You could advise her—"

"No, Lesley." His voice was quiet. Not sarcastic, curt or even frosty. It was quiet. He shut off the water, dried his hands on a dish towel and turned back to her. "There is nothing I can say that Coby doesn't already know or that her mother hasn't already lectured her about. Between Ceil and Coby's own tendencies toward overachievement, my daughter has more than enough pressure on her."

He rested his hands on her shoulders. "I know a little about pressure and how it affects teenagers, Lesley. You forget what happened to my own brother over this same kind of thing."

His eyes clouded for a moment, then a soft smile curved his mouth.

"I know you've brought this up because you care about Coby. And you don't know how happy I am that you do. But, trust me on this, okay? I know my daughter. I know what does and doesn't work where she's concerned. Any more tension or stress in her life right now will not motivate her, it'll only make things worse.

"I don't want to rehash our differences either," he said, his fingers combing back one side of her hair so he could place whisper-light kisses across her cheek. "We've worked past those differences, haven't we?"

"Yes. Yes, we have," she answered, her hands going to his waist when he pulled her body closer to his. She tilted her head back to look at him. "You're Coby's parent, Gil. I'm sure you know what works best with her. I was just hoping...well, I think it would be a crying shame if she were to miss out on the play.

"But you're probably right," Lesley continued, remembering Coby's reaction when she'd broached the subject with the girl just last night. "I brought this up when I talked to her at the football game, and she didn't want to discuss it."

He nodded. "Her mother's been riding her about it, which only serves to make Coby mad. Believe me, Coby's going to bring up that grade, but not because of anything that any of us say to her. She'll do it because she wants to be on that stage with all her drama friends."

Lesley hoped Gil was right. She hoped that his sit-back-and-let-matters-take-care-of-themselves attitude would work in this case. As he'd said, he knew his daughter better than she did; he knew how to handle the situation. She just wished there was a way she could be more sure of the outcome.

"I don't know about you," he said, his lips grazing her ear, "but I'm ready to shelve all conversation and take an after-game nap."

Lesley smiled, tightening her arms around his waist as his mouth sought her throat. "Only a nap?" she asked, pretending disappointment.

"An... energetic nap."

CHAPTER THIRTEEN

LYING ON THE BED in her room at her mom's house, Coby gripped the phone receiver hard and stared at the ceiling. "Devin, I've told you. I need more time for studying."

"I understand that, Coby. But a couple of hours away from the books won't matter. Come on, you'll have the rest of the day to study."

"And I'll need every minute of it. Besides we were just out with all your football buddies last night after the game. Didn't we do enough celebrating the district win then?" she asked, not bothering to mask the edge in her voice.

There was silence for a moment. "Well, I didn't realize it was such a chore for you to be with me and my football buddies. Or maybe it's not just my friends you don't want to be with?"

"What's that supposed to mean?"

"I think you know. You've hinted that you've been wanting to cool things off between the two of us for some time now. I may be a jock, but I'm not stupid, Coby."

She rolled her eyes. It seemed that the closer Devin came to making a choice between drama and football, the more defensive he became about being an athlete in the first place. He'd also started wanting them to spend more and more time with his friends on the team. It was time that Coby couldn't spare right now. "Will you quit it with that stupid 'jock' business? I've never called you that, and you know it. I just need more time by myself so I can pull up my English average. Can't you understand?"

His sigh was audible over the line. "It's other things I don't understand."

"What other things?" she asked in an exasperated tone.

"Okay. Since you asked... we've been going together long enough that... certain things, certain physical things, are just naturally going to happen between two people who care about each other, and—"

"Oh, I see!" Her expression quickly escalated to anger, and she sat bolt upright on the bed. "All that stuff about not wanting to pressure me, about giving me time to decide what *I* wanted was for a limited time only. Well, I may be female, but I'm not stupid, either. Women have been wise to that prove-you-love-me line for a long time now."

"Oh, for God's sake, I'm not asking you to prove anything. I'm just saying that if you were as committed to us being a couple as I am, you'd at least be a little more open to—"

"That really rips it! Since you see nothing wrong with us just falling into bed together, you're more committed to us being a couple than I am. That is the biggest load of crap I've ever heard."

"Would you just let me finish what I'm trying to tell you? I'm not talking about us falling into bed together. And by the way, giving you time and room to decide was not on a limited-time-only offer. I'm just saying that, jeez, it seems like I can't even kiss you anymore without you freezing up on me. And God forbid that I should try to touch you unless I just want to hold your hand. Do you think I haven't noticed that?''

"I do not—"

"Yes, you do. And what am I supposed to think about it? That you're head over heels about me? Admit it, Coby, you're having regrets that we ever pushed things past friendship. You're wishing that we were still just study partners.''

"Well, at least we never fought then.''

"You see! You do admit it.''

Coby clenched her eyes shut. She stood up and paced around the room, dragging the long phone cord behind her. Why was Devin doing this to her? It seemed as if in the past couple of weeks there had been one pressure stacked on another. Her mother's nagging. Extra drama rehearsals. Grades. College entrance requirements. She wouldn't have thought that Devin would want to get in on the whole stress-fest, too, but apparently she was wrong.

She plopped back down onto the bed. "I don't regret that we're more than friends,'' she said. "I just have lots of things going on in my life right now. I might 'freeze up' when we're alone together, but it's not because I want to cool things off, it's because I can't handle making a decision about going any further with you right now, Devin. I have too many other things on my mind. I thought you understood that.''

"Too many other things on your mind. It doesn't sound like I'm very high on your list of priorities these days, does it?"

"Oh, Devin." Coby shook her head. Why couldn't he be more supportive of what she was going through instead of taking everything she said wrong? Looking at the stack of books sitting on her desk, she felt a jolt of impatience. "I don't have time for this," she said desperately. "I've got three papers due tomorrow."

"Yeah. Right."

She ignored his harsh tone. "I'll talk to you tomorrow after second hour, okay?"

Devin snorted. "Sure you can squeeze me in?"

"Goodbye, Devin." She didn't wait to hear his goodbye before hanging up.

"HEY, THOSE PEPPETTE GIRLS are out there painting your car again," Devin's twelve-year-old sister said from the door of his room. "I think they *like* you," she singsonged.

Devin glanced up from the floor he'd been staring at since the call from Coby. He rubbed a hand over his face. "Don't you have something better to do, Shelly?"

"Nope." She waltzed into the room, stopping next to his window and peering out through the mini-blinds. "I'm gonna be a peppette when I go to WHS. I like those neat shoes they wear with the jingle bells on them."

"Come on, Shelly. Vamoose."

"Oh, no. One of them got shoe polish on your car again."

"Shelly. . ."

"Gee, what's got you so weird? Usually you get mad when they get polish on the paint."

Wanting to be miserable in peace, Devin went to the window, turning his younger sister around by the shoulders. "Out, Shelly. Give me a little privacy here, huh? Go. . . practice being a peppette or something."

"All right, all right. Jeez, you don't have to be so rude."

She closed the door behind her, and Devin pushed at one of the slats on the blinds to see out. Upset or not, Shelly was right, he did get mad when the peppettes got shoe polish on his Firebird. When he saw what was written on the back window, he had to wonder if the girls with the neat jingly shoes were into ironic jokes.

Lucky Senior.

Oh, yeah, he was the luckiest. He was the lucky football star who liked playing the game less and less. He had parents who would never be able to understand that, friends who thought he'd gone around the bend and a girlfriend he was crazy about who seemed to care less and less about him. Lucky. He was supremely lucky.

"You know," Gil said, his lips twitching into a smile, "you're supposed to be the organized one. So why is it that you are never ready when I come to pick you up for a date?"

"Oh, close the door and get in here," Lesley said. "I'm freezing."

Gil did as she ordered, then grabbed at the belt on her short terry-cloth robe to pull her close. "You wouldn't be freezing if you'd been dressed on time," he said against her mouth, then sealed her lips with his in a long, luxurious kiss.

"Mmm. It's your bad influence that—Ahh! Your hands are like ice!"

"Yes, but that's only because you're so warm beneath this robe." He caressed the planes of her back, smoothing his hands over her spine, then moving to the curve of her waist as he took up the kiss again. "I think I've discovered the real reason you're always late," he murmured.

"What's that?" Her mind was beginning to swirl with the heavenly sensations evoked by his hands and mouth.

"You figure if you're half-undressed when I get here, you'll drive me so crazy with lust that I'll undress you the rest of the way. Admit it, woman," he growled against her neck. "You want me. You want me all the time."

Lesley smiled, her pulse escalating when he strung kisses down her throat... then lower. He nudged her robe aside. "I can't decide whether all that... ego comes from... oh, Gil... the football coach or... the Texas male."

Gil raised his head, his eyes glazed with desire and his breathing, Lesley was gratified to discover, as shallow as hers. "It's both. What time does this barbecue start?"

"You told me seven-thirty."

"Good," he said, scooping her up into his arms to carry her to her bedroom. "We've got an hour to waste, then."

"Not that I'm complaining," she said after Gil had lowered her to the bed, "but how do you figure we have an hour when it's seven o'clock now?"

"Thirty minutes for love, thirty minutes for you to get dressed. That'll make us fashionably late." Pulling her to her knees on the edge of the bed, he unknotted the belt at her waist and brushed the robe off her shoulders. His gaze flicked downward, and he took a deep breath. "Make that forty-five minutes for love . . . no, an hour . . ."

"GIL?"

"Hmm?"

"I admit it. I do want you all the time."

He raised up on one elbow, looking down at her. "That's a good thing," he said softly. "It's the same with me, you know."

"And that doesn't . . . frighten you at all?"

"No," he said, slightly puzzled. "Does it bother you?"

She nodded, then reached for his hand, entwining her fingers with his. "I . . . don't exactly know why. I do know that it's definitely *not* because I'm afraid we haven't known each other long enough to be considering a serious relationship, and it's not because we're such different people. I think I've gotten past all that. But sometimes, I'm . . . scared."

Gil frowned, and he laid his head back onto the pillow, gathering her body close to his. She was scared, all right. And he had a hunch that it was the very things she'd said she wasn't afraid of that were the root of the problem. He reached for the sheet and blankets they had kicked aside and tucked them around both of them, thinking it was only natural that she hadn't gotten past all that surface stuff yet. She'd trained herself from an early age to pay attention to details that could muck things up. That much he'd learned from her reaction to her sister Kelly's wedding announcement.

"But there are some people who would say those are things we definitely should be afraid of," he mentioned.

"What people?"

"Oh, you know, psychologists, marriage counselors, people who write books about relationships."

"Oh, yes. I guess you're right. Did you and Ceil see a counselor before your marriage broke up?"

"No. You have to remember we divorced more than fifteen years ago. The relationship industry wasn't going full guns then." He propped his chin on top of her head, smoothing a hand over the silken tumble of black hair. He chuckled wryly. "Last year I was laid up in bed for about a week and a half with a mean case of mononucleosis that had been going around school. I learned everything you'd ever want to know about modern male-female involvements from all the talk shows. Let's see, there are women who love too much, men who don't love enough and men who'd like to love more but their women have careers and simply don't have the time or patience to teach them. Then there are the women who love men who like to dress up in dresses. Those women had a real problem with sharing their wardrobes."

Lesley laughed. "Got an education, did you?"

"Yeah. But it was strange. Listening to all those people with their complicated definitions of what a relationship is supposed to be, I came to a conclusion of my own. It's simple, but then again, no one'll ever accuse me of being terribly complicated."

She raised her head to look up at him, one brow arched. "Are you telling me that you think of yourself as 'simple'? That's not true. You're direct. Straightforward. You don't put up with a lot of external junk, you cut through to the heart of a matter, then deal with it. I really admire that about you."

"You do, do you?" he asked with a grin. "Would you go so far as to say that you *love* that about me?"

"I most certainly would," she stated emphatically. "Among other things. Like your sense of humor and your honesty, which is related to your directness, and what Coby calls your 'tough on the exterior, teddy bear on the interior' act." She reached up to touch his face. "Then there's the way I feel whenever I'm with you. Or for that matter, whenever I even think about you. You...make me happy."

Gil hugged her tight, never realizing before how mere words could lift someone's heart so high. "I admire and love lots of things about you, too." He placed a kiss on her forehead, her cheek, her mouth. "I admire you for holding strong to your beliefs as you have with no-pass, no-play. I admire your intelligence and how together, how organized you are. I love your smile, your laugh and the fact that you're so grown-up and dignified but at the same time you can come out to play with overgrown kids like me. You make me happy, too, Lesley. Very happy.''

"Gil . . . you'll make me cry." She lowered her head to his chest again.

"I've never had the chance to test the simple conclusion I came to. That is . . . until now. But I think it's a good one.''

"What is it?" she whispered.

"It's that people concentrate on the differences in their mates that they don't like, so much so sometimes that they forget all about the differences they do like and admire and love.''

A slow smile dawned on Lesley's lips. Their lists of what they both loved and admired *were* composed of differences. For a man who referred to himself as simple, he was pretty insightful, in her opinion. "You're saying you think I *am* afraid of all those things?''

"Maybe. If I'm right, if you are frightened of what the differences you don't like could do to us, then there's a simple solution, right?''

"I should concentrate on the differences I do like?''

"You're such a quick study," he said with a grin.

THEY ARRIVED at Wayne Thomas's sprawling ranch house outside of Warren fashionably late.

"Isn't this beautiful," Lesley said as she unbuckled her seat belt. "It looks like something you'd see in Santa Fe.''

"It's great, huh? Wayne bought it from an oilman who had to alter his life-style a bit after the bust.''

Lesley nodded. "How is it that you know Mr. Thomas, Gil?"

"He was a good friend of my brother, Greg." Gil undid his seat belt and opened his car door. "They were roommates in college."

Hand in hand they walked to the front door of the impressive home. "Hey, if it's not the next Sam Walton," Gil said when they were greeted at the door by their host. Grinning, the man ushered them into a large foyer that continued the pueblo-style dwelling's motif with large Navajo wall hangings and beautiful Indian pottery on rough-hewn side tables.

"I'm a few dollars and several shares of stock behind old Sam," Wayne said as he shook Gil's hand.

"Sure you are," Gil scoffed, glancing around the entry and into the large, exquisitely appointed living area. "He and Sam," Gil said to Lesley, "why they're just a couple of good ol' boys."

Lesley smiled, shaking Wayne's outstretched hand. "It's nice to meet you, Mr. Thomas. I'm Lesley Tyler."

"Yes, yes. I've heard a lot about you from this guy here. And the first rule with good ol' boys is that you've got to call them by their first names. Wayne, please."

"Wayne then," she said.

"Let me take your coats. Wait here and I'll stash 'em in the closet down the way."

He returned moments later to walk them through the house to a large game room at the back where the party was in full swing. Several of the guests were eating barbecue at a long table while others were gathered around a pool table watching a game in progress; still others were stationed along a massive saloon-type bar.

"So," Wayne said as he led them toward the buffet where all the food was laid out, "you're the principal at that school with the crackerjack football team."

Lesley chuckled, by now more than accustomed to being referred to that way by most of the citizens of Warren. "Yes, I am."

"Watch it there, Wayne. You'll get me in trouble. She likes to think that more than just football goes on there." Gil picked up a plate and handed it to Lesley with a wink.

"I thought that *was* all that went on there," a male voice from the other side of the table piped up.

"Hey there, Don. Good to see you," Gil said jovially. "Lesley, this is Don Michaels, Devin's father. Don, Lesley Tyler. She's your son's principal."

Lesley nodded goodbye to Wayne, who excused himself to see to other guests, then smiled at the man Gil was introducing. "Nice to meet you Mr. Michaels. You must be very proud of your son. He seems like a fine young man."

"Thank you, Miss Tyler, I am. Right now, however, he's a depressed young man," Michaels said as he filled up a plate of his own. "What's the matter, Coach, you couldn't get your daughter to wait until after the football season to start bickerin' all the time?"

The man's tone was light, but Lesley noticed that the grin he wore didn't extend to his eyes. Gil had told her about Coby and Devin's recent squabbles. She could understand how the pressure they both felt and the fact that Devin seemed interested in getting serious could lead to arguments. Obviously Mr. Michaels didn't understand that.

"Oh, you know how it is with women, Don," Gil joked as he filled his plate with ribs. "They have no concept of the importance of a state championship."

"All I know is that he's been mooning over all of this like it was a divorce instead of a high school infatuation. Louise and I are worried that it'll affect his performance through the rest of the season."

Affect his performance through the rest of the season? Lesley glanced up at Mr. Michaels, hardly believing she'd heard him correctly. He sounded more concerned about his son's performance skills than he was about his current mental state.

"Aw, I don't think you have much to worry about, Don." Gil speared a jalapeño pepper and placed it on the side of his plate. "Devin's a good, consistent player. There's not much that rattles him once he hits the field."

"I sure hope so. I also hope this little depression of his doesn't screw up his grades. I wouldn't like to see his chances for recruitment ruined by romance problems."

Placing a hot roll on her plate, Lesley glanced up at Gil. She was glad to see the telltale tightening of his jaw. It meant that he wasn't thrilled with the man's attitude any more than she was.

"Well, Don, I don't know what to tell you about that, except that even if he missed every other game in the season, Devin would still stand a good chance of being recruited by any number of colleges who've had their eye on him."

"Probably. But I know he'll want to end his high school career on an up note. And it sure would be a shame if Warren lost out on a chance for the state championship because Devin wasn't playing."

This time it was Gil's grin that didn't reach his eyes. "Devin's good, Don, but no one's indispensable. Guess he'll just need to crack those books a little more if he wants to finish his senior year on an up note, huh?"

Lesley had only seconds to be pleased with Gil's response before the boy's father made another remark that had her temper flaring.

"That might be easier if I could get him to drop that damned drama class he got talked into. For the life of me I can't see why he's interested in that crap—"

"Listen, Don, you know I could discuss football all night long, but I want to get to this barbecue before it gets cold. What do you say we pick up this conversation later, huh?"

"Uh...sure. You go on and eat. I'll catch you later."

Their plates filled, Gil and Lesley walked over to a long table that had been set up for diners. "I can't believe that man," she said once they were seated.

"He's a real sweetheart, isn't he?"

"Have you had many dealings with him before?"

"Only since Devin's been in high school," Gil said as he placed his napkin on his lap. "Don't judge him too harshly, though. He's usually not that bad."

"Not that bad? Gil, he's only upset over Devin's emotional distress because it might hurt Devin's playing ability!"

Gil picked up a rib and took a bite, then shrugged. "Same thing's crossed my mind."

"Well...yes. I'm sure it has," she said. "But that's not your only concern. You've told me how down Devin has been since he and Coby have been fighting, and how worried you've been about both of them. And besides, what was all that stuff about no one being indispensable if you weren't more concerned about Devin's depression than his being able to play the rest of the season?"

"I did tell Michaels that," he said with a slight frown. "And I truly hope that's the case."

"You mean it might not be?"

"I can't be sure. Devin's played an instrumental part in our success this season. While no one player can take all the glory, the loss of one talented player can still make a big difference. And you have to remember that we're not competing with run-of-the-mill teams now. We're playing the best of the best, and we need all the help we can get."

"I...guess I can understand all that, but as a father I would think you'd be a little offended by the man's attitude toward his son. It's clear that he's no better than some...some fanatical stage mother wanting only what's best for the boy's performance on Friday nights. Didn't it upset you in the least that he wants Devin to drop drama? I mean, Devin's a wonderful actor, and according to Coby, he loves the class and—"

He reached across the table for her hand. "Lesley, here's one of those differences that we were talking about earlier. And it's one of the ones you're not going to like." He squeezed her hand and gave her a little smile. "Kindly remember the differences you do like as I tell you this.

"I'm a football coach. It's vital to my job security to deliver a winning football team. Because of no-pass, no-play, grade-watching has become a major part of my job for the past several years. And when one of my better players is in danger of being cut because of a course that isn't necessary for graduation, I'll advise that player to drop the course. In fact—and you're not going to like this a bit—I've advised Devin to do just that."

"You're right," she said, her voice cool as she slid her hand from his. "I don't like it at all. Gil, how could you? You were in that auditorium the same day I was, and you saw what a good actor he is. What about what he wants? Does that make any difference to you and his father? He desperately wants to be in the play, Coby has told both of us that."

"He's also a good football player, Lesley. Good enough that he can take his pick of colleges. On full athletic scholarship, I might add—if he wants it badly enough. And that translates into a better-than-average chance that he can go pro."

Gil reached for her hand again, even though it was apparent she didn't want him to. Clasping it in his, he said, "It's not that I don't care about what he wants. I told him that the decision was his. He can either play football or be in the play. But this is like the situation with your sister Kelly. Sometimes young people don't always think about consequences until it's too late. And the consequences for Devin, if he lets this acting bug take over, could be the loss of a lucrative career."

Lesley shook her head. "If he's that good a player, then what will it hurt if he pursues his acting bug this year? You yourself just told Don Michaels that Devin has so many recruiters after him that even if he didn't play another game, he'd still—"

"Lesley, I said that because Don was getting under my skin with all those veiled remarks about Coby being responsible for Devin's chances at a career. I wanted to shut him up.

"The truth of the matter is that Devin has a good chance of being recruited without playing anymore, but only a *good chance*. That chance is considerably better if he's able to play the rest of this season. When you add in the fact that the NCAA is putting more and more pressure on college football programs as far as their players' SAT scores and grade point averages are concerned, you've got good cause to worry over Devin's situation."

"If a career in football is what Devin, not his father, wants," Lesley pointed out.

"Well, of course he has to want it. I'm not arguing that point. I'm just telling you what my position is. And don't think for a minute that his drama teacher isn't operating from the very same position I am, Lesley. After all, if his grades go any further south, he won't be participating in either drama or football, will he?"

"No," she said with a sigh. "No, he won't. I just wish..."

"What? That he could have it both ways? That's not possible, Lesley."

She closed her eyes briefly, her frustration level heightening. "I know, I know. No-pass, no-play makes it impossible."

"Right."

"Well, you don't have to look so smug. I've never denied that there was a downside to the law." Resigning herself to the situation, she reached for her fork and took a mouthful of coleslaw. "That doesn't mean that it isn't valuable for the most part. Grade point averages have gone up since we've cracked down on this issue."

"I have to agree, Madame Principal," Gil said, buttering his roll. He looked up with a grin, pointing at her with the roll. "That doesn't mean I have to like it."

A grudging smile made its way to her lips. "No, that doesn't mean you have to like it."

"WHAT'S HARD FOR ME to believe," Michaels said, propping a foot on the brass railing that surrounded the bar, "is that you didn't automatically get the job when Moore retired last year. You've been vice principal at Warren for what, two years now? I just assumed the principal's job would go to you, Collins."

Dwight held up his glass to signal to the bartender that he was ready for a refill. He'd be needing it, he decided, if he were going to stand here listening to this obnoxious man much longer. "Yes, Mr. Michaels. I thought so, too."

"Well, I wonder what the hell was going through old Jack's mind when he hired someone outside of the district?"

"Don't know." Dwight glanced around the room, looking for his date. When she'd mentioned that the superintendent of schools was a good friend of her boss, Wayne Thomas, and would probably be in attendance at this barbecue, Dwight had jumped at the chance to come. It never hurt to do a little politicking when a job opportunity was at stake. So far, however, he hadn't seen the superintendent. For that matter, he hadn't even seen much of his date.

"Guess she must have had more years on the job," Michaels said after taking a swig from his long-neck beer. "Sure hope Jack doesn't regret hiring her."

Dwight shifted his eyes sideways to Michaels. "Why would he regret hiring Lesley Tyler?"

"Oh, you know. Over all this House Bill 72 business. Jack was telling me the other day that she's not even in charge of it at Warren anymore. Said she handed it over to you."

That caught Dwight's interest. "You know the superintendent pretty well then, Mr. Michaels?" he asked.

Don chuckled. "Jack and me go way back. We played football together at SMU."

"You don't say?" Michaels and Jack Standifer were old football chums? That was a tidbit Dwight hadn't been aware of. Suddenly this get-together didn't seem like such a washout. "So you say he mentioned my name to you?"

"Indeed he did. I got the impression that he's pretty impressed with you, son. I believe he said something along the lines of 'Collins can be counted on to do the right thing.'"

Dwight's brow creased in a slight frown. "Do the right thing, Mr. Michaels?"

"Well, this is just my opinion, you understand, but I figure he's referring to the football program. Jack's as big a football fan as me, you know. He's fairly bustin' with pride over Warren's success this season. I sure would hate to see anything happen to trip up the team. You know what I mean, boy?"

Dwight nodded slowly, eternally grateful now that Lesley Tyler had given him the extra responsibility for no-pass, no-play. It was going to get him that principal's job he wanted. "You bet I do, Mr. Michaels. You bet I do."

WATCHING COBY STORM away from him and down the hall, Devin shoved his arms into his leather jacket, then slammed his locker door shut. Would their arguing and fighting never stop? It had been three weeks since their first big blowup over the phone, and the end didn't seem to be in sight.

He flipped up the collar of his jacket and did some storming of his own in the direction of the gym, glad for once that he had practice to attend. Physical activity was just what he needed to blow off a little steam.

Fed up didn't begin to describe how he felt about his and Coby's relationship. It seemed the further her grades slipped, the worse it became between the two of them. A few moments ago, she'd as much as laid the blame for her English grade at his feet.

"Women," he muttered to himself. They really knew how to lay on the guilt. And it wasn't as if his grades were any better. They'd fallen to dangerous depths, and the worst part about it was that he didn't give a damn. He didn't care that he was close to being sidelined for the rest of the season. He was even starting to feel as apathetic about the play.

No, he thought. That wasn't the truth. He did want to be in the play. He just wished things could be good between Coby and him again. And he wished everyone would quit riding him about playing football.

Stopping at a water fountain to get a drink, he heard a female voice call his name. He glanced over his shoulder.

"Hi, Stacey," he said as the office secretary drew up beside him. "What's up?"

"I'm so glad I caught you before you went to football practice. I have a message from Mr. Collins for you. He'd like to see you—before practice if possible. If it's not, then before school starts tomorrow morning."

"Thanks," he said. "I guess I can spare a few minutes now."

Thirty minutes later, Devin closed the door to Dwight Collins's office behind him and headed down the hall for the gym again, all his problems solved. All his problems with grades, at least. He pocketed the class schedule change, wondering if he should ask the man to fix his personal problems while he was at it. When it came to impossible situations, the VP certainly seemed to know his way around.

What was it Collins had said? "There is nothing illegal about what we're doing with this schedule change, Devin. It's simply a loophole in the law that we can take advantage of. Coach Fielden needs you for the remainder of the season, and House Bill 72 says if you're in honors classes, your grade can be one letter lower and you'll still be allowed to participate in extracurricular activities. And there's no need for you to worry that you won't be able to handle honors class assignments. I've already assigned someone to...uh, *tutor* you in that area."

Devin knew that he might not be smart enough to qualify for honors classes the honest way, but he wasn't so stupid that he'd failed to get the man's drift. He wasn't going to be tutored; he was going to have his assignments done for him.

He stopped short, feeling a stab of guilt. What was he doing going along with this business? It was cheating, plain and simple. And it was being done to allow him to remain on the playing field, something he didn't even want to do anymore.

He changed directions, going not to practice but his car in the parking lot. This was *his* life they were screwing around with. Coach Fielden and the vice principal might feel that this was the best thing for him to do, but he should have some say in it, dammit.

He unlocked his car door and climbed inside, then switched on the ignition and waited for the car to warm up. He had two courses of action here. He could either go along with what everyone else wanted for him and reap all the benefits—such as being able to act in the play. Or he could take control of his own life for once, make his own decision and possibly lose out on being in the play and the chance for recruitment. Staring through the windshield at the school, he gave a harsh chuckle. Taking control, making his own decision, doing the honest thing really sucked.

CHAPTER FOURTEEN

LESLEY STARED at the slip of paper Devin had handed her, wishing more than anything that it was a computer error. But she had a feeling that it wasn't. She reached into a desk drawer and pulled out a folder with the words House Bill 72 printed on the front, glanced up at Devin's serious expression, then thumbed through the pages of the bill until she found the page dealing with exceptions to the no-pass, no-play law.

As she had thought, Devin's schedule change wasn't a computer error at all. It was a clear violation—by way of a loophole—of the law.

She'd known that something was up when he arrived at her office before school had started minutes ago. The look in his eyes, the sound of his voice when he'd handed her the paper and said, "There's something you should know," had tipped her off to the seriousness of the situation.

Looking at Dwight Collins's signature at the bottom of the schedule change, she pressed her fingers against her temples. She didn't understand why Dwight would try this. He had nothing to gain by attempting to bend the rules. He didn't stand to—

At the realization that someone besides Dwight was behind it, Lesley's heart went cold. No, Dwight had nothing to gain by bending the rules in this manner...but someone else did.

That someone was Gil.

No. Lesley couldn't, wouldn't believe it. Gil might be the most logical person to suspect, but believing he would actually do something this devious meant that the trust she'd given him when she'd given her heart was a one-way street. And if that were true, what did that say about their love?

He'd taught her to finally rely on what her heart told her. And what it told her now was that she was wrong to suspect him.

She looked up at Devin. He was sitting in the chair in front of her desk, his fingers nervously tapping his knee as he looked out the window to the parking lot.

"Thank you for bringing this to my attention, Devin. I'll get to the bottom of it."

His fingers stopped tapping and he looked directly at her. "Look, Miss Tyler, I'm not trying to get anyone in hot water or anything. I just..."

"You did the right thing. I'm proud of you for stepping forward."

His eyes lowered. "It's weird. I thought I'd feel good about it, but..."

"I think I understand."

"Yeah? Well, I don't." He shook his head. "I thought about this all night. I thought about how this past year everyone else has been making my decisions. My dad won't hear of me wanting to do anything other than play football for the rest of my life.

Coach wants the same thing. But I . . . I don't want to do it if the only way I can play is to cheat. . . ." His words trailed off. "I just want some control over my own life," he added quietly. "I thought refusing to go along with this would be a good start. Now I don't know."

"It is a good start, Devin."

"You don't sound so sure of that."

"I'm just upset that it's happened, Devin, not that you've come to me with it."

He nodded. "Look. I don't want Coach Fielden to get in trouble over this. Could I just refuse to go along with the schedule change and, you know, leave it at that? I mean, if my grades slip below C's, then I'll forfeit football and drama, but no one has to be the wiser, okay? We can just act like it never happened."

"Devin, I'm not sure that Coach had anything to do with this. Do you . . . have a definite reason to believe that's the case?"

His expression was guarded.

"Devin?" she prompted, dread inching up her spine.

"Yeah," he said finally, blowing out a breath. "Mr. Collins said that Coach needed me on the field for the rest of the season. That's why he was changing my class schedule."

The dread she'd felt seconds ago became a cold, sharp pain that sliced at Lesley's heart. "I . . . see," she said, but she didn't. How could Gil have done it? Knowing what this could do to her, to their relationship, how could he have taken the risk? Was a winning season so important that it was worth the loss it could incur?

Obviously it was.

"Devin, I'm afraid, as much as you and I would like to ignore it, we can't."

He nodded again, then stood. "I had a feeling you'd say that."

Lesley rose from her chair and walked him to the door. "Your instincts are good," she told him. "Only you can know what you want and need out of life. You might not feel good about coming to me with this right now, but in the long run, I promise you will."

"I'll try to remember that," he said before leaving.

Lesley watched him disappear through the outer office door.

She stepped around the corner to Stacey's desk and waited for the girl to get off the phone.

"Hi, Les. What can I—"

"Stacey, I want to see Dwight Collins in my office immediately."

OVER. Thank God this day was over, Gil thought, dropping his damp towel into a bin and switching off the lights in the showers. He ambled toward the bench in the locker room where he'd left his clothes and slipped into underwear and jeans.

The shower hadn't helped. He still felt wasted. Pulling his polo shirt over his head, he wondered when a practice had ever gone so badly. It had to be the pressure of these post-district games that was getting to his players. Not one of them seemed to remember how to kick, pass or even hold on to a ball without fumbling. Not one of them seemed to remember what he told them for more than five minutes at a time.

And then there was the fact that Michaels hadn't been at practice. Gil frowned, propping his foot on the bench to tie his court shoe. This was the second day the boy hadn't shown up. Yesterday Gil had just figured Devin was out with a cold or something. Today he'd checked with admissions and found that Devin had been in school both days.

Something was up. Either he and the boy's father had pressured Devin too much about his grades, or the depression over Coby had done just what Don had feared it would. In any case, Gil would need to call Devin after dinner tonight and find out.

Dinner with Lesley, Gil remembered, and he felt the fatigue and frustrations of the day magically fade. Funny how just the thought of her did that for him. Funny how something he'd almost decided didn't exist was now such an integral part of his life.

Love. It did exist. It lived in the anticipation he felt when he knew he'd be seeing her again after days or hours apart. In the feeling of wholeness that engulfed him when they were together; in the desire he felt to make sure they would be apart less and less.

He thought of the ring he'd seen in the window of Grant's jewelry store last week and the commitment he now wanted to make.

Marriage. Since his divorce so many years ago, the subject had been one that had rarely crossed his mind. Lately he'd been able to think of little else. Lately he'd begun to wonder if Lesley's mind was similarly occupied.

It would be easy enough to find out, he decided as he strode out of the locker room to his office. All he had to do was ask.

SHE WAS WAITING for him in his office when he got there, sitting in the chair across from his desk with her back to him. His mouth curved in a smile as he came up behind her and placed his hands on her shoulders.

"God, you smell good," he whispered, leaning down to plant soft kisses on her neck. One hand snaked under the collar of her blouse, and he rubbed his fingers over the velvet skin of her shoulder. "There's no gym class outside the window watching us today, you know."

"Gil, we need to talk," she said.

"Yes, I know." He straightened up and walked around her to the desk, grabbing his car keys. "We need to decide where we're going to eat."

Her dark expression brought him up short. "You look like your day might have been worse than mine, babe."

She said nothing, holding out a wrinkled slip of paper instead.

"What's this?" he asked, reaching for the paper. He frowned when he saw Devin's name and the class changes. "Honors classes?"

"Yes, honors classes," she said, her voice deadly quiet.

Gil glanced up, perplexed at her tone. "What's it mean?"

"According to House Bill 72, it means that Devin won't have to maintain a C in his classes in order to play football."

Gil glanced down at the slip of paper again. "But why would Collins care one way or another about Devin playing football? And why are you acting so... wait a minute. You don't think that *I* had anything to do with this, do you?"

The stony look in her eyes indicated that she most likely did. "Good Lord, Lesley. That's not my name signed at the bottom of the page. Have you talked to him?"

"Yes, Gil, I had a talk with Dwight."

"And what did he do, tell you I talked him into this crap?"

"No. As a matter of fact, he refused to tell me who was behind it." Her lips tightened into a grim line. "But then, he didn't have to, did he?"

He couldn't believe what he'd just heard. Angry, he propped his hands on his hips. "What the hell is that supposed to mean? Someone fiddles with your precious no-pass, no-play law and I'm automatically to blame?"

"Who am I supposed to blame, Gil?" She rose from her chair and paced to the window looking out into the gym. Glancing over her shoulder at him, she said, "Just give me a name."

"Well, hell, I don't know!" He plowed a hand through his hair, feeling cornered and hating it.

"That's what I thought."

"That's what you thought! That's what you thought?" He gave a mirthless chuckle. "This is flooring me. Did you even stop to imagine that someone else might be responsible?"

Her gaze fell to the windowsill. "Yes, Gil. At first I refused to believe otherwise. I thought there would be no way that you'd endanger what we have together, not even for a state championship."

"Well, you're right. There is no way. I love you, Lesley, you've gotta know that."

"I thought I did."

Thought. She had *thought* she did. His chest tightened with a bleak emotion. "For God's sake, what changed your mind?" he uttered.

She raised her eyes to his. "Devin. He told me that Dwight had seen the need for the changes because you want Devin on the team for the rest of the season."

Gil closed his eyes. He was simply amazed at how easy it had been for Collins to lay the blame at his feet. But, wait a minute. Collins hadn't blamed him. Lesley had just said that Collins had refused to name names. She had assumed, *assumed* after what Devin had said, that Gil had masterminded it. Heavy circumstantial evidence to be sure, but still only circumstantial. It hurt like hell to think that she had only needed to hear the words from Devin to convince her.

Opening his eyes, he studied her profile. Her lips were trembling slightly, her eyes watery with unshed tears. He curbed the urge to go to her and take her in his arms. He was hurt, too, dammit! Hurt that her trust didn't extend far enough to give him the benefit of the doubt.

"I knew something like this would happen," she said, her voice sad and oddly self-berating as she continued staring out the window into the empty gymnasium. "I told myself over and over again that it wouldn't work for the two of us because of this very thing. Guess I should have listened."

At her remark, Gil shook his head slowly, realization dawning. For her, this wasn't so much a matter of trust as it was a self-fulfilled prophecy. As she'd said, she'd convinced herself early on that an involvement with him would be a mistake. He'd thought he had managed to get her past whatever doubts she'd had. Obviously there'd never been a chance for that.

"Yeah, you told yourself, didn't you, Lesley? And you kept on looking and looking until you found something that would prove your little hypothesis correct." His short bark of laughter lacked humor. He plopped down in his chair. "Well, you wanta know something? I've got a hypothesis of my own. I think that for the first time in your life, you've come across something that you can't handle."

"And just what is that, Gil? The fact that I can't stomach being lied to, or that I can't simply turn my head long enough for your football team to win a state title?"

"You haven't been lied to."

"Right, you didn't really lie to me, you just neglected to tell me about it. The old what-she-doesn't-know-won't-hurt-her theory."

Gil's jaw tightened, but he refused to let his temper get the better of him. "What you can't handle is the fact that something you have no control over has come along and turned your life upside down. It can't be put on a schedule or a list of things to do. You can't rationalize it, categorize it or analyze it to death, so you don't know how to handle it." He lowered his voice. "You fell in love. So did I. The difference between the two of us is that I quit fighting it. You didn't."

"Stop it. Just stop it." She whirled around, her green eyes flaring with anger as she stalked toward his desk. "Don't you dare pull that think-with-your-heart-and-not-your-head business. Because I did stop fighting it, damn you!" A tear rolled down her cheek, then another, and she slashed at them with her hand. "I stopped fighting and let it happen until all I could see, hear, think or do was wrapped up in you. I wanted to be with you, talk to you, *love* you to the exclusion of everything else in my life, Gil."

He stood, emotion washing over him at her words. He grasped her hand. "Lesley. Love, there's nothing wrong with—"

"Don't." She wrenched away and Gil's heart twisted in his chest. She glanced down at the slip of paper that had so effectively rent the fragile fabric of their relationship, her tears rolling freely now. "Don't tell me there's nothing wrong with mindlessly letting go, Gil. Don't tell me I was right to ignore my instincts, all those warning bells in my head. Not while that piece of paper sits on your desk telling me otherwise."

Fighting the anger and desperation he felt, he paced his words evenly. "There's a chance for us, Lesley, if and only if you ignore those instincts."

Indecision flashed in her eyes for the briefest of moments. It was immediately replaced by her former accusing look. Pointedly glancing at the paper he held, she said, "My instincts seem to be the only thing I can trust, Gil. I won't ignore them ever again."

Her gaze fell away from his then, and she walked out of his office, closing the door firmly behind her.

"DAD, I KNOW what I'm doing."

Don Michaels's jaw clenched, and he pounded his fist on the dining room table for the third time. "You don't know nothing, boy! Not if you think passing up the opportunity that vice principal offered you makes any sense. How are you going to catch recruiters' attention? How are you going to get into the right college's sports program if you don't play through the rest of this season? You got an answer for that?"

Devin nudged at his salad with his fork, then set the fork down. He was no more interested in his dinner now than he was in discussing this. But his father had brought up the subject by asking about his grades, and Devin wasn't going to lie by not telling him what Collins had done. Knowing his father's obsession with Devin's football career, the man would find out about the schedule change one way or another anyway.

"I shouldn't get special privileges because I'm a good athlete, Dad. And if I don't make the grade—"

Michaels snorted. "You won't. You're too damn busy with that drama crap and mooning over your fights with Fielden's girl to pay attention to schoolwork. But that's beside the point. Collins had fixed it so you don't need to worry about grades. You just show up for those classes he's got you assigned to and keep your attention on the important thing—football."

Devin glanced at his mother, who sat opposite his father at the table. Her expression told him that she'd be of no help to him in this argument. As always, she would defer to his father's wishes. Devin sighed and looked his father straight in the eye. "I'm not going to do it, Dad. It's wrong."

"It's wrong," Michaels said mockingly. "Listen to me, son. Situations like this, wrong or not, have been going on in this town—hell, for that matter, all over the country—for as long as anyone can remember. Wrong has nothing to do with it. That's just the way it is. If you're going to play ball in college, you might as well know right now that things aren't always done on the up-and-up. If you're smart, you'll keep your mouth shut and go along with the program whether you agree with it or not."

"Well, I don't agree with it. And maybe I don't want to go along with the program if they have to bend the rules for me. Haven't you always said I should take pride in my accomplishments, Dad? How can I be proud if I have to cheat to get anywhere?"

His father shook his head, then rubbed the bridge of his nose with his fingers. "Devin, I do want you to take pride in yourself, but you need to learn that there are going to be times in your life when you have to swallow your pride. This is one of those times. Now there's a lot at stake here. If you're on the bench for the rest of the season, you might miss out on a scholarship. If you lose that chance, you've lost the chance for a career in pro ball. And playing professional football is what you've always wanted, isn't it?''

Was it? Devin used to think so. But this past year he'd found out that a professional football career was what everyone else wanted for him, from his father and mother to all the coaches he'd ever had, including Coby's father. "No, Dad. It's not what I want," he said, scooting his chair back from the table and tossing his napkin beside his plate. "I decided that today when I took the schedule change to the principal and blew the whistle on Collins."

"You did what?''

"I turned him in," Devin said in an even voice. "And tomorrow morning I'm going to withdraw from football."

His father's face paled. "Son, you made the biggest mistake of your life. You're wasting your natural ability."

"I know you won't understand it, Dad, but I finally made the right decision for me. Maybe I do have natural ability, but I don't want to play ball. I haven't for some time now, but you haven't listened when I've tried to tell you."

"That's because it's nonsense."

"No, it's not. I'm old enough to know what I want to do. I won't be miserable for the rest of my life doing what everyone else wants. Giving up football is going to give me time to pull up the rest of my grades so I can act in the play. That's what I want, Dad."

"Let me get this straight. You're giving up the chance for a college scholarship for some damn high school play?''

"No, I'm giving it up for the chance at a drama scholarship."

Michaels gave a harsh laugh. "You gotta be kidding me."

"No. I'm serious. If I can't get a scholarship, then I'll work my way through college. Drama's going to be my major."

His father rested his head in his hands. "You don't know what you've done," he warned in a weary voice.

"Yes, I do, Dad. I've finally taken the initiative. I've taken some long-overdue control of my life."

STACEY POKED HER HEAD into Lesley's office. "I come bearing the gift of caffeine," she said, lifting a mug for Lesley to see.

"I accept," Lesley said, waving her in. She placed her coat and purse in the closet and walked to her desk, not knowing if she was ready for the long day ahead, but realizing it couldn't possibly be longer than the night she'd just suffered through.

Stacey gave a sympathetic smile. "Didn't get much sleep last night?"

"No." She took a sip of the coffee, thinking of all the hours she'd spent tossing and turning. And crying. "Not much at all."

"It must be going around. Dwight looked like hell when he first got here this morning. He's been in his office pacing back and forth and looking miserable for the past thirty minutes."

"I'm afraid Mr. Collins's misery has just begun." Lesley might not have accomplished much in the way of sleep last night, but she had come to a decision as to what she was going to do about Dwight. At Stacey's questioning look, she said, "Tell him I'd like to speak to him, Stacey."

"Sure."

Stacey left, and Lesley settled behind her desk to wait for him.

Thinking up a suitable way to handle Dwight Collins's punishment hadn't been what had kept Lesley awake most of the night. Gil was responsible for her sleeplessness. And for her tears. Funny, she thought now as a new image of him brought another painful rush of emotion to the surface, it had been memories of time spent together... things he'd said to her, how he'd touched her, both physically and emotionally, that had torn at her heart through the night. Funny, she thought, that it hadn't been his involvement in the scheduling violation that had weighed on her mind.

"Lesley?"

She looked up. "Dwight," she said coolly. "Have a seat. We have business to discuss."

His eyes were wary. And Stacey had been right, he looked like hell. He dragged a hand through his hair and took a chair opposite her. "About Devin Michaels?"

"Indirectly. I want to tell you what I plan to do about your part in this mess."

"Before you start, let me just say that I know how angry you are and—"

"You couldn't possibly know how angry I am, Dwight," she said, cutting him off with a glare. "Because when you came up with your little plan to keep

Devin Michaels on the football team you not only endangered your job, you endangered *mine!*"

"I'm sorry, Lesley. I guess I was just so anxious to...well, to please the right people so I'd have a better chance at the new principal's position that I wasn't thinking about that."

His contrite facade had no effect on her. "No, Dwight. The only thing you didn't think was that you'd get caught. You didn't care about anyone but yourself. You let your ambition override your good sense."

"Yes. You're right," he said nodding his head. "And again, I'm—"

"I know," she said tightly. "Sorry."

"Well, I am. You don't know how bad I feel. I was awake all night thinking about it. I'm truly sorry."

"Well, my friend, you're about to be a whole lot sorrier."

A bleak look crossed his face. "You've...taken this to the superintendent, then? Had me fired?"

"No, Dwight. I haven't taken this to him. Not yet, at least."

Relief flashed in his eyes, but only momentarily. "Contingent upon?"

"First," Lesley said, "I want to know who put you up to this."

He squirmed in his chair. "I, uh...I'd still rather go down alone on this one, Lesley."

"You'll excuse me if I'm not impressed with your sterling sense of honor, Dwight, but I don't give a damn about what you'd rather do. I want to know who else is involved in this."

He stared down at his hands resting on his knees. "I'm the one who changed the schedule, Lesley. I don't see why you can't just dole out whatever punishment you feel is necessary and leave it at that."

Dwight's loyalty to Gil puzzled Lesley. They weren't close friends, and she couldn't think of anything that Gil might have to hold over Dwight's head that would keep the man so closemouthed.

"Dwight, you're trying my patience. You don't have to worry that I won't get around to doling out punishment. I will. But in order for this type of fiasco never to have the chance to happen again, I want to know the name of this person. You may have been the one who changed the schedule, but you and I both know that it wasn't solely your idea, don't we? You didn't have enough to gain by doing this to justify the risk, but someone else here at Warren did. I want to know who that someone is."

"The person involved wasn't someone at this school," he said in clipped tones.

Lesley's eyes widened. "Not someone at...?"

"He was the parent of one of the football players, okay?" His eyes darted from side to side. "Considering the circumstances, I think you can figure out who that parent was. He's... he told me he's a good friend, an old college buddy of the superintendent's."

Dwight gave her a pleading look. "Earlier it sounded like you might be thinking of sparing my career, Lesley, but don't you see? If you jump down this person's throat... well, I could lose my job anyway. Believe me, this man will find a way to get me fired."

Dwight's bombshell had Lesley's heart pounding in her chest. Devin's father. Dwight was telling her that Don Michaels, not Gil Fielden, had been behind this. Remembering how the man had acted at Wayne Thomas's house the night of the barbecue, she had no trouble believing that he'd pressured Dwight into doing whatever was necessary to keep his son playing football. "And no one else...no one on faculty at Warren...?"

"No. Just me, Lesley." Dwight looked away again, his fingers nervously drumming on his knees. "I've been going crazy ever since you talked to me about this. I didn't sleep more than an hour last night wondering if I'd still have a job today." He looked up again, pinning her with a desperate look. "If you could just tell me where I stand, Lesley. Tell me what to expect."

Still reeling from Dwight's announcement, Lesley struggled to concentrate on the matter at hand, Dwight's part in this business. "Dwight, I'm not completely unsympathetic to your jangled nerves. I...just had thought...well, never mind that." She sat up straight, pushing the implications of what he'd admitted to the back of her mind for the moment.

"You made a big mistake in judgment. Thank heavens Devin Michaels had the character to want no part in it. He saved your backside, Dwight. I hope you realize that."

"Yes," he said quietly. "I do."

"And you also realize that if I take this matter to the superintendent, you'll most likely be fired. It will be a blot on your record, making it difficult for you to find another job teaching or as an administrator."

"Yes. But, Lesley, I made one mistake. One. Surely all the hard work I've put in negates that. Surely—"

"Dwight, I don't intend to go to the superintendent over this." She held up a hand when his shoulders slumped in relief. "Don't get too excited. You're not going to be thrilled with what I *am* going to do."

Lesley rose from her chair and walked to the front of her desk. She folded her arms across her middle and looked down at him. "Before the scheduling violation, I was prepared to give you a good recommendation for that principal's position you wanted to apply for. You might have guessed that all hopes for it died when I found out about this."

His mouth tightened and he nodded. "Yes, I assumed that."

"Good. Because I'm taking it a step further, Dwight. Recommendation or not, I don't want you to apply for the job. If you do, I'll go to the superintendent with this. Not only will you not get that job, but the job you hold now will be in peril."

Dwight frowned. "I know I should be grateful that you aren't going to turn me in, but—"

"You should be."

Dwight shook his head. "I'm more than qualified for that job, Lesley."

"Are you? I used to think so."

His gaze lowered again and he exhaled a long breath. "So... how long before I can redeem myself? How long before I'm *allowed* to make career decisions for myself again?"

Ignoring his sarcastic tone, Lesley walked back to her chair. "That depends on you, Dwight. All that's ever been required of you is that you do your job well and without the influence of special-interest groups. I expect you to keep your nose clean in the future. If you do, a couple years more in the vice principal's chair is all you're looking at. If not—"

"Yeah, I know. The superintendent will hear of it."

"Precisely."

Dwight rose from his chair. "Guess that's that, then."

"Dwight, I wish things hadn't turned out this way. You know how I felt about the job you'd been doing as vice principal."

"Right. But, as they say, I have no one to blame..." His words trailed off. "If you have nothing else, I should be getting to work," he said dispiritedly.

There was nothing more to say, so Lesley dismissed him.

She watched him leave, the usual enthusiasm that bordered on cocky gone from his demeanor. She allowed herself a moment of worry. It wasn't her plan to break the man, merely to teach him a lesson. It was crucial that he understood just how far he'd stepped out of line and that he'd pay a great deal if he ever attempted it again.

By taking away Dwight's opportunity for advancement at this point, she wasn't ruining the man, Lesley reminded herself. She was giving him a second chance to prove himself. To regain her trust.

Trust.

ALL THE RIGHT MOVES

Her thoughts careened to Gil and the trust she'd accused him of breaking. Guilt washing over her, she recalled each and every word of that accusation. She also remembered the things Gil had said to her.

He'd told her that she couldn't handle falling in love and that she'd been looking for something like the alleged violation to use as an excuse to end their relationship.

Had she? Had her refusal to believe him been a way to fulfill her own prophecy?

Lesley didn't think so. She might have been wrong to suspect Gil, but that didn't mean their differences were nonexistent. Their contrasting personalities, even their opposition on the no-pass, no-play situation issue had caused problems between them. Wouldn't those things continue to drive them further and further apart?

Emotionally Lesley wanted to believe that they wouldn't. Her instincts told her differently.

One thing was clear, though. Lesley owed Gil an apology. She reached for the phone, then dialed his extension. When his voice came over the line, Lesley's heart lodged in her throat, making speech impossible for a moment. But only for a moment. Then a strength that Lesley didn't know she possessed took over, and she found herself apologizing for her mistake.

CHAPTER FIFTEEN

"GET LESLEY," Linda said. "She'll know what to do."

Lesley stepped inside the bride's dressing room, closing the door behind her. "Get Lesley for what?" she asked. "What's wrong?"

"Oh, thank God you're here." Dressed in a slip, her hair in electric curlers, Kelly rushed forward and clasped Lesley's upper arms. "The flowers. They haven't arrived yet, and look at the time!"

"Calm down, honey. I just came from the sanctuary and the flowers are in place. The poinsettias look lovely, Kell."

"No, I'm not talking about those flowers. Our bouquets and the groomsmen's boutonnieres! The florist was supposed to leave them when he left the others, but he didn't! I can't get hold of him by phone, all I get is a recording. 'We're closed now. Our regular business hours are Monday through Saturday...'"

Lesley bit her lip. "Oh, my. We do have a problem."

At the dressing table, Gayle calmly applied blusher to her cheeks. "I'm not worried. Lesley will figure something out."

Lesley truly hoped that would be the case. Her recent powers of concentration, however, hadn't been up to par. She racked her brain. "Okay. Where's your appointment book, Kelly? Surely you have the florist's home number in it."

Kelly shook her head, her expression, if possible, even more panicked. "No, Lesley. If *you* had been in charge there would be an appointment book with home phone numbers. I'll be lucky if I can remember the man's last name."

"Oh, Kelly. Honey, you should have made sure—"

"I know, I know! But should haves aren't going to help me now! What am I going to do?"

Lesley sighed, turned Kelly by the shoulders and led her to the dressing table. "First of all—get up, Gayle— you're going to finish your makeup. Secondly, tell me that florist's name."

"Les, I said I don't know—"

"You know it if you want to carry a bouquet down that aisle," Lesley said firmly.

"Oh, it's . . . it's . . . Ramirez. Yes, that's it!"

"Good. Linda, hand me that phone book."

"Here you go," Linda said, passing her the book. "Too bad his name couldn't be Smith. Might be easier than finding the right Ramirez in a Texas phone book."

"Never mind that," Lesley said, flipping to the *R*s. "Kelly, think. What is the man's first name?"

"Oh, God. I . . . just don't know."

"Come on, Kelly. I can't dial up every one of these listings in forty-five minutes."

"Wait a minute. I remember his son's first name. He works at the shop and it struck me as strange because his first name was Norwegian, not Mexican. It's Erik, of all things."

"What good will his son's name do?" Linda asked with a chuckle.

Lesley's index finger sped down the page. "Here it is, Erik Ramirez. And right here is an Enrique Ramirez with the same address." Lesley grabbed a nearby phone and quickly punched in the number. "Mr. Ramirez? You own a florist's shop? Good. I'm Lesley Tyler, Kelly Tyler's sister. We've run into a problem. Yes. Yes, they neglected to leave the bridal bouquets and groomsmen's... yes, that's right, it'll begin in forty-five minutes. Thank you. We'll see you in about twenty minutes. That's fine."

Lesley hung up the phone. "No problem," she said.

Kelly closed her eyes in relief. "Oh, Lesley, thank you."

"You're welcome. Now, get that makeup on," she ordered.

Gayle slipped into her satin pumps. "Kell, surely you didn't doubt that big sister would save the day."

"You're right. I should have known not to panic."

Linda presented her back to Lesley, and Lesley began fastening the row of tiny pearl buttons on her bridesmaid's dress. "I didn't save the day. You would have come up with the name on your own. What is it that you guys have been telling me so much lately? 'We're adults now, we can handle our own lives just fine...'"

"But we miss having you around to make sure everything goes smoothly," Gayle said. "You, sis, are the one who inherited the organizational gene. We three got a gene that breeds chaos."

Lesley's hands stilled on the buttons. Her sisters had been reminding her of that fact ever since she'd arrived in Austin four days ago. It had been a joke they'd enjoyed for years now. In the past, Lesley hadn't minded it. These days, the truth hurt. "That's nonsense and you know it. Have you stopped to look at how well all three of you are doing these days? Shock of the century, you're doing it all without my scheduling skills."

Linda glanced over her shoulder at Lesley. "Scheduling skills? That's putting it a little lightly, isn't it? You're one of the few people I know who has made a science out of lists."

Lesley finished with the buttons. "The term 'science' is a bit much, Linda," she said tightly.

"She's teasing, Les," Kelly said, stroking her lashes with mascara.

"To a certain extent, I am." Linda lifted piles of clothing, looking for her pumps. "But unlike you, Gayle, I don't think it had anything to do with heredity in Lesley's case."

Gayle shot Linda an amused glance. "And what is your theory, Dr. Linda?"

Linda found her shoes and put them on. "I think anyone who'd gone through the same circumstances at such a young age would have become as . . . careful as Lesley is."

"That's a crock," Kelly threw in. "I know lots of people who are just naturally more together. None of them suffered through childhood traumas to become that way."

"I don't know," Gayle added. "I myself may not have become more 'careful,' as Linda put it, as a result of Mom's illness. But I've often stopped to wonder, even worry at times, that I could, you know, go crazy the way she did. I'm sure that, along with all the responsibility Lesley had to take on, the same thing must have worried Les."

Lesley could stand no more. Her temper, usually slow to rile, flashed. "Got it all figured out, have you?" she asked the three of them sarcastically. "Well, when you've finished psychoanalyzing my neuroses, you can find me outside in the narthex. I'll be the one putting military creases on all of next Sunday's church bulletins."

Ignoring her sisters' astonished expressions, she left the room, angry—no, furious—that they'd discussed her as though she hadn't even been there.

The tears that blurred her eyes were a surprise. She'd figured she'd used up her allotment in the past three weeks since...

Gil.

Sorrow slowed her steps, and she blinked back the tears. It seemed that along with all those excellent organizational skills she possessed, she'd also been blessed with a sharp memory. A memory so keen, in fact, that she couldn't seem to put Gil and the mistake they'd made by becoming involved behind her. Images of him haunted her.

She entered the narthex and strolled to one of the windows that looked out over the church grounds.

Lesley had come to realize that everything he'd said that afternoon in his office had been on target. She did categorize and schedule things to death. Control was an important aspect of her life. And even though she'd lost her temper with her sisters just now, they'd been right, too. Growing up as she had, she'd found security in a rigid, calculated life-style.

Security. If she was so damned *secure*, then why did she feel so empty? Since she and Gil had split, the organized details of Lesley's day-to-day life had begun to seem trivial. Where once she'd reveled in accomplishing lists of tasks, she now felt as though she were merely marching in place, accomplishing little of value save the fact that she was filling time. Time. Why, if she was so secure, did the days seem overwhelmingly long, why did the nights fill her with dread?

Obviously, her rational mind concluded, she wasn't secure. But there was no help for it. She might have harbored the secret hope that Gil would come barging back into her life, insisting that they try again, but that hadn't happened. When she'd apologized after learning of his innocence, he'd remained cool toward her. A colleague. Since then he'd treated her as a colleague and nothing more every time they met.

Lesley spun around when she felt a hand on her shoulder.

"I was elected as group apologist," Gayle said. "Lesley, we're sorry. We didn't mean to—"

"No, Gayle. No apology necessary." She placed her hand over her sister's. "It's not what you guys said that caused me to lose it back there. It's . . . just some residual sensitivity, I guess. Obviously I'm not back up to full speed yet since . . . well, you know."

Gayle's expression was full of concern. Lesley had filled the girls in on all that had happened between her and Gil. "Lesley, are you sure that it's not too late for you and the coach? Maybe if you guys simply give it some time . . ."

Lesley shook her head. "No. I don't think so, Gayle."

"But—"

"Is she still mad at us?" Linda asked as she approached them from behind.

Lesley managed a smile. "No. She's not still mad."

"Good. Because Kelly's freaking in there. Says she doesn't know if she can go through with this. You have to talk to her, Les."

Lesley's smile widened. "Come on, you two," she said, looping her arms through theirs. "We'll all talk to her."

As it turned out, Lesley was the only sister Kelly wanted to discuss it with. It was understandable; Kelly needed a parent. Lesley had been that parent for most of Kelly's life.

"It's only natural that you're nervous," Lesley said once they were alone in the dressing room. She took Kelly's hand in hers. "This is a big step."

"I know, I know. The cliché of all time—prewedding jitters. But this is different. I just keep thinking about the last fight Stephen and I had. We never did fully resolve it, Lesley. We both just sort of decided to ignore it. There's something disturbing about that, don't you think?''

Lesley placed a hand on her sister's shoulder, gently pushing her into a chair. She pulled up another chair and sat down across from her, marveling again at how beautiful her younger sister looked in the simple candlelight-lace wedding gown.

"Was the argument one that you and Stephen had had before?"

"No. No, it wasn't." Distraught, Kelly rubbed her temples with her fingertips. "But, Lesley, we're so different. He has all these big dreams and plans for our future. I'm happy with the travel agency. What if...what if life with me just doesn't measure up for him? What if—"

"Stephen loves you, Kelly. Have you forgotten that?"

Kelly shook her head. "I haven't forgotten. And I love him. But all of a sudden I wonder if it will be enough."

Lesley sighed. What could she possibly tell Kelly to reassure her? Lesley had wondered the very same thing. She'd ended up discovering that sometimes it wasn't enough. She'd ended up with her heart in pieces.

"Kelly, I don't know the answer to that. What do you think?"

"Oh, I don't...know." Her voice broke and Lesley could see that she was close to tears. "I mean, I'm terrified. Now that this day has finally arrived, I'm terrified."

"What frightens you most, baby?"

"That I'll lose him." She looked Lesley in the eye. "That I'll do something stupid, something—"

"You don't do stupid things, Kelly."

"You're my sister. Of course *you* feel that way."

"He loves you, Kelly. He feels that way, too."

"No, Lesley. There are things about me that I know drive him nuts. I'm so impulsive, so—"

"Kelly, listen to me." Lesley leaned forward, taking her sister's hands in hers. "I don't know Stephen as well as I'd like to, but I'd be willing to bet that the differences you're so afraid of are some of the very reasons he fell in love with you in the first place, honey."

"Well, maybe." Kelly frowned. "But that's now, Lesley. What about later? What will I do if—"

"Stop trying to second-guess things. What you'll do is this: both of you will refuse to dwell on the differences you don't like about one another and you'll concentrate on the differences you do love."

Kelly's frown became skeptical. "It sounds too simple."

It's simple, but then again, no one'll ever accuse me of being terribly complicated.

The realization that she'd just quoted Gil's theory to Kelly hit Lesley with a staggering intensity. It was accompanied by a quick mental image of the two of them as they had lain together on her bed that night. He'd held her in his arms, and they'd listed all the things they loved about each other... and all the differences....

"Lesley?" Kelly prompted. "Don't you think that's oversimplifying it?"

She hesitated for a moment. Then, with a clarity of thought that had been absent for some time now, she shook her head. "No. Who said it has to be complicated?"

LESLEY PULLED HER CAR into the space next to Gil's and killed the engine, then got out. A wave of anxiety swept through her, but she ignored it resolutely and marched up the walk to his apartment door. She knocked firmly on the door, willing herself to remain resolute.

"Well, hi there," Coby said, her eyes wide when she answered the door. "Come on in."

"Hello, Coby." Lesley stepped inside, her nerves surfacing again as her gaze took in the familiar room.

"This is a...surprise," she said. "A nice one, I mean."

Lesley smiled at the girl. "How have you been?"

"Good, good." She hooked her thumbs in her back pockets. "How 'bout you?"

"Oh, as good as could be expected."

"Dad...said you were at your sister's wedding over the holidays. Was it...you know, okay?"

"It was very nice," Lesley said. She remembered then that Coby had failed to bring her English grade up enough to be in the play over the holidays. "I...hope the holidays weren't too much of a disappointment for you, Coby."

"Oh. The play, you mean. Well, as you can guess, I was pretty down on opening night. I wasn't even going to go, but I'm glad I did. Devin was killer." She smiled sadly. "It hurt a little, not being up there on stage with him and all the others, but I got over it."

Lesley smiled. "Good for you. It sounds as if you might be on better terms with Devin now," she ventured.

Her smile broadened. "Yeah. We think we might even be going to the same college next fall. Listen, do you want me to get Dad? He's out back in the courtyard shooting baskets."

"Oh, no. I'll just...go out there myself." Lesley reached for the doorknob.

"Ms. Tyler?"

Lesley looked back at her. "Yes?"

"He's missed you a lot."

Lesley's heart beat quickened. "I've missed him, too. A lot."

GIL DIDN'T BELIEVE it was her at first. The woman walking toward the cement basketball court might have looked like Lesley, but it wasn't possible that it was actually her. He'd accepted the fact that he wouldn't be seeing her here again, wouldn't see her anywhere but at school, and only on a professional basis.

A mild breeze ruffled her hair, blowing several long black strands across her face, and his heart began to beat erratically. It was her. He stood stone-still, holding the basketball on his hip as she approached.

"You forgot to concentrate on the differences you love," she said when she stopped in front of him.

"I forgot to—"

"That day in your office you told me that I categorize, rationalize and analyze things to death. Fine. I admit it. That's me. It's the way I handle things."

"Lesley, *I* never had a problem with—"

"No, let me finish. Control has always been important to me. You were right about that. But it's something that I can't change overnight."

"I don't want—"

She held up a hand, cutting him off. "Then, at the wedding, Kelly almost backed out at the last minute. She told me she was afraid of her and Stephen's differences. And when I found myself telling her to concentrate on the differences that they *do* love about one another, the thought hit me. You forgot, Gil."

"No, Lesley." His palm went to her cheek. "I didn't have a problem in the world with your lists or the fact that you needed control in your life. Not until it threatened what we had together."

What we had *together.* Hearing him speak the words aloud brought tears to her eyes. "I was afraid, Gil."

"Like Kelly?"

"Yes, like Kelly." Her voice was husky with emotion. "And, like Kelly, I was foolish, wasn't I?"

Gil held his breath, a cautious hope stirring in his chest. "Were you?"

She nodded. "And ever since I left Austin, all I could think about was getting back here to you. I wanted to tell you again how sorry I was for doubting you. And I wanted to tell you I wouldn't make lists, that I'd never allow anything to come between us again. I wanted to promise that the love I feel for you will always be stronger than my fear."

She looked away and Gil's spirits sank. Dear God, surely she wasn't going to do this to him again.

"But I can't make those promises, can I?" she asked, a tear escaping and sliding wetly over his thumb. "Because standing here in front of you now, I'm more afraid than I've ever been. And I . . . I don't know how to get rid of this emotional baggage I carry around. It's so much a part of me, so ingrained in my personality that I just don't . . . know . . . how."

He caressed her cheekbone with his thumb. "Lesley, all of us carry emotional baggage from childhood into our adult life."

"Not you, Gil. You're strong."

Gil shook his head, a wry smile tugging at one corner of his mouth. "What about all of my hang-ups over Greg?"

Lesley covered his hand with hers. "Your brother?"

"Yeah. It tore me up, you know?" He turned his hand, lacing her fingers with his.

"But I'd always felt that I had dealt with his suicide a long time ago. That the anger I've always had inside was normal because I'd lost him to suicide, not just death. But the other night I realized that I hadn't come to terms with it."

"What made you decide that?"

"I was at Wayne Thomas's house. And after I'd cried in my beer over you for about two hours, the conversation drifted to Greg. Wayne was Greg's best friend—he knew him better than any of us. When I told Wayne that I held my parents partially responsible for Greg's death because of the pressure they put on him to succeed, Wayne was shocked.''

"*Did* they pressure him, Gil?''

"Yes. But, as Wayne said, both he and Greg were overachievers. Both he and Greg had pressure from their families to succeed. The difference was that Greg couldn't take the pressure. Wayne was spurred on by it. I'd never thought about it like that. I'd gone around angry at my parents for years before they passed away. Lord, I'd even let my anger affect the way I've been raising Coby.''

Lesley frowned. "What are you talking about? You're an excellent father. You—''

"Refused to say a word about her grades when they started to slip,'' he said. "Remember?''

"That was because of Greg?''

"Yes. And because I refused to step in and put any pressure on her, she screwed up her chances of being in the play. Think about it, Lesley. My *not* wanting to step in and control her life was just another form of control in itself.''

"I ... think I see what you mean.''

"Do you, love?'' He brought their clasped hands to his lips, brushing a kiss across her knuckles. "What I'm trying to say is that we're all weighed down, one way or another, with emotional baggage. But the fact that it exists doesn't mean we have to throw up our hands in defeat. And it doesn't have to come between us, not if we don't want it to. We can confront it.''

We. Not just *you,* Lesley thought, but *we.* She swallowed, not certain she could speak again without crying.

"Together, Lesley. We can confront it together. How does that sound to you?" He let the ball go then and, not waiting for her answer, pulled her into his embrace.

Her arms wound around his back and the tears came freely. "Oh, Gil. Can we?"

He leaned back to look at her, the cocky grin that had always been her undoing on his lips. "You're damn straight we can."

Laughter mingled with her tears and she nodded her head. "Yes, we can. I love you so much. I thought I'd go insane missing you."

He tilted her face up. "I love you, too. Always will."

She stroked his jaw with her palm. "I'm sorry that you lost the state game."

"Yeah, me, too. But I pretty much figured we would when Michaels pulled out of the program." He shrugged. "I had more important things to be upset about."

"Did you?" she asked with a grin.

His arms tightened around her. "Oh, yes."

She peered up at him. "Gil, if I hadn't come here today...were you going to—"

"Your plane got in at 2:53. I was going to allow you an hour to unpack, then I was coming over."

She wrapped her arms around his neck and stretched up on tiptoes to kiss him. "You know what really turns me on about you?'' she whispered in a sultry voice. "You're so aggressive, *so* take charge."

He laughed. "Yeah, right." Then he shrugged and leaned down to brush his lips against hers. "I can't help it," he said in a husky voice. "It's all part of the coach thing. I know all the right moves."

CHRISTMAS

STORIES · 1991

Bring back heartwarming memories of Christmas past
with HISTORICAL CHRISTMAS STORIES 1991,
a collection of romantic stories
by three popular authors.
The perfect Christmas gift!

Don't miss these heartwarming stories,
available in November
wherever Harlequin books are sold:

CHRISTMAS YET TO COME
by Lynda Trent
A SEASON OF JOY
by Caryn Cameron
FORTUNE'S GIFT
by DeLoras Scott

**Best Wishes and Season's Greetings
from Harlequin!**

XM-91R

Reach for the stars with

Harlequin Superromance®

in a new trilogy by award-winning author Pamela Bauer

Family ties...

Seventh Heaven (title #481)
Kate Osborne feels she needs to watch out for her
daughters. But it seems she isn't the only one
watching! Police Commissioner Donovan Cade
appears to have a telescope trained on her oldest
daughter's bedroom window! Protest leads to passion
as Kate discovers Donovan's true interests.
Coming in December

On Cloud Nine (title #484)
Kate's second daughter, Juliet, has old-fashioned
values like her mother's. But those values are tested
when she meets Ross Stafford, a jazz musician and
teaching assistant... and the object of her younger
sister's affections. Can Juliet only achieve her heart's
desire at the cost of her integrity?
Coming in January

Swinging On a Star (title #487)
Meridee is Kate's oldest daughter, but very much her
own person. Determined to climb the corporate
ladder, she has never had time for love. But her life is
turned upside down when Zeb Farrell storms into
town, determined to eliminate jobs in her company—
her sister's among them! Meridee is prepared to do
battle, but for once, she's met her match.
Coming in February

SPB

Harlequin Superromance®

COMING NEXT MONTH

#478 TROUBLE IN EDEN • Elise Title
Gillian Haverford had worked hard to establish her resort
inn at Big Sur, California. Now a saboteur was threatening
her livelihood—and her life. Police chief Joe Devlin felt out
of place among the rich and famous, yet he found himself
drawn to Gillian. He soon realized she meant much more to
him than just another case....

#479 OVER THE HORIZON • Kaye Walton
Gail Montgomery never knew she had a twin sister. Yet,
now she was being asked to impersonate her. As if that
weren't enough, she had to juggle two men—her twin's
fiancé and Alex, the man Gail herself was falling in
love with....

#480 THREE WAIFS AND A DADDY • Margot Dalton
If they hadn't found the three orphaned children, Sarah
Burnard was sure she could have gotten away with it. But
now that she was helping Jim Fleming take care of the three
waifs, how could she keep her secret? Jim was bound to not
only learn her name, but to find out she was pregnant—
with his child.

#481 SEVENTH HEAVEN • Pamela Bauer
Even though her three daughters were all grown-up,
Kate Osborne felt she had to watch out for them. But it
seemed that she wasn't the only one watching! Her oldest
daughter's mysterious neighbor appeared to have a
telescope trained on her bedroom window! Protest would
finally lead to passion as Kate discovered Police
Commissioner Donovan Cade's true interests.

"INDULGE A LITTLE" SWEEPSTAKES

HERE'S HOW THE SWEEPSTAKES WORKS

NO PURCHASE NECESSARY

To enter each drawing, complete the appropriate Official Entry Form or a 3" by 5" index card by hand-printing your name, address and phone number and the trip destination that the entry is being submitted for (i.e., Walt Disney World Vacation Drawing, etc.) and mailing it to: Indulge '91 Subscribers-Only Sweepstakes, P.O. Box 1397, Buffalo, New York 14269-1397.

No responsibility is assumed for lost, late or misdirected mail. Entries must be sent separately with first class postage affixed, and be received by: 9/30/91 for the Walt Disney World Vacation Drawing, 10/31/91 for the Alaskan Cruise Drawing and 11/30/91 for the Hawaiian Vacation Drawing. Sweepstakes is open to residents of the U.S. and Canada, 21 years of age or older as of 11/7/91.

For complete rules, send a self-addressed, stamped (WA residents need not affix return postage) envelope to: Indulge '91 Subscribers-Only Sweepstakes Rules, P.O. Box 4005, Blair, NE 68009.

© 1991 HARLEQUIN ENTERPRISES LTD.

DIR-RL

"INDULGE A LITTLE" SWEEPSTAKES

HERE'S HOW THE SWEEPSTAKES WORKS

NO PURCHASE NECESSARY

To enter each drawing, complete the appropriate Official Entry Form or a 3" by 5" index card by hand-printing your name, address and phone number and the trip destination that the entry is being submitted for (i.e., Walt Disney World Vacation Drawing, etc.) and mailing it to: Indulge '91 Subscribers-Only Sweepstakes, P.O. Box 1397, Buffalo, New York 14269-1397.

No responsibility is assumed for lost, late or misdirected mail. Entries must be sent separately with first class postage affixed, and be received by: 9/30/91 for the Walt Disney World Vacation Drawing, 10/31/91 for the Alaskan Cruise Drawing and 11/30/91 for the Hawaiian Vacation Drawing. Sweepstakes is open to residents of the U.S. and Canada, 21 years of age or older as of 11/7/91.

For complete rules, send a self-addressed, stamped (WA residents need not affix return postage) envelope to: Indulge '91 Subscribers-Only Sweepstakes Rules, P.O. Box 4005, Blair, NE 68009.

© 1991 HARLEQUIN ENTERPRISES LTD.

DIR-RL

INDULGE A LITTLE—WIN A LOT!

Summer of '91 Subscribers-Only Sweepstakes

OFFICIAL ENTRY FORM

This entry must be received by: Nov. 30, 1991
This month's winner will be notified by: Dec. 7, 1991
Trip must be taken between: Jan. 7, 1992—Jan. 7, 1993

YES, I want to win the 3-Island Hawaiian vacation for two. I understand the prize includes round-trip airfare, first-class hotels and pocket money as revealed on the "wallet" scratch-off card.

Name _____

Address_____ Apt. _____

City _____

State/Prov. _____ Zip/Postal Code _____

Daytime phone number _____
(Area Code)

Return entries with invoice in envelope provided. Each book in this shipment has two entry coupons—and the more coupons you enter, the better your chances of winning!

© 1991 HARLEQUIN ENTERPRISES LTD.   3R-CPS

INDULGE A LITTLE—WIN A LOT!

Summer of '91 Subscribers-Only Sweepstakes

OFFICIAL ENTRY FORM

This entry must be received by: Nov. 30, 1991
This month's winner will be notified by: Dec. 7, 1991
Trip must be taken between: Jan. 7, 1992—Jan. 7, 1993

YES, I want to win the 3-Island Hawaiian vacation for two. I understand the prize includes round-trip airfare, first-class hotels and pocket money as revealed on the "wallet" scratch-off card.

Name _____

Address_____ Apt. _____

City _____

State/Prov. _____ Zip/Postal Code _____

Daytime phone number _____
(Area Code)

Return entries with invoice in envelope provided. Each book in this shipment has two entry coupons—and the more coupons you enter, the better your chances of winning!

© 1991 HARLEQUIN ENTERPRISES LTD.   3R-CPS